## "Sometimes I think you forget which one of us *owns* this ranch

and which one merely works on it," Maris hurled at him.

"Why don't you just tell me why you're out here trying to pick a fight?" Luke took a step toward her. "Is that what you want, Maris, a no-holds-barred fight? Maybe I've been doing something that's been rubbing you wrong. Or maybe I *haven't* been doing something you want done real bad."

Luke yanked her toward him. His arms closed around her. Maris gasped. "I didn't come out here for this!"

He was breathing into her hair, his nearness arousing unwanted reactions from her traitorous body. "*I* think this is exactly what you came out here for. *I* think you were lying in your bed all alone and picturing me out here alone in mine." His voice had grown husky. "It's a terrible waste, isn't it, you in one bed, me in another?"

# Jackie Merritt

and her husband live just outside of Las Vegas, Nevada. An accountant for many years, Jackie has happily traded numbers for words. Next to her family, books are her greatest joy. She started writing in 1987 and her efforts paid off only a year later with the publication of her first novel. When she's not writing or enjoying a good book, Jackie dabbles in watercolor painting and likes playing the piano in her spare time.

# Jackie Merritt

# THE WIDOW AND THE RODEO MAN

Silhouette Books

Published by Silhouette Books
America's Publisher of Contemporary Romance

Special thanks and acknowledgment to Jackie Merritt for her contribution to the Montana Mavericks series.

Text and artwork on page 8 is reprinted with permission from NEVER ASK A MAN THE SIZE OF HIS SPREAD: A Cowgirl's Guide to Life, by Gladiola Montana. Copyright © 1993 Gibbs Smith Publisher. All rights reserved.

 SILHOUETTE BOOKS

ISBN 0-373-50166-8

THE WIDOW AND THE RODEO MAN

# MONTANA
## Mavericks

*Welcome to Whitehorn, Montana—*
*the home of bold men and daring women.*
*A place where twelve rich tales of passion and*
*adventure are about to unfold under the Big Sky.*
*Seems that this charming little town has some mighty*
*big secrets. And everybody's talking about...*

**Floyd Oakley:** A stranger to Whitehorn—but not for long. Once his body was found during the Kincaid wedding, the whole town was buzzing. Was he a friend of the groom or...

**Mary Jo Kincaid:** Not even a dead man could spoil her big day. And now that she was the wife of the richest heir in town, she didn't have a worry in the world. As long as she stayed away from...

**Winona Cobbs:** This wily old woman had lived in Whitehorn most of her life and she knew *everyone*. Some called her eccentric, but no one ever questioned her psychic vision. Winona knew things others couldn't even fathom—not even...

**Sheriff Judd Hensley:** This rugged lawman was hot on the trail of a murderer. And he wasn't gonna let up until the town of Whitehorn was safe again. That meant all newcomers were suspect—no matter how harmless they seemed....

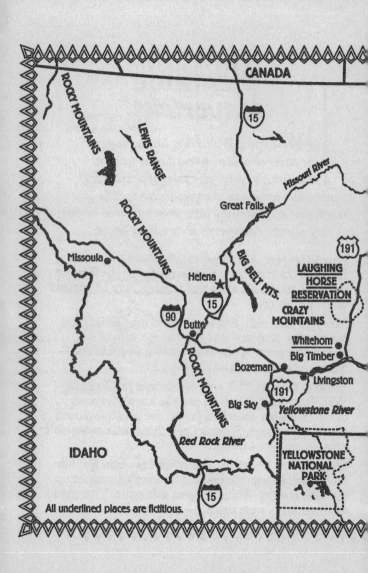

CANADA

ROCKY MOUNTAINS

LEWIS RANGE

ROCKY MOUNTAINS

15

Missouri River

Great Falls

Missoula

BIG BELT MTS.

191

Helena

15

90

LAUGHING
HORSE
RESERVATION

CRAZY
MOUNTAINS

Butte

Whitehorn

Big Timber

ROCKY MOUNTAINS

Bozeman

191

Livingston

Big Sky

Yellowstone River

Red Rock River

IDAHO

YELLOWSTONE
NATIONAL
PARK

15

All underlined places are fictitious.

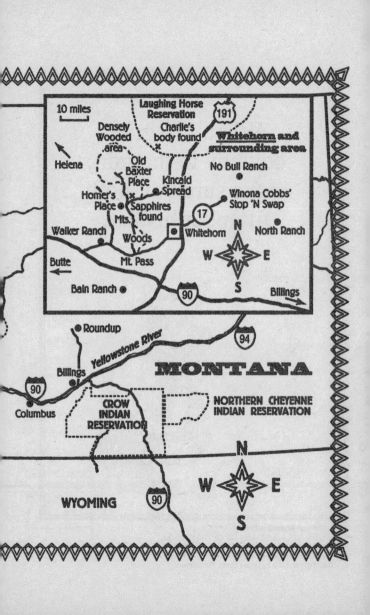

10 miles

Helena

Densely Wooded area

Laughing Horse Reservation

Charlie's body found

**Whitehorn and surrounding area**

191

No Bull Ranch

Old Baxter Place

Kincaid Spread

Homer's Place

Sapphires found

Mts.

17

Winona Cobbs' Stop 'N Swap

Walker Ranch

Woods

Whitehorn

North Ranch

N

W E

S

Mt. Pass

Butte

Bain Ranch

90

Billings

Roundup

Yellowstone River

94

Billings

**MONTANA**

90

Columbus

CROW INDIAN RESERVATION

NORTHERN CHEYENNE INDIAN RESERVATION

N

W E

S

**WYOMING**

90

# When kissin' a cowboy in the rain, make sure you both fit under his hat.

Quote and Illustration from:
NEVER ASK A MAN THE SIZE OF HIS SPREAD:
*A Cowgirl's Guide to Life* by Gladiola Montana.
Illustration by Bonnie Cazier.
Copyright © 1993 by Gibbs Smith Publisher.

# One

Maris Wyler disliked unexpected visitors. The black pickup truck that had pulled into her front yard was definitely unexpected and the man who got out was a stranger. She shielded her gaze from the strong afternoon sun to get a better look at him. He was tall and broad shouldered, a black Stetson shadowing his face as he headed toward the house. Maris had just come off the range, having tended her small herd of cattle on horseback for most of the day. She felt sweaty, gritty and in no mood for a caller. Nevertheless, she stepped off her front porch and walked out to greet him.

Something about the man seemed vaguely familiar, she thought as she drew closer. Though even face-to-face she couldn't quite place him.

"Can I help you?"

Her caller flashed a charming smile. "Hello, Maris. How are you?"

His familiar greeting put her a little off-balance. She tried, but her own smile faltered some. "Apparently we've met."

"Apparently you don't remember." His amused expression suggested that he'd rarely heard a woman say she'd forgotten meeting him. "Name's Luke Rivers. We met in Casper, Wyoming. A bunch of us from the rodeo had joined up in a little bar—"

Maris's hand jerked up. "I remember now." Her deceased husband's behavior that night wasn't a memory to elevate a widow's spirit. Ray had followed a flashy-trashy girl around like a panting puppy dog, embarrassing and angering Maris. Luke Rivers had broken the whole thing up by persuading Ray it was late and time to leave. Maris never did know if Luke had gallantly come to her rescue to save her from further humiliation, or simply because it really was late and the woman Ray had been hitting on was Luke's date. Certainly they hadn't discussed it, and, in fact, had never seen each other again until this very moment.

"What are you doing in Montana? Is there a rodeo in the area?" Maris wasn't speaking with any great amount of friendliness. Ray's obsession with rodeo had been one of the poisons that had destroyed their marriage, long before his fatal accident. Luke Rivers—if she remembered correctly—was a rodeo man through and through, a substantial enough reason to keep a very wide chasm between them.

Luke leaned his hips against the front fender of his truck. Maris Wyler was nice to look at, even with that guarded expression on her face. She had long, sun-streaked, honey-brown hair, restrained at the back of her neck by something he couldn't see. Her skin was as tanned and smooth as honey, and he would bet anything she wasn't wearing any makeup. Her leanness and long legs were accentuated by her worn jeans and red T-shirt. She didn't look soft or at all helpless; rather, she impressed him as a tough, no-nonsense woman. That was okay; she was still nice to look at.

"I came to see Ray. Is he around?"

Maris stiffened. This was the second time an out-of-state pal of Ray's had dropped in, the second time she was going to have to explain why he wasn't "around."

"Ray's dead." The first old pal had gotten tears in his eyes, Maris recalled. Luke Rivers looked as though someone had just punched him in the belly.

"He can't be!" Luke heard his own ludicrous denial and shook his head to clear it. "I'm sorry. What happened?"

Maris recited without emotion. "He got drunk and ran his truck into a cement pier at an underpass out on Highway 191."

"Damn." Frowning, Luke moved away from the pickup and paced a small circle. He pulled off his hat and ran his hand through his hair. "Damn," he repeated. "Now what am I gonna do?"

"What are *you* going to do?" Maris didn't care what Luke Rivers did about anything, but his remark was so quixotic that she repeated it with some sarcasm. "I can't see why Ray's death should have any effect on your life."

Maris watched him scowling and pacing. He was a tall, rangy, good-looking man, with thick black hair and vivid blue eyes. A lady's man, she'd bet, if the women who made themselves so blatantly available to rodeo men could be called ladies. They were in every town, hanging on the corral fences while the men took care of their horses, cracking jokes, laughing too loudly, trying to catch the men's notice.

Ray had noticed too many times to count, each occasion driving the spike in Maris's heart a little deeper. Luke Rivers would notice. She could tell just from his good looks that he was cut from the same cloth as Ray. Two peas from the same damned pod. Overly macho, strutting peacocks who thought the sun rose and set in their hind pocket just because they risked their stupid necks in the rodeo arena.

Luke stopped pacing and faced Maris with his hands on his hips. "Ray owes me three thousand bucks."

Maris's left eyebrow shot up. "Oh?" She almost laughed. Luke couldn't have known Ray all that well, or he would also have known that collecting that debt would be next to impossible. The only time Ray had ever repaid a loan was when the lender had harangued it out of him. Maris gave her head a brief, negative shake. "All I can tell you is that you're out the three thousand, Mr. Rivers."

"I have an IOU." Luke dug for his wallet and fished out a ragged piece of paper, which he handed to Maris.

She read it—IOU three thousand dollars. Ray Wyler—then handed it back.

"It's none of my affair," she said calmly.

Luke's face darkened. "I need that money."

Maris smirked. "I hope you're not thinking of collecting it from me. I'll tell you right now that I don't have three thousand dollars, but even if I did I wouldn't use it to pay off one of Ray's gambling debts."

"It wasn't a gambling debt. Ray came to me about two years ago and all but begged for that money. He said something about using ranch money…" Luke stopped. What Ray had told him had been in confidence. *Luke, I took money out of the ranch account, and I've got to put it back before Maris gets the next bank statement. She'll brain me for sure if she finds out I gambled again.* It had been all but impossible for Luke to refuse. He had just earned a big purse in a bronc-riding contest, and only the day before Ray had saved him from being gored by an ornery old bull. He'd never been particularly fond of Ray Wyler, but the man had risked his own life to save Luke from certain injury.

"He used ranch money?" Maris asked suspiciously. "Two years ago, you said?" There were so many incidents of Ray depleting the ranch bank account for some inane reason, to pay a gambling debt or to buy another piece of junk, to name two. There were acres of old cars, trucks and odd pieces of junk out behind the barn, and Ray had said the same thing every time he brought home another unnecessary and foolish purchase: "I'm gonna fix it up and sell it for a big profit."

He had never fixed anything. Ray Wyler had been a dreamer and a schemer, a gambler, a womanizer and, something that only Maris knew, an insurance-company swindler. But she wasn't thinking of her deceased husband's amoral character right now, she was thinking of that three thousand dollars. In the back of her mind was a bank statement with a mysterious withdrawal and deposit, each for three thousand dollars. Ray had sworn he knew nothing about it and had finally convinced Maris that the bank had made a mistake and merely corrected it. Since it hadn't affected the account's balance, Maris had let it go.

"Let me see that IOU again," she said to Luke. He handed it over and she studied the date and thought about that peculiar bank statement. It was easy to put together: Ray had withdrawn the three thousand, wasted it on something, probably gambling, and borrowed the money from Luke to maintain the correct balance in their account to keep her from finding out that he'd lost so much money.

She wilted inside. Was she responsible for Ray's reprehensible schemes? For his conniving and manipulating Luke Rivers into giving him a loan? Obviously the IOU was genuine, and Luke had every right to expect repayment.

But she had to look after herself, and while she could probably scrape together the three thousand, she wasn't going to hand it over to Luke Rivers.

She passed the IOU back to him. "Sorry, I just don't have that kind of money."

There was a rising panic in Luke. A year ago he'd had a bad accident in the arena, resulting in a broken leg and collarbone. But worse than his own injuries was the death of Pancho, his horse. Pancho had broken his neck in that freak fall and had to be put to sleep, and everyone who had ever seen Pancho work knew he was one of the best cutting horses in the business. For Luke, losing Pancho had been like losing a piece of himself. His broken bones had healed, but would he ever find another Pancho? Especially when he didn't have the money even to start looking?

About two weeks ago he'd remembered that old IOU from Ray Wyler. Though it wasn't nearly enough to buy a horse of Pancho's talent and experience, three thousand would give him the means to get started again. He'd used all of his savings since the accident, and he was as close to being busted right now as he'd ever been. His current status was very little money, no horse and some aches and pains that would probably stay with him for the rest of his life.

But rodeo was all he knew, rodeo or getting a job on a ranch, which sure as hell didn't appeal to him. Anyway, he'd packed up and driven to Whitehorn, Montana, to find Ray Wyler and collect on that old debt.

Instead he was standing in the Wyler yard and being stared down by a woman whose stubborn expression suggested that he had a snowball's chance in hell of seeing that money again. Whether she had the money or not really wasn't the issue, Luke realized. She wasn't going to pay Ray's IOU, and that was final.

Well, it might be final to Maris Wyler, Luke thought irately, but it wasn't final to him. He began looking around, taking in the house—a modest home—the barn and corrals, a number of other outbuildings and last, but certainly not least, a large pasture containing about a hundred horses. His gaze went further out to the snowcapped mountains he could see on the western horizon. The view was spectacular, in his opinion adding enormous value to this ranch. Grimly, he looked again at the horses. Money on the hoof, he thought. And plenty of it.

"I'll take some of those horses for payment," he said brusquely, turning around to look at Maris.

Her back became rigid. "You'll do no such thing. You will not touch one thing on this ranch, and if you try I'll call Sheriff Hensley, who happens to be a personal friend."

Anger was in the air now. Luke felt it, Maris felt it.

"You're not even going to try to make good on any part of that debt, are you?" he accused.

"Why did you wait two years to collect on it?" Maris spoke harshly. "Ray probably put it out of his mind five minutes after you gave him the money. Didn't you know him at all?"

Luke was staring at the horses. They were mostly quarterhorse stock, good-looking animals. "I thought Ray raised cattle. I don't remember him mentioning horses."

Maris wasn't going to get into that dismal story with Luke Rivers. "Like I just said, didn't you know him at all? Look, you might as well take your IOU and go on about your business. I'm not paying it, and—"

"The law might say otherwise."

Maris sighed wearily. "Take your best shot, cowboy. Frankly, I don't give a damn what you do about it. Your piddly little IOU is nothing compared to what else I'm facing." Maris turned to walk away.

Luke's eyes narrowed angrily. "It might be nothing to you, lady, but it's a hell of a lot to me. You don't have it so bad, and your whining isn't impressing me in the least. You've got a damned nice little ranch here, a home, a—"

Maris whirled. "I was *not* whining! And your judgment of my situation doesn't impress *me* in the least. So why don't you just climb back into that fancy truck and take yourself off of my land?"

Fancy truck? Luke looked at his only asset, a six-year-old pickup that he'd kept in good repair and just happened to be clean and shiny from the recent wash and wax he'd given it. He was down to practically nothing, and Maris Wyler was taking slams at his one possession of any value?

Anger burned his gut. He wasn't giving up on that IOU, damn it, not when *her* assets were everywhere he looked. "I'd take payment on an installment basis, half now, half in a month or so," he said flatly.

Maris threw up her hands in exasperation. "Have you heard one word I've said?"

"Have you heard one word *I've* said?" he shouted. "I'm flat broke, busted, and you're acting like I'm trying to steal something's that's mine in the first place. If you really don't have the cash, why not let me have a couple of those horses? At least I could sell them and eat until I figure out what to do next."

"Sell them?" Maris scoffed. "They're green, Luke, unbroken, wild as March hares. Who would buy them?"

"They're green?" Frowning, Luke walked away, moving to the fence. The animals appeared docile, grazing on the lush grass in the pasture. "Mind if I take a closer look?" he said over his shoulder.

"They'll run right over the top of you," Maris drawled with some sarcasm, at the same time thinking that might be a picture worth seeing. "Go ahead. Be my guest."

Luke took off his hat to crawl between the strands of barbed wire, then settled it back on his head. Watching Luke closely, Maris heard footsteps behind her and then Keith's voice. "What's going on, Maris?"

Keith Colson was the one employee Maris was able to keep on the ranch. Keith had been in trouble of one kind or another since childhood. An alcoholic, abusive father and no sensible adult supervision had left their marks on the sixteen-year-old, but since Maris had put him to work on the ranch, Keith hadn't been in even one small scrape with the law.

He was a handsome boy, dark and lanky, and he was willing to work hard at whatever chore Maris suggested. She had developed a genuine fondness for Keith, thinking on occasion that he could be her own son. Ray had been adamant about not wanting kids, and, in fact, had gone and had a vasectomy without Maris's knowledge. Months later, when he'd been drunk one night, he'd told her about it. She had wept for days, and then, as always, she had regathered her courage and carried on.

Keith was watching the man on the other side of the barbed wire. "What's he doing? Who is he?"

"His name is Luke Rivers, and I don't think he believed me when I told him those horses are green."

"Dang, Maris, he could get hurt."

"Yes, I expect he could," she agreed quietly. "But I think he's one of those men who do exactly as they want, when they want. In other words, no woman is going to tell Luke Rivers what to do.''

Keith gave her a curious glance, but what was going on in the pasture was too interesting to miss and he quickly brought his gaze back to Luke Rivers.

Luke was walking very slowly. Any time he got within twenty feet of a horse, the animal kicked up its heels and ran off. Maris was right; these horses were completely wild, too spooky to let a human get near them. But some of them looked good, very good. As he'd already noticed, most were quarter horses, and they had marvelous symmetrical and muscular conformation. They were heavily muscled in their hindquarters, necessary for quality cutting horses. Generally, Luke knew, quarter horses had a gentle disposition, but these broncs had been completely ignored, maybe allowed to grow up on some isolated range without human contact. Then, obviously, someone had rounded them up and sold them to Ray Wyler.

Who was going to break them for Maris? Glancing back to where she waited, he saw a young fellow wearing a huge hat standing next to her. Maybe *he* was going to do the breaking.

Maris was watching Luke's every move and was impressed in spite of herself. He showed absolutely no fear, and though she wasn't normally afraid of horses, she gave the group in this pasture a wide berth.

Luke Rivers. The awful evening at that bar in Casper returned to Maris's mind. Ray had been drunk and disgusting, and she, with her very own eyes, had seen him take that girl out on the dance floor, his hands moving all over her and the rest of his body moving against her as if they were already checked-in at a cheap motel.

Maris had figured that she'd seen just about everything there was to see in life, but her own husband just about bedding a woman in a public place and obviously not caring that his wife was one of the witnesses, was a new low. Teary-eyed, she had scrambled to her feet, knocking down her chair in her haste.

Suddenly Luke had been there, righting her chair, getting Ray off the dance floor and that girl, talking and talking and talking to Ray, and finally escorting her and Ray out of that bar and to their motel, where he even offered, Maris remembered now, to help put Ray to bed.

She had thanked him but said no, that she could manage to pull off his boots and put him to bed on her own. She had sat up the rest of that night, Maris recalled with the pain of old bitterness, seeing again and again her husband standing there with that idiotic look of drunken ecstasy on his face. The next morning, after feeling just a little bit glad that Ray was sick as a dog with a hangover, she had brought their suitcases out to the car, helped Ray from the motel to the vehicle, gotten behind the wheel and started the long drive home. Not a word had ever been said about the night before, not during the drive or anytime after. As was her way, she had put the whole awful incident out of her mind, and to tell the honest-to-God's truth, she had never thought of Luke Rivers again.

But here he was, testing her word on the horses, and perhaps doing a little more than that. Wasn't he studying them rather intently?

After Luke had seen all he wanted, he returned to the fence and crawled through it. "They're green, all right. Where'd they come from?"

"I have no idea," Maris replied. "Ray bought them and they were delivered by a trucking firm." She glanced at Keith. "Keith Colson, Luke Rivers."

Keith offered his hand. "Pleased to meetcha."

"Same here." Keith was a mere boy, Luke realized. If he knew how to break those horses it would be the surprise of the century. "Do you work here, Keith?"

"Yes, he does," Maris answered before Keith could. But she feared the boy might try to explain how he'd come by his job, and Maris didn't think Keith's sad and sorry background was any of Luke's business.

"Who else?" Luke questioned.

Maris gave him a well-aren't-you-the-nosy-one look, but decided to be truthful. "No one else right now. I had a few more hands, but I had to let them go."

Luke's gaze moved from woman to boy and back again. "And which one of you is going to break those horses?"

Keith's smooth, whiskerless cheeks got pink. "I could break 'em if someone showed me what to do."

"Don't let Mr. Rivers's question throw you, Keith," Maris said with a frosty glare at Luke. "He's only attempting to prove how superior he is to you and me."

"That's a mighty narrow-minded attitude," Luke stated gruffly. "Maybe I've got a good reason for asking about what help you've got on the place."

Her golden hazel eyes flashed. "I understand the reasoning behind any question you might ask," she said sharply. "But let me say it one more time. I do not have three thousand lying around gathering dust. I do not have three thousand gathering interest. *I do not have it!* Now, if there's any other way that you would like me to express my financial situation, name it and I'll be glad to comply."

Luke stared at her for several long moments, then turned on his heel and walked away. Startled, Maris watched him reach his pickup truck and get in.

Keith said, "He's madder 'n a wet hen, Maris. How come?"

She sighed. "Ray borrowed money from him two years ago and never paid it back. He came here today to collect, not knowing that Ray was gone."

"Jeez, that's tough," Keith murmured. "Seems like an all-right guy. He probably needs the money."

"Don't we all," Maris drawled. But as Luke Rivers's truck sped away and she was walking to the house, her own innate sense of fair play began to pinch. She could have handled the situation with a little more diplomacy, maybe explaining just how bad things really were for her right now.

Wearily she rubbed her forehead as she went into the house. How did a woman remain kind and considerate when her very foundation was crumbling a little more every day? There were payments on the ranch's mortgage to worry about, and utility bills, gas and oil for her car, groceries for her and Keith, Keith's small wage, and on and on. Right now the horses and few re-maining cattle were faring just fine on natural feed, but come winter there would be hay and grain to buy, and what would she use for money?

Luke Rivers showing up and demanding payment for an old IOU she hadn't even known existed really was a final straw. Small wonder she hadn't been diplomatic, she thought on her way to the kitchen to scare up some supper. Keith, bless his heart, was a bottomless pit. He didn't care what she put on the table to eat as long as there was lots of it. Tonight it would be a dish she had grown up calling "goulash," a filling concoction of ground beef, macaroni and canned tomatoes. Bread and butter and milk would round out the meal, and for dessert there were still a few of those peanut-butter cookies she had baked the other day.

Luke drove away steaming. True, that IOU wasn't Maris Wyler's debt, but it sure as hell had been Ray's, and obviously Maris had control of the family assets. Didn't one inherit liabilities right along with assets in an estate?

Luke shook his head. He knew beans about legal matters. He could take the IOU to a lawyer and get some answers, but the idea of getting into a legal hassle with Maris Wyler rubbed him wrong. There had to be another way to collect that money. He didn't think she doubted the authenticity of the IOU, and maybe she was as short of cash as she'd said. But she had other assets, such as those unbroken horses, and if he was willing to take the animals in lieu of cash, why was she so stubbornly opposed?

On the other hand, suppose she had agreed to giving him two or three of the horses? What then? They were all but valueless as they were, and he sure didn't have a place to take them for the breaking process. Turning untamed broncs into good cutting horses, which was what he would want to do with them, took time and patience. Well, he had the time and he had the patience, but that was all he had. In retrospect, he was lucky Maris had refused to give him the horses.

Reaching Whitehorn, he drove around and decided it was a pleasant little town. It had a courthouse, a police station, a library, a movie theater, two schools, two churches, a fire station, and various restaurants, food markets and a couple of saloons. He noticed the Hip Hop Café on Amity Lane, and the Amity Boarding House at the intersection of Amity Lane and Cascade Avenue.

But he bypassed the boarding house and drove around until he located a small motel on the highway leading to Interstate 90, where he rented a room for the night.

This wasn't over yet, he told himself as he stretched out on the bed with his hands locked behind his head, staring at the ceiling. Someway, somehow, he was going to collect that three thousand. Leaving Whitehorn, just driving away and forgetting that IOU, wasn't going to happen. He could be as stubborn as Maris Wyler, which she was going to find out.

Lying on that lumpy motel bed, Luke's expression became hard and determined. What he had to do now, tonight, was figure out his next step.

There had to be one. All he had to do was think it through.

# Two

The following morning Maris woke up with a throbbing headache. Dragging herself out of bed, she went into her bathroom and took two over-the-counter pain pills. Then she eyed the bottle and wondered how many it would take to put her out of her misery for good.

Tears filled her eyes. Never in her life had she had such a horrible thought, and never in her life had she been a quitter. What was happening to her? There was a solution to every problem, and by all that was holy she was going to find the one that fit her situation. Returning the bottle of pills to the medicine chest, Maris turned on the shower full blast, dropped her nightgown and stepped into the stall. The water hadn't yet warmed up, but she felt she needed an icy shock this morning.

Fifteen minutes later, she was dressed and ready to face the day.

Maybe something good would turn up for a change, she thought hopefully on her way to the kitchen.

Luke went to the Hip Hop Café for breakfast, which, he discovered, wasn't at all what he'd expected before walking into the place. Nothing matched. There was a long chrome counter straight out of the fifties, and then a bunch of tables and chairs that had to have been picked up at garage sales, since none of them were the same. Some were constructed of old oak, some had red vinyl seats, some were painted in startlingly vivid colors. The café's walls were crammed with objects. He spotted an oval mirror with a seashell frame, baskets overflowing with ivy or straw flowers, posters by the score and hand-stitched fabrics in frames, one that read Home Sweet Home and another advising everyone to Have A Good Day.

The many objects, along with the many patrons occupying the place, gave Luke the impression of clutter. But the country music coming from the garish jukebox in a far corner and the buzz of conversation and laughter invited him in, and he walked to the counter and slid onto an empty stool.

The man on his left nodded. "'Morning."

"'Morning." Luke reached for the menu standing on edge between a sunshine-yellow plastic napkin holder and a container of sugar. "What's good in here?" he asked his neighbor.

"Everything's good at the Hip Hop. You must be new in town if you haven't eaten in here before."

The activity of the place was astounding. The waitresses not only delivered food from the kitchen with speed and efficiency, they chatted and joked with their customers. Luke's foul mood began lightening up, and he even smiled at some of the conversations he could hear going on around the room.

Then a young woman came through the swinging doors from the kitchen. Her dark, almost black hair was arranged in a French braid that hung down to the middle of her back. She had vibrant blue eyes and a trim figure, and was wearing a flowing skirt that nearly reached her ankles and a bright-pink blouse. Luke looked her over real good as she passed behind the counter, smiling and commenting to people as she went.

"That's Melissa Avery, the owner," Luke's friendly neighbor volunteered. "Real nice gal."

Melissa Avery not only looked like a "real nice gal," she was pretty enough to draw any man's attention. At any other time, Luke would have pursued the topic, such as asking the fellow next to him if Melissa was married. But this morning his mind was on more important matters than pretty women. Granted, Maris Wyler was damned attractive, but her looks weren't the reason he couldn't stop thinking about her. His stomach cramped every time he thought of hounding a woman for money, even though there was no other way to collect on that IOU.

He mentally counted the cash in his wallet—two twenties, a ten and three ones. Fifty-three bucks. In a secret compartment in the wallet was also an old, sharply creased hundred-dollar bill. That bill had been in that compartment for at least seven years, which was the last time Luke had been down to nothing. The first money he'd earned after being dead broke for nearly two weeks, he had folded that hundred and secreted it in that compartment, and ever since, knowing it was there had given him a modicum of security.

But that was all the money he had left, one hundred and fifty-three bucks, and the thought of using that hundred gave him a sinking sensation, as though he were going down for the count.

He *had* to collect that three thousand.

"Ready to order, mister?"

Startled, Luke looked up at the waitress. He'd been staring at the menu without absorbing anything written on it. "Uh...ham and eggs and some hash-brown potatoes. And coffee."

"Sure thing. How do you want your eggs?"

"Over easy."

"And what kind of toast? There's wheat, rye, white and sourdough."

"Sourdough."

The waitress stuck her pencil behind her ear and smiled. "I'll get your coffee. Your order will be up in a few minutes."

"Thanks."

"Bread's homemade," Luke's neighbor remarked. "Melissa turned this old place into a fine eating establishment."

A cup of coffee was set in front of Luke. "Thanks," he said to the waitress, then turned to his neighbor and offered his hand. "Luke Rivers."

"John Tully. I own the drugstore between here and the boarding house."

John Tully was around fifty, Luke figured, with a balding head and smelling of antiseptic. "Know of any jobs in the area?" Luke asked.

Mr. Tully frowned. "Well...can't think of anything right off. What kind of work are you looking for?"

Though he had initiated it, the topic depressed Luke. He didn't want a job, damn it, he wanted his three thousand dollars so he could get back on the rodeo circuit. "Ranch work," he said grimly.

"In that case you shouldn't have a problem. There are a lot of ranches around Whitehorn. Let's see now. You might try the Kincaid place first—it's the biggest. Then there's the Walker ranch, and Wyatt North's spread, and . . ." The man's eyes lit up. "Hey, I bet you could get a job at the Circle W." Then he started to chuckle.

Luke couldn't see that anything funny had been said, so he took a swallow of coffee—very good coffee, he realized—and gave Tully a chance to simmer down.

Then he stiffened. The Circle W was Ray Wyler's ranch! *Maris* Wyler's ranch, he reminded himself with an inward wince.

John Tully stopped laughing, though his round, chubby face still bore an amused grin. "You couldn't know, being new and all, but Mrs. Wyler changed the name of her ranch right after her husband died." For a moment Tully's grin vanished. "Fatal highway accident. Tragic business." His smile returned. "Anyhow, she took down the old Circle W sign and put up one that says No Bull Ranch. It's got everyone around here trying to figure out what she means by that name." Tully chuckled again. "No Bull Ranch. Could signify a lot of things, couldn't it?"

Luke wasn't laughing. "Could mean there's no bull on the place."

"Or no man?" Tully suggested with a masculine twinkle in his eye.

The waitress delivered Luke's breakfast. "Here you are, sir. Enjoy."

Luke picked up his fork, wondering why he hadn't seen that sign yesterday. He'd found the Wyler ranch by asking directions from a gas-station attendant in town, and he'd been anxious to see Ray. Then, too, maybe the sign wasn't in a prominent location. At any rate, he'd missed it completely, and besides, he didn't think it was nearly as funny as John Tully did.

"Anyway," Tully continued, "Mrs. Wyler is undoubtedly in need of a good ranch hand. You might speak to her about a job."

"Yeah, I might. Thanks." Luke was glad to see John Tully picking up his check.

"Nice talking to you, Luke. Be seeing you again, I'm sure."

"Probably will," Luke muttered as the chatty druggist walked away. He dug into his food, which was hot and as tasty as any ham and eggs he'd ever eaten. Out of the corner of his eye he could see John Tully paying his check and talking to Melissa Avery, who was tending the cash register.

Depressed again, Luke concentrated on his food. He was just finishing up, when the café's door opened for another customer.

"Hi, Judd," Melissa called from the opposite end of the counter, where she had sat down for her own breakfast, a cup of coffee, a glass of orange juice and a plate of toast.

Luke paid no attention to the newcomer until someone else greeted him. "Hello, Sheriff." Then Luke slowly swiveled on his stool to get a look at the man Maris Wyler had used to threaten him with yesterday. So, he thought dryly, that tall, dark, muscular lawman was Maris's personal friend. That was what she had said. *The sheriff is a personal friend.*

For some reason Luke's lips thinned, probably because he didn't like the sheriff at first sight and it made no sense. Grabbing his check, he ambled past the sheriff, who was heading for an empty stool, and stopped at the cash register.

Melissa hurried over. "I hope you enjoyed your meal."

Laying down the check and his ten-spot, Luke looked directly into her stunning blue eyes. "It was the best breakfast I ever had."

Melissa smiled. "That's what we like to hear." She rang up the sale and gave Luke his change.

Remembering that he hadn't left a tip, Luke walked back to where he'd been sitting and dropped a dollar on the counter.

Then he sauntered out of the Hip Hop as though he hadn't a care in the world, just in case Melissa Avery was watching.

As he climbed into his pickup, however, his dark mood returned and Ms. Avery was completely forgotten. Sighing heavily, he started the engine and tried very hard to resign himself to making the rounds of the local ranches to inquire about work.

Right now life stunk. Big time.

Luke did a lot of driving. The Kincaid ranch was seventeen miles northwest of Whitehorn; the Walker ranch lay twenty-five miles west; and the North ranch was in the opposite direction entirely, thirty-five miles east. Then he crossed Interstate 90 and took a look at the Bain spread. When he turned around and reached the interstate again, he pulled his pickup to the side of the road. He'd found the major ranches in the area without too much trouble, but he hadn't stopped at even one and asked about a job.

All during the driving and the looking he'd been doing some heavy-duty thinking. John Tully was right; Maris Wyler *did* need a good ranch hand. He himself had realized yesterday that she needed someone with the know-how to break those broncs. If he had any genuine talent, Luke knew, it was in working with horses. He'd grown up on a ranch in Texas and there'd been plenty of green horses to train to the saddle. Of course, he'd loved rodeo a whole lot more than ranch work, and once he was old enough to take off on his own, he'd pretty much left the Rivers ranch to his parents.

Then his father died. He'd been notified and had made a mad dash for home. His mother was naturally devastated, but within a month she was pretty much her old self and noticing her son's increasing restlessness.

"I know you want to get on with your own life, Luke, so it probably won't bother you none that I'm selling the ranch and moving to town. Am I wrong in that assumption?"

He'd been so relieved that his knees had gotten weak. "That's a great idea, Ma. Just great."

Lila Rivers had smiled wryly. "That's what I thought."

Luke saw his mother about once a year. His visits always co-incided with the rodeos scheduled in East Texas, but Lila never seemed to mind. Once in a while, though, she made subtle references to him getting married and settling down like the rest of the world. Luke's standard response was always a big laugh, a hug for his mother and a cocky "Heck, Ma, think of all the unhappy gals there'd be out there if I settled down with just one."

Though he was thirty-five years old, settling down wasn't in Luke's plans, certainly not in his immediate future. The thought of tying himself to a steady job actually pained him, but he was in a financial bind and had to do something. Still, he'd driven on past a half-dozen ranches today. He might have a job right now if he could get Maris Wyler, her unbroken horses and that three thousand dollars out of his mind.

Sitting alongside that vacant stretch of road, with the interstate on ramp no more than a hundred feet ahead, Luke pondered his options. His things were in the back of the pickup, and he could kiss goodbye that three thousand and leave Whitehorn and Maris Wyler in the dust right now. The interstate went west to Butte and east to Billings. He could find out where and when the next scheduled rodeo with any kind of decent purses would take place in either city.

So...why in hell didn't he do that? Why fight with a woman over money? Why worry about her being straddled with a hundred wild broncs and, apparently, no money to hire someone to break them?

He rubbed his mouth and then his jaw, scowling intently. He tugged on his left ear and glared at the interstate, at the traffic it bore, the eighteen-wheelers hauling freight, the motor homes, the pickups and cars.

After about ten minutes of deciding first one way and then another, he muttered a vicious curse, slapped the shifting lever into Drive and took off.

He drove under the interstate and headed back for Whitehorn.


Maris had been bending over and pulling weeds from her vegetable garden for at least two hours. Straightening her back with a muffled groan of relief, she wiped her sweaty forehead with the back of her forearm and eyed the neat rows of weed-free plants. A garden was always a must for Maris, but this year's crop was going to see her and Keith through the winter and seemed more important than usual. She would can and freeze everything that was possible to can and freeze, and come fall she would have Keith haul one of the steers to Grayson's Meat Packing Plant, which would supply them with beef to eat with the vegetables. They would make it through the winter— providing, of course, she managed to scare up enough cash to meet the mortgage payments on the ranch each month.

The movements of the horses in their pasture drew Maris's attention, and she chewed on her lip while considering their present value, certainly not for the first time. Unbroken, they might bring a hundred dollars apiece, and there were ninety-three horses. Finding buyers for ninety-three unbroken horses in the Whitehorn area was a fantasy, however, so anticipating ninety-three-hundred dollars was nothing more than a futile exercise.

Besides, they were fine animals, and with the proper training should be worth at least five times that amount. She had been delaying asking around about a good horse trainer, because anyone with experience and knowledge was bound to come high, and where would she get the money to pay his or her wage? It was a vicious circle, Maris decided bitterly for about the hundredth time in the past several weeks. No money, no trainer. No trainer, no money. Why in God's name had Ray thought selling the cattle to buy a herd of green horses made sense? That was what he'd done, with absolutely no warning—sold their best cattle and used the money to buy those horses. Maris hadn't understood Ray's motive for doing something so impractical at the time and she still couldn't figure it out.

"Maris, look what I found!"

It was Keith, and Maris turned around to see him coming toward her with a scruffy, skinny black dog on his heels. "You *found* a dog?" she said dryly. "Where?"

Keith shrugged. "She just showed up out of nowhere. Maybe someone dropped her off on the road."

People did that, Maris knew, just stopped their cars and kicked a poor little kitten or dog out to fend for itself. A stray of that nature raised her hackles. Some pet owners behaved abominably.

She left the garden to inspect the pitiful dog. The animal cringed and trembled and then lay down with its head on its paws. "She's skinny as a rail," Maris said angrily. "Keith, go into the house and fix a bowl of bread and warm milk. This poor little dog might even be too weak to eat, but we'll give it a try."

Uncertain about touching the sad-eyed pooch until it knew her better, Maris sat down in the grass to await Keith's return. "Life dealt you a dirty blow, too, huh, girl?" The dog's tail weakly thumped the grass. "You'd like to be friends, wouldn't you? Well, maybe we will be." Maris shook her head in dismay. The last thing she needed right now was another mouth to feed, particularly one that couldn't possibly benefit the ranch.

But chasing off a poor hungry animal just wasn't in her. She pulled off her canvas garden gloves and examined her dirty, broken fingernails. "Might as well go without gloves," she mumbled dejectedly.

It was just that everything seemed to get her down these days, and she realized that she could easily shed tears over that sad little dog and her own work-worn hands.

Keith came striding up. "Here we go, girl." He set the bowl down in front of the dog, but the little pooch just lay there listlessly. "Come on, girl, you have to eat."

Keith, Maris saw, wasn't at all wary of the dog, as she'd been, and he scooped up a piece of milk-soaked bread from the bowl and held it to the dog's mouth. The animal's tongue flicked to wipe it away, and then she seemed to realize what it was. Struggling to her feet, she stuck her nose in the bowl and began eating.

"That's it, girl," Keith said soothingly. "Eat it all up."

"She probably needs water, too," Maris said while getting to her feet. After locating an old pan in the toolshed, she returned to fill it with water from the garden spigot and brought it to the dog.

"She didn't eat all the bread and milk," Keith said.

"She'll probably finish it later. Here, girl, have a drink of water."

The dog lapped up some water, then lay down again. "Do you think she's sick, Maris?" Keith asked worriedly.

"I think she's half-starved, Keith. But she ate a little, and now she needs to rest. She'll probably be fine in a day or two."

Keith was on his knees next to the dog, petting its matted back. "She's real pretty, don't you think?"

Maris almost smiled. This piteous, bony mutt certainly wasn't pretty. But Keith had had so little love in his young life, and if he felt some fondness for the stray it was fine with Maris. "She'll be a handsome dog, once she's fattened up," she said agreeably.

They both heard the vehicle approaching the compound. Keith saw it first. "Oh-oh, guess who's back."

Maris turned to see Luke Rivers's pickup pulling to a stop near her own truck. Her face turned stony. "Great. Another go-around with that man will certainly complete my day."

"Want me to talk to him?" Keith asked, willing, as always, to help Maris whenever he could.

"Thanks, but I think I'd better do it myself. Apparently he hasn't given up on that IOU Ray gave him." Maris had been sitting on the grass again, and she pushed herself up to her feet. "Do this for me, Keith. Stay within listening distance, and if Mr. Rivers gets too belligerent, call Judd and ask him to come out here, on the double."

Keith's youthful features turned hard right in front of Maris's eyes. "Do you think he'll try something funny, Maris? If he does, I'm gonna tear into him."

"No, Keith, no! Just do as I said about calling Judd. Luke Rivers is twice your size, and I don't want you getting hurt."

"Size ain't everything," Keith mumbled. "I ain't scared of him just 'cause he's bigger."

"I know you're not. If it makes you feel any better, I'm not scared of him, either. It's just that I'm not going to be harassed every day by Luke Rivers. If that's going to be the case, then Judd should be brought in to set him straight. Do you understand what I'm saying?"

"Guess so," Keith said rather sullenly. He wanted to protect Maris, and *would* protect Maris from any threat or danger. Calling the sheriff probably made good sense, but he wished Maris would realize that he wasn't a helpless little kid.

Drawing a deep breath, Maris detoured around the garden and walked toward the parking area of the ranch, where Luke was getting out of his truck.

"Before you start yelling," he said with the same scowl he'd worn all day, "give me a chance to say one thing, okay?"

"If that one thing is about Ray's IOU, the answer is no," Maris said flatly.

"It's not. Well, in a way it is, but mostly it's about something else."

Maris folded her arms. "Very well. Shoot."

Clearing his throat, Luke turned his gaze on the horse pasture. "You need someone to break those horses and I need a job. Here's my offer." His eyes connected with Maris's. "You give me room, board and a few bucks a week, and I'll put a smile on every one of those horses' faces. Some of them look to me like good cutting stock, which will take more work than the others. But when they're all broken to the saddle and acting as sweet as sugar, you'll get a good price for them. Then you pay me the three thousand, give me my pick of the lot for a bonus, and I'll get out of your hair for good."

Maris was slightly stunned. "Seems to me your offer is pretty heavily weighted in your favor. Why should you end up with the best horse in the herd, which I'm sure would be the case?"

"Because you won't have to pay me during the breaking process, except for a place to sleep, meals and, like I said, a few bucks a week so I've got a little spending money. Look, you already owe me the three thousand, so you can't count that as pay. The horse would be my fee for doing the job."

Maris stood with her arms folded across her chest, frowning at this overbearing man and his outrageous offer.

But was it really that outrageous? As he'd said, he was already owed the three thousand, although she really hadn't intended to pay that debt of Ray's. But fair was fair, and that aspect of Luke's offer wasn't out of line. There were other considerations, however.

"How do I know you can do the job?" she asked.

"Because I'm telling you I can," Luke said gruffly. "I grew up on a ranch. I understand horses and I'm damned good with them."

Luke's macho confidence annoyed Maris. Ray had thought he'd been an expert in every possible field, when, in fact, his knowledge on any given subject had been extremely limited. Luke Rivers could be the same kind of person, all bluster and brag.

"How long would it take?" Maris asked, unable to keep the suspicion and doubt in her system from influencing her tone of voice.

Luke heard the suspicion but ignored it. Again his gaze went across the fence to the grazing horses. "There are about a hundred horses..."

"Ninety-three."

"All right, ninety-three." Luke did some figuring in his head. Breaking a horse took time and patience, but a handler didn't pull only one animal out of a herd and work solely with it until it accepted humans and their commands. He would be working with seven, eight horses a day—one at a time, of course. Some would break easily and require only a few sessions; some would be stubborn, balky and mean and require dozens of repetitive sessions. But he knew how to spot the outlaws and would begin with the more docile animals. The whole thing shouldn't take more than ten weeks.

"I'll be out of here by the end of September," he told Maris.

Her eyes widened. "Less than three months?"

Luke nodded. "That's fact, not boast. By the end of September those horses will be ready to sell." The corner of his mouth turned up in a crooked half smile. "Maybe you can throw a big whoop-de-do and have an auction."

"An auction," she repeated slowly, though her blood was definitely flowing faster from Luke's promises and comments. An auction would be a dramatic way to sell her horses. She could advertise the event all over the area, using the newspaper and strategically placed signs.

But jumping into anything, however good it sounded, wasn't her nature. "Let me think about it overnight," she said.

Aw, hell, thought Luke. "Overnight" meant laying down another thirty bucks for a motel room.

"Come back in the morning and I'll give you an answer," Maris added.

Frustration made standing still impossible for Luke. He walked a small circle, rubbing the back of his neck, then took a breath and began again. "What's the problem? Do you think I can't do it?"

"I only have your word on that, don't I?"

"That's all you'll have in the morning, too. Maris, today was the pits. I drove about two hundred miles looking at the other ranches around Whitehorn, trying to work up the desire to ask one of them for a job. I *need* a job, but I don't want a job. Do you get my drift? This arrangement would benefit both of us. Your horses would be salable by the end of September, and I could get back to what I do best."

"Rodeo," Maris said, icicles dripping from every syllable.
Her tone stunned Luke. "Something wrong with rodeo?"

"Too many things to mention."

"But Ray—"

"Loved it, just as you seem to do. Forget it. Your prefer-
ences are none of my affair, nor are my attitudes of any interest to you. Getting back to your offer, I really do need tonight
to think about it."

Luke's face hardened. "Fine. But would you mind if I bedded down in your barn while you're doing your thinking?"

"In my barn! You mean spend the night in there?"

"I have a bedroll."

Maris took a breath. Was he *that* broke? The boarding house
in town didn't charge exorbitant rates, and she knew there was
a little motel on the road to the interstate. But if he didn't even
have enough money to pay for a room for the night . . . ?

She groaned inwardly. Two strays in one afternoon. Keith
was still sitting beside his half-starved friend, petting the dog's
head and back, and now this, Luke Rivers asking to sleep in her
barn because he couldn't afford the cost of a room.

"Fine," she said tiredly. "You can stay. But you don't have
to use your bedroll. There's a room in the loft of the barn with
a bed, and a small bathroom. I'll have Keith show you the
way."

Shaking her head, Maris turned and walked away. Watching her go, Luke admitted total and complete perplexity about
Maris Wyler. She was wearing cutoff jeans, an old T-shirt and
sneakers, and the dirt on her clothing, hands and legs evi-
denced a day of hard work. For certain she wasn't the kind of
woman Luke was usually drawn to. Melissa Avery, with her
gorgeous blue eyes and long dark hair was much more his type.
But it was Maris he felt in his loins, not Melissa. How in hell did
a man figure that one out?

Well . . . at least he had a free bed for the night. And maybe
by morning Maris would realize what a good deal he had offered her.

Like he'd said, it would benefit both of them.

# Three

Maris did give Luke's offer a lot of thought that night, and there was one aspect of the arrangement that kept popping into her mind and turning her off on the deal: the fact that Luke Rivers, rodeo bum, would be living on the ranch. Forcing herself to remember the details of that night in the bar in Casper, she finally recalled the woman who had to have been Luke's date for the evening—a vivacious young blonde wearing tight, tight jeans and a low-cut blouse that displayed her ample cleavage. It was a disturbing image, indicating quite clearly the type of woman Luke Rivers preferred.

The problem, of course, was that she had no alternative solutions to choose over Luke's. If Luke wasn't just bragging and throwing his machismo around and he actually got those horses ready for sale by the end of September, her financial worries would vanish in the fall. Or most of them, at least.

Maris walked the floor half the night. There was so much to consider. Money for this, money for that. Putting the ranch up for sale had occurred to her, of course, but she loved the place, which had been in Ray's family for several generations. Ray had been the first Wyler in decades who hadn't been completely contented with his lot as a rancher. There'd been a restlessness in Ray, Maris had always known, some kind of inner force that made him seek excitement . . . such as the rodeo circuit . . . and gambling . . . and other women.

Despondent at the turn of her thoughts, Maris snapped off the light, crawled into bed and drew the covers up to her chin. A bright moon shone through the window, and she thought of Luke Rivers in that little loft bedroom. Did she want him in that room every night for weeks and weeks? Did she want him at the table with her and Keith, meal after meal? Then her thoughts flipped. Was she judging Luke too harshly because he reminded her of Ray? Oh, not in looks, for pity's sake. The two men looked nothing alike. Ray had been a slight man, not much taller than her, with light hair and pale brown eyes, and Luke was ... Luke was ...

Well, he was just too darned good-looking, that's what he was. And he made her ... uncomfortable. Yes, that was the word. Luke Rivers made her *very* uncomfortable. Now, why do you suppose that was? she thought with a perplexed frown. Certainly he wasn't apt to make a pass when he preferred leggy blondes with overdeveloped chests.

That entire subject was unnerving to Maris. Punching her pillow into a different shape, she grumpily told herself to put Luke Rivers out of her mind and get some sleep.

Luke didn't sleep well, either. His mind wouldn't shut down, and nearly everyone he'd ever known paraded through his brain. The specter that bothered him the most was the one of Ray Wyler. Why in heck had Ray bought so many unbroken horses? Luke was positive Ray hadn't been an experienced handler, and Ray's personality had been erratic and sometimes downright unstable. Luke would bet anything that Ray's idea of breaking horses had been to tie down the animal, throw a saddle on its back and ride it to exhaustion. He probably would have used the whip on the balky ones, too, beating them into submission. Luke hated cruelty to animals, and more than once had stepped between a man with a whip and a horse.

It was odd then the way his thoughts moved from Ray Wyler and horses to Ray Wyler and Maris. But Luke had seen for himself how Ray had treated Maris. The embarrassing episode in that Casper tavern could have been an isolated incident for the Wylers, but Luke really didn't think so.

Maris puzzled him. She conveyed determined independence and female vulnerability, both at the same time, and he'd be willing to bet that she'd huff up and do battle with anyone who dared to mention her vulnerability. Maybe she wasn't even aware of it herself.

Luke had one more point to ponder about Maris Wyler. He had the impression that Ray's fatal accident hadn't happened that long ago, but she honestly didn't appear to be a grieving widow. True, she had a lot to deal with—the ranch, very little money and no help other than Keith. But she had told him about Ray's accident without a dram of emotion, and wouldn't a woman who had loved her husband be devastated for months after his death?

On the other hand, his own mother hadn't mourned openly for any great length of time after his father had died, and Luke was positive his parents had had a good and happy marriage. Maybe some women recovered more quickly than others. Or maybe they did their crying when they were alone.

He frowned at the possibility of Maris crying into her pillow after dark when no one could see her. The idea of her crying at all was surprisingly discomfiting.

"Aw, hell," he mumbled, and turned to his side to get more comfortable. Maris Wyler's emotions or lack thereof were none of his business. All he wanted from her was an agreement on the deal he'd offered. She wasn't all that great, anyway. Hadn't she let him drive to town for supper, rather than inviting him in to eat with her and Keith?

That was all he wanted from Maris Wyler, he thought again, getting drowsy, an agreement on his offer. Then he would break her horses, collect his three thousand dollars, pick himself a good cutting horse out of the herd and leave the Wyler ranch and Whitehorn, Montana, for good.

He'd be back on the rodeo circuit in October. It was a satisfying thought to fall asleep with.

Keith was preparing to leave the kitchen with a bowl of bread and milk for the stray dog, which had been bedded down on an old blanket in the toolshed.

Maris was stirring a pot of oatmeal on the stove. "Keith, please go by the barn and tell Luke that he's welcome to join us for breakfast."

"Okay." Keith stopped at the door. "Uh . . . are you gonna take his deal?"

Maris hesitated, then nodded. "I think so." She threw a hopefully brave smile at her young friend. "It's the only game in town right now, Keith."

"Yeah, guess it is."

From the kitchen window, Maris watched Keith go into the toolshed with the dog's breakfast. Before he came out again, she spotted Luke walking from the barn. "At least you're not a slugabed," she mumbled. It wasn't yet 6:00 a.m., and Luke's early appearance was a good sign.

Keith came out of the toolshed with the stray pooch on his heels. Luke veered directions to meet the boy halfway. "'Morning, Keith. Who's your friend?"

Bending over, Keith scratched the dog's ears. "I don't know her name. She's a stray. Someone probably dropped her off on the highway. She looks a lot better this morning than she did last night."

Luke grinned down at the scruffy animal. "Looks like she could use a bath."

Keith straightened. "Yeah, she does. I'm hoping Maris will let me keep her. I'd buy her food with my own money."

Luke could see that the boy was fond of the motley little mutt. "Can't think of any reason why Maris wouldn't let her stay."

Keith suddenly remembered what Maris had asked him to do. "You're invited to breakfast." Keith's cheeks got pink. "If you wanna eat with us, that is."

"Sure, thanks."

"Come on in, then. Breakfast was almost done when I came outside a few minutes ago."

Luke followed Keith into the house. The dog tried to follow, as well, but Keith stopped her at the door. "Stay, girl," he said, and the little dog sat down next to the steps.

"'Morning, Maris," Luke said. She was dressed in worn jeans and a white T-shirt, and she looked as fresh as the morning dew. He caught himself staring at her pretty, sun-streaked hair and abruptly turned his gaze.

"Good morning. Everything's ready. You two go ahead and sit down while I pour the coffee."

Luke waited until Keith sat at his place, then decided that the one nearest the stove would be Maris's spot at the table and sat in the third chair. In front of him was a large bowl of steaming oatmeal, a glass of orange juice and a cup awaiting coffee. The center of the table contained a pitcher of milk, a sugar bowl, a jar of peanut butter, a small bowl of jam—strawberry, it looked like—and a plate heaped with toast.

Maris came around the table and filled his cup with coffee, then went to her place and poured her own. Keith, Luke noted, had a glass for milk along with his glass of orange juice.

Maris took her seat. "Dig in," she said while looking at Luke. "It's not fancy but it's filling."

"It looks... great." Oatmeal was not his favorite breakfast food, but he would never say so. Maris got up to switch on the small radio on the counter. "For the weather report," she explained, resuming her place at the table.

They ate with very little conversation. Keith, Maris realized, was shy around Luke, and since she couldn't think of any small talk that made sense, they mostly listened to the morning news and finally the weather report. "Scattered clouds, with the temperature reaching ninety degrees. A great day, folks."

Keith devoured the last toast on the plate after slathering it with strawberry jam, then got up and carried his dishes to sink. "Want me to work on those fences again today, Maris?"

"Later, Keith." Maris stood up and began gathering her own dishes. "First I'd like you to drive to town and buy that skinny dog some regular dog food."

Keith's face broke out in a big grin. "Then she can stay?"

She smiled. "I think we need a dog on the place, don't you?"

"Yeah, I sure do."

"Remember, though, Keith, someone might come along and claim her. She could have merely strayed away from home on her own."

"I'll remember. I've been thinking up names for her, but I bet she's been called 'Blackie.' What do you think?"

"Seems appropriate," Maris said with a laugh. She dug out a ten-dollar bill from a pocket in her jeans and held it out to Keith.

"I'll buy her food, Maris," Keith said with a prideful lift of his chin. "I'd like to do it."

She studied the young boy. Keith's eyes contained a joyful light that touched her deeply. Nodding, she tucked the ten back into her pocket. "Drive carefully."

"I will. And thanks, Maris." Keith grabbed his big hat from the hook by the door and eagerly bounded out.

Luke started to get up and Maris reached for the coffeepot. "We need to talk. Would you like more coffee?"

He'd been wondering when she would get around to telling him her decision. Sinking back to his chair, Luke nodded. "Yes, thanks."

After their cups were refilled, Maris sat down and regarded Luke across the table. Impersonally, she hoped, since impersonal was the only way she wanted their relationship. "I'm going to accept your offer, if you accept my conditions."

His hopes ignited. "What are they?" he asked casually, pretending that his gut wasn't tied in a knot. This deal was maybe the most important of his life, the new start he desperately needed.

Looking directly at Luke's handsome face made Maris nervous, and she dropped her gaze to the table in front of her. "No drinking on the place. Not even beer. And should you overindulge somewhere else, don't come back here to sleep it off."

"Agreed," Luke said quietly. He wasn't much of a drinker— a few beers once in a while—so this condition was no hardship. "What else?"

"No women." Maris's face colored. "I mean, of course, no women on the ranch. What you do in your own time is of no concern to me. I just don't want you bringing a woman here. Keith is at an impressionable age, and—"

Luke broke in brusquely. "Don't worry about it. There won't be any women."

"Fine. Thank you," she said stiffly. "I won't expect you to work seven days a week, but I would like as much of your time spent working with the horses as you can manage."

"I don't need any days off. I probably will work seven days a week." He leaned forward slightly. "Maris, I want this job over and done with as soon as possible. Don't worry about me goofing off when I should be working."

"You want it over with so you can get back to rodeo," she said tonelessly.

"I know you don't like rodeo, but I'm not going to be embarrassed every time it comes up in conversation. It's what I do, Maris, what I've done since I was old enough to leave home."

Maris mustered up a shrug. "It's nothing to me." Her gaze sought Luke's across the table. "Well . . . do we have a deal then?"

"We do as far as I'm concerned." Relieved and elated that it had gone so easily, Luke shaped a tentative smile. "Should we shake hands on it?"

Maris got to her feet and began clearing the table. "I don't think that's necessary. We've struck a bargain and I'm sure we'll both abide by it."

Luke stood up. "If it's okay with you I'd like to look around the ranch. Snoop through the barn and the other buildings and take stock of what equipment you have."

"Do whatever you think necessary." At the sink Maris rinsed her hands and picked up a towel to dry them. "Wait a minute. There is one point we haven't discussed."

Luke was already on his way to the door. He stopped and turned. "What's that?"

"Your wage. You said something about a few dollars a week. I think we should agree on the amount, don't you?"

Luke tugged at his ear. "Well...yeah, guess we should. I was thinking about fifty a week. Is that all right with you?"

Maris's stomach sank and her face flushed to a dark crimson. "I...can't pay fifty a week."

This aspect of their discussion didn't set right with Luke. Pressuring a woman for money made him feel like a damned parasite. The only thing he really needed money for was gas for his pickup, and he probably had enough in his wallet to keep him going until the job was done.

"Let's forget that part of the deal," he said, wishing he hadn't mentioned a wage at all yesterday. He'd embarrassed her by suggesting fifty bucks a week, and he realized that he didn't like embarrassing her.

But Maris shook her head rather adamantly. "No, a deal's a deal. I can't pay fifty a week, but I can pay..." She hesitated, praying to God he wouldn't be insulted by such a paltry sum. "Twenty-five."

Luke saw the pride in her pretty golden eyes, the independence, whether natural or forced by circumstances, and he vowed on the spot to do the best job possible and pray that the sale of those horses would make things easier for her.

"Twenty-five is fine. Thanks."

Maris breathed a quiet sigh of relief. She was putting all of her eggs in one basket by relying on Luke Rivers, and only time would prove her right or wrong.

But even if he was all brag and bluster and she ended up with only half-broken horses, would she be much worse off than she was today?

Luke gave one sharp, definitive nod of his head. "Guess that's it then. I'll go to work now."

"Yes, go ahead," Maris said faintly as he again started for the door.

This time he stopped on his own. "I have a condition, too, Maris."

Startled, she looked at him. "What is it?"

"It's this. I know what I'm doing with horses, and I don't want you or anyone else interfering with my methods."

"Oh." *His* condition riled her. This was her ranch, after all, and her horses. A noticeable coolness crept into her voice. "I'm sure no one will interfere. If I knew how to do the job I wouldn't need you at all, would I?"

"Good point. See you later." Luke left the kitchen and went outside. The first thing he did was suck in a huge gulp of fresh air. Making a business deal with a woman was an unnerving undertaking. Walking to the barn, he remembered that he'd never worked for a woman before, other than his mother.

But then, he hadn't worked for men very much, either. His entire life had been dedicated to rodeo, and there'd been five, six years back a ways that he was damned proud of. He'd won lots of money and earned a slew of trophies. Luke frowned. The money was gone, his mother had the trophies and thirty-five was an iffy age in the arena. He was paying the price of too many bad falls and this latest accident. Every morning he awoke with some new ache in his bones he'd fight to ignore. Some cowpokes seemed to go on forever, but most of the competitors were young, tough and full of vinegar. But what the hell else would he do if he didn't jump back into the rodeo circuit?

Grim-lipped, he decided that he couldn't worry about his age, or his aching bones. What the young guys lacked he had plenty of, and that crucial component was called experience. And he also had a reputation, a damned *good* reputation. Once he got hold of another great cutting horse, though there would probably never be another Pancho, he'd do all right. The steer-roping event had always been his specialty, and he'd rise to the top again with the right horse. He'd find the right horse in Maris's herd, and he'd train him to perfection exactly as he'd done with Pancho.

Feeling better about his future, Luke walked into the barn.

Maris did the dishes and tidied the kitchen, moving at a snail's pace. Ordinarily the job took no more than ten minutes; this morning she fiddled around for a good half-hour.

But the arrangement with Luke changed everything, and she kept thinking of the additional cooking, the extra food to buy and how strange it felt to have a man like Luke living on the ranch. How would he and Keith get along? How would *she* and Luke get along? She felt disruptive undercurrents when she was with him, odd little sensations within herself that she couldn't pin down.

Maris stopped at the clean and shiny sink to stare out the window. What should be her chores for the day? What was Luke looking for down at the barn? Equipment, he'd said, but what sort of equipment? She should have asked, and maybe saved him some time and effort by explaining that she did or did not have what he needed.

Deciding that she could water her garden while lining out her day, she went outside to the garden area. She had just gotten started with the water hose, when she heard a vehicle approaching. It couldn't be Keith back so soon, she thought, and turned off the spigot to walk around the house to see who was coming.

Smiling at the sight of Judd's official black utility vehicle she continued walking to greet him as he got out. "'Morning, Judd."

"'Morning, Maris."

Judd was a tall, dark and mostly silent man. Since Ray's death he had stopped in quite a few times, and Maris appreciated his thoughtfulness. Twice he had asked her out for supper and they'd eaten at the Hip Hop Café. The evenings had been pleasant diversions, and Maris recognized and admired Judd's strong and honest outlook on life. He was everything

Ray hadn't been—a complete opposite, to be perfectly accurate. A woman could do a lot worse than to take up with Judd Hensley.

"Everything all right on the Wyler ranch?" Judd asked.

Maris laughed with some wryness. "As right as can be expected."

But Judd, she saw, had become more interested in Luke's pickup than in her answer and was giving it a thorough once-over. "Got company?"

"A hired man, Judd. He's going to break the horses."

"Anyone I know?"

"I doubt it. He's not from Montana. Actually, he knew Ray and came here to—" Maris stopped short of blurting out the whole story. That old IOU really wasn't anyone else's business. "See Ray." Maris's voice became quieter. "He didn't know Ray was gone."

"Too bad," Judd said. "Must be hard on you to tell old friends about it." Judd was still looking at Luke's pickup, which he was sure he'd seen in town yesterday. "What's this guy's name?"

"Luke Rivers. He knew Ray from the rodeo, Judd. That's what he does ordinarily." Maris could see Judd's wheels turning and decided to change the subject. Her financial situation really wasn't open for discussion, and as of this morning, Luke Rivers and her pitifully small bank account were oddly intermingled.

"Any news on that man who died at Mary Jo and Dugan's wedding?" she asked.

"He didn't just die, Maris. He was murdered."

"Murdered!" Maris's eyes got very big. "But I heard he was a stranger. Why would anyone murder a total stranger? And how come he was at the wedding in the first place? People don't usually crash weddings."

"All we've been able to discover so far is that his name was Floyd Oakley. Neither Mary Jo nor Dugan admit to inviting him to the wedding, so maybe he was just a transient looking for a free meal. We're working on it. That makes two strangers in our little town now, doesn't it? Floyd Oakley and Luke Rivers."

Appalled at Judd's implication, Maris rushed to defend Luke. "Oh, but Luke didn't arrive until after the wedding, Judd."

Judd cocked an eyebrow. "Maybe he didn't show his face out here right away. Maybe he'd been hanging around town for several weeks. Mind if I talk to him?"

Maris drew a nervous breath. "Well, no, of course not, but..." She couldn't believe that Luke could be a murderer. As hard-nosed as Luke could be, the idea struck her as utterly preposterous. But Judd Hensley wasn't a man to waltz around on a subject, either. She could see on his stern face that he was determined to talk to her new hired man. She wondered if Judd really suspected Luke, or was simply feeling protective of her and maybe even rankled at the news that a stranger was going to be living on the ranch.

"He's in the barn, Judd. Let me run down there and get him."

"No...let's just walk down to the barn together," Judd said calmly.

"Uh . . . fine. That's fine." All sorts of things ran through Maris's mind during the short trek. Luke *had* come directly to the No Bull Ranch when he'd gotten to the area, hadn't he? But what if he hadn't? Would his presence in the area at the time of that murder automatically make him a suspect?

Uneasily she led Judd into the barn, calling "Luke? Are you in here?"

Luke stepped out of the tack room with a bridle in his hand. "Do you need me for something?" He saw the sheriff and involuntarily stiffened. "'Morning, Sheriff."

"Judd, this is Luke Rivers. Luke, Sheriff Judd Hensley."

They didn't shake hands. Maris sucked in an exasperated breath. It was all too obvious that Judd and Luke weren't going to be friends, though she wasn't vain enough to suppose their immediate animosity had anything to do with her. It was a male thing, she thought, an instantaneous clash of personalities.

"Didn't I see you in the Hip Hop yesterday morning?" Judd questioned evenly.

"I saw you," Luke replied. "So guess you could have seen me, too."

"How long you been in the area?"

"Three days. Why?" Luke looked at Maris for an explanation, but she was merely standing by and chewing on the inside of her bottom lip with a worried frown.

"You have proof of that, I suppose," Judd said.

"Proof? Why would I need proof? I drove into Whitehorn two days ago, asked directions to Ray Wyler's place at a gas station and came directly here. What's this all about, Sheriff?"

"We had a little trouble around here a few weeks back. Where were you on . . ." Judd named the date in late June of Mary Jo and Dugan's wedding.

Luke's forehead creased in thought. Then his expression cleared. "I was in Denver, visiting friends." It was the truth. After his release from the hospital, most of his recovery time had been spent in Texas. Then, with that IOU in mind, he had started working his way north to Montana. Since he'd been out of commission for nearly a year he had made several stops during the trip to see old friends.

Judd decided to believe him . . . for the time being. Floyd Oakley, if that was his real name, thus far seemed to be a man without a past. His wallet had been empty except for a few dollars, a snapshot of a woman and an outdated Wisconsin driver's license. That license had provided Oakley's name, but Judd has his suspicions about its authenticity. Of course Judd knew he was a naturally suspicious person.

Regardless, Oakley had been murdered in his jurisdiction, either by one of the wedding guests or by someone who had slipped into the group unnoticed, done his dirty deed and then slipped away again, and he intended to identify the culprit, whatever it took.

He spoke to Luke again. "Are you planning to make Whitehorn your home?"

Luke's voice was cold and unfriendly. "This is my home, but only until Maris's horses are broken and salable. I'll be moving on then."

Maris could tell that Judd didn't like Luke calling the No Bull home. But the belligerent look on Luke's face said rather plainly that he didn't like Judd Hensley period. It struck her that they were squaring off right before her eyes, as stubbornly and determinedly as two bulls did in the presence of a juicy young heifer. The only elements missing were the lowered heads, snorts and the pawings of the ground.

But it was so dumb. She certainly wasn't a juicy young heifer, not by any stretch of the imagination, and her relationship with Judd so far was only friendship. As for Luke, he couldn't even claim that. He was her employee and that was all he would ever be.

Maris cleared her throat, loudly, hoping these two macho men would get the picture that she wasn't very pleased with their attitudes. "Luke," she said deliberately, "are you finding the equipment you need to get started with the horses?"

Both men shifted their weight, breaking their staredown to look at her. Judd said, "Guess I'll be running along. You two have work to do."

"Yes, we do," Maris replied rather coolly.

But she walked Judd to his car. "Thanks for stopping by. You're welcome here anytime, Judd. I hope you know that."

Judd's dark eyes still contained suspicion. "How well do you know Rivers? You said he was Ray's friend, but did you know him, too, before he showed up?"

"I...knew him." It wasn't a total lie, Maris told herself. But she was not going to get into a long dissertation on when and how she and Luke had met. "Judd, I really don't think he's going to be any kind of problem."

Judd slid into his car. "Probably not, but just to be on the safe side, I'm going to check him out, see if he has a record. Anything's possible."

As the sheriff's car sped away, Maris heaved a sigh. Luke wasn't any fugitive from the law. Maris knew it instinctively. He was just a rodeo cowboy—one who was going to break her horses and help her get out from under a load of debt. She sure didn't need Judd chasing Luke out of town, at least not until his job was done.

# Four

Luke entered the horse pasture with a coiled rope clasped in his right hand and held down around his thigh. He walked slowly, studying the horses, looking for one with a gentle disposition. Horses had personalities just as people did. Some were meaner than rat poison and never would gentle down enough for a novice rider. Others were easily trained, and that was what he wanted to start with, an animal that wouldn't throw a fit at every step of the process.

He spotted a gray mare with good lines and a well-shaped head. She lifted her head when she became aware of Luke, and he got a clear, unobstructed look at her eyes, which were constant and calm with no white showing. Quick, darting eyes that displayed a large amount of white on a horse usually indicated a spooky, erratic animal.

Cautiously and slowly he moved closer to the mare, uncoiling the rope as he went. When she didn't bolt and run, as the other horses had been doing if he got too close, he began talking in a quiet, soothing voice. "There's a nice girl. Stay steady, girl. No one's going to harm you." The chant continued, soft and singsong, until Luke was within roping distance. He didn't move quickly until he threw the loop, and it landed precisely where he'd aimed it, squarely over the mare's head.

She squealed and reared in an attempt to get rid of the noose around her neck, but Luke dug in his heels, wound his end of the rope around his leather-gloved hands and hung on.

Maris was watching from outside the fence, utterly fascinated. Ray had practiced roping quite a lot, but he had never attained the expertise she had just witnessed. Luke began walking up the rope, getting closer to the mare. He was too far away for Maris to hear what he was saying, but she could tell he was talking to the horse. Gradually the mare calmed; gradually Luke got closer. When there was about six feet of rope between him and the animal, he started urging her to follow him. The mare took a step and stopped. Luke tugged lightly on the rope. "Come on, girl," he crooned. The mare took a few more steps, and then Maris shook her head in amazement: Luke was leading the mare toward the gate in the fence!

Quickly she ran over and opened the gate. Luke and the mare passed through it and she closed it again. Luke had left the corral gate open, and he led the mare into the corral as easily as anything Maris had ever seen. Though Luke had issued no instructions, other than for her to bring out a sack of apples, Maris closed and latched the corral gate.

"Toss me one of those apples," Luke said softly. Maris dug one out of the sack and threw it to Luke, who caught it deftly in his left hand. Using the apple as a bribe—the mare ate it directly out of his hand—he loosened the loop around the mare's neck and released her.

Recoiling the rope, Luke walked over to Maris. "This one's going to be easy. Give me a couple more of those apples." He stuck the apples in his shirt pockets, giving him the appearance of breasts and causing Maris to laugh.

Then he walked over to the section of corral rail where he'd earlier placed an old feed sack and slowly walked back to the mare. First he offered her another apple, which she willingly took from his hand, then he began tentatively and gently rubbing the sack over her neck. She turned her head, looked at him and snorted, but she stood still and let him rub her with the sack. Patiently he rubbed the sack over her hind quarters, her belly, her neck and finally her head.

"Why is she letting you do that?" Maris asked, keeping her voice down so she wouldn't startle the mare.

"Probably because it feels good," Luke said quietly. "Rubbing and touching is the first step to familiarity."

Maris equated his comment to humans and flushed hotly. She hadn't had any rubbing and touching for a long, long time. Ray had been gone so much, and during the year just prior to his death, he had seldom come near her. When he had, it had been quick and emotionless sex and she had received no pleasure from it. That mare was receiving more loving, tender, patient caresses right now than Maris Wyler had gotten in longer than she cared to remember.

And the man doing the caressing, the rubbing and the touching was truly a sight for any lonely woman's eyes. His wide shoulders stretched the seams of a blue chambray work shirt, and then his torso tapered to a flat, firm belly. Everything below his belt was equally magnificent—his tight behind, his long, muscular thighs. Oh, God, Maris thought frantically. Am I having a sexual fantasy in broad daylight? And about Luke Rivers?

Suddenly she felt as though she couldn't get enough air, and she hopped down from the corral fence where she had perched herself and walked away. As intriguing as watching Luke work was, it had set off something ridiculously sensual in her system, and the last thing she wanted was another rodeo man muddling up her life.

Keith drove into the yard at about the same time Maris reached the house. She veered directions to see Blackie jumping out of the pickup right behind Keith. "Everything go okay?" she called, glad of any diversion to get her mind off Luke.

From the back of the pickup Keith picked up a huge sack of dry dog food. "Everything went fine. How's it going here?"

"Luke's in the corral, working with the first horse, and Judd stopped by for a few minutes."

Keith swung his gaze to the corral and saw what was happening. "Luke's a fast worker."

"Could be," Maris agreed dryly, recalling her hot flash a few minutes ago. "Anyway, looks like you've got Blackie all set."

Keith hoisted the bag of dog food to his shoulder. "These large sacks were marked down. Thought I may as well take advantage of the sale."

"Put it in the toolshed," Maris called as Keith walked off with his twenty-pound burden.

"Okay," he called back. Blackie was no more than six inches behind her newly adopted master's bootheels. In watching the boy and dog, Maris nodded with fond approval. Keith had needed something of his very own, and maybe Blackie, stray, straggly little pooch that she was, was it.

Maris didn't immediately proceed into the house. Instead she stood with her hand splayed at the base of her throat and endured a peculiar throbbing in the pit of her stomach. Automatically her gaze slipped back to the corral and its occupants. Never would Luke throb over her, and her doing so over him was the height of foolishness, especially when she really wanted nothing but hard work from him. Actually, his deadline was rather ludicrous. How could any one person tame ninety-three wild horses in less than three months?

But that gray mare was responding incredibly well, she had to admit. Was Luke's touch special? He was still rubbing the animal, and talking to it. What was he saying? What magic was he breathing into that pretty mare's ears?

Sighing, slightly disgusted with her own lurid imagination, Maris turned her back on the corral, Luke Rivers and the mare. She had her own work to do . . . if she could only think of what it was.

By supper, Luke had moved the gray mare and three other horses into another pasture. Seated at the table with Keith and Luke, Maris said, "Please explain why you're moving the horses." She paused then added, "And don't take my curiosity as interference."

Luke looked at her sharply, then nodded. "Right. I'm picking out the calmest horses from the herd, one by one. Today's sessions with the four I moved to that other pasture went well, and I don't want them relearning bad habits from their pals. By the way, do either of you ride?"

"I do," Maris volunteered. "We used to have several good horses, and I enjoyed riding each of them. There's only one on the ranch now, though."

"What happened to the others?" Luke asked.

"Ray traded them for a car. It's behind the barn with the rest of the—" she stopped short of the word *junk* "—things he purchased over the years."

Keith's eyes lit up. "It's a Corvette, Luke, a Sting Ray Coupe. Sure wish I knew how to get it running. It's really cool."

"A Corvette, eh? Out behind the barn? Maybe I'll take a look after supper." He glanced at Maris. "If you don't mind, of course."

She shrugged. "Why would I mind?"

Luke returned to his original question. "Do you ride, Keith?"

The boy's cheeks got pink. "I've only been on a horse a couple of times, Luke, but I really liked it."

"Why, Luke?" Maris questioned.

"Well, in a few days some of those horses are going to be ready for a rider. I'll ride them first to make sure they'll obey commands and won't try to throw the person off their back, but then they're going to need a lot of riding."

"Heck, I'll do it," Keith exclaimed excitedly.

Maris frowned. She didn't want Keith getting hurt riding half-broken horses. "Will it be dangerous?"

Luke glanced over at her and thought she'd never looked prettier than she did this evening in that red blouse she was wearing. "I wouldn't put anyone on a dangerous horse, Maris. There are some in that pasture that will never be calm enough for either of you to ride. Here's my plan. Mother—that's the gray mare—will be the first horse I'll be riding. When she's ready for some real action I'm going to use her to move the three stallions from the main pasture to another. Probably the one with the cows. That big red bozo is the head honcho of the herd, and getting him and the younger stallions away from the other horses will calm them all down. It's going to have to be done from horseback, and Mother's going to be my mount."

"Interesting," Maris commented. She was smiling. "Are you going to name every horse?"

"Probably," Luke admitted with a grin. "That tan gelding I worked with after Mother has a curly tail, so his name is 'Curly.'"

"Naturally," Maris said with a laugh. "And the other two?"

"Zelda and Mickey."

Both Maris and Keith were laughing now. "So, we have Mother, Curly, Zelda and Mickey so far," Maris said.

"And Bozo," Luke reminded.

"Oh, yes, the big red stallion."

"You can sure count on me to ride 'em when they're ready," Keith said with unabashed enthusiasm.

"I'll do it, too," Maris said, though she cast a concerned glance at Keith. "Just be certain it's safe, Luke."

Taking a swallow of coffee, Luke saw and recognized Maris's affection for Keith. Was he a relative? The son of a friend who'd needed a summer job? He was a nice kid, Luke felt, and eager to get involved. Keith could be a big help with the horses, but from the protectiveness he detected in Maris's attitude toward the boy, he had better discuss it with her before mentioning it to Keith.

"It'll be safe, Maris," he told her. "You have my word on it."

His word. Maris fell silent. How good was Luke Rivers's word? Ray's "word" had been wasted breath, his promises forgotten the second they came out of his mouth. She had learned not to count on anything Ray said, but what about Luke? Regardless of the two men's common obsession with rodeo, she probably shouldn't be too hasty in judging them as being alike.

"I'll hold you to that," she told Luke with a steady look across the table. Luke returned the look, and their gazes suddenly locked in a brand-new and disturbing way. Maris felt that unnerving throbbing again; Luke admired her red blouse and the startling color of her hair and eyes. Keith was eating and noticed nothing, but both Luke and Maris were all too aware of the attraction between them. Both dropped their eyes and awkwardly began eating.

An unfamiliar nervousness sprang to life in Luke's gut. Maris Wyler was off-limits. He sent her a quick, furtive glance. She *was* off-limits, wasn't she?

Maris's appetite was gone. She'd eaten about half the food on her plate, but it suddenly looked as tasteless as sawdust. She sat there, however, and pretended to eat by pushing the food around on her plate and occasionally bringing a teensy bite to her mouth.

Finally Luke and Keith were finished. "There's pudding for dessert," Maris announced tonelessly, wishing they would say they were too full for dessert. That look exchanged with Luke had put her on edge, because now she wasn't sure that he *wouldn't* throb for her.

At long last—it seemed an eternity to Maris—the meal was over. Luke pushed back his chair and got up to take his dishes to the sink. Keith and Maris did the same, and then the two men left the kitchen to go outside and Maris was alone.

Weakly she leaned against the sink counter. That "throbbing" business could be getting out of hand. How could she stop it? There must be a way to put an end to it.

Outside, Keith said, "Want to take a look at that Corvette, Luke?"

"Yeah, I'd like to see it." They began walking—with Blackie right behind them—toward the barn. "I didn't know there was a car parked back there."

Keith let out a whooping laugh. "There's a lot more than a car back there, Luke. Wait till you see."

Luke had figured that he'd explored the ranch pretty well, but obviously he'd missed the acreage behind the barn. His eyes widened with outright shock when he and Keith rounded the back corner of the barn and he saw what was out there: cars, trucks, tractors, a row of old refrigerators, electric motors rusting on the ground, a riding lawn mower, and much more, too many items to take in at one time. Knee-high weeds had grown up so thickly as to obscure some of the smaller objects.

"Good God," Luke muttered.

"The Corvette's over there," Keith said excitedly, starting to plow through the weeds and debris to a particular location.

Luke followed the boy to a red car propped up on blocks, its tires missing. There were rust spots in the red paint, but the body wasn't banged up. "I tried to start it one day," Keith confessed. "But nothing happened. The engine looks okay to me, but I'm not much of a mechanic. Do you know anything about engines, Luke?"

"Very little." He opened the Corvette's door and peered inside. "It has a four-speed manual transmission." The interior of the car was black leather and in pretty good condition. An idea was taking shape in his mind. He wasn't interested in old cars, but he knew someone who was. Maris just might pick up a sizable piece of cash for this baby.

"I'm going in to talk to Maris, Keith. There's a good chance that a fellow I know might be interested in buying this car."

"Really? Hey, that'd be great."

Blackie was sniffing around, and Keith began throwing a stick for Blackie to chase and bring back. "She's a real smart dog, Luke. Knows lots of tricks."

Grinning, Luke walked off. "See ya later." He hurried around the barn and to the house, where he walked in without any warning.

Maris jumped a foot. "Good Lord, you scared the stuffing out of me. I thought you were down by the barn with Keith."

"I was." She was just finishing up at the sink, Luke saw, wiping down the counters. "Maris, that Corvette has some value. Maybe some of that other stuff does, too, but I know a guy who collects old Corvettes and he just might be interested in yours. What do you say I give him a call?"

Holding the dishcloth, Maris turned. "You mean someone might actually pay good money for that junk?"

"That Corvette isn't junk, Maris. If my hunch is right, it's worth a good sum of money."

"And you know someone who might be interested? Well, yes, by all means, give him a call." It had never occurred to Maris that some of Ray's old junk might have any value. None of the vehicles ran, she knew, and everything was dirty and rusted and half-hidden by weeds. The place was an eyesore, and one of her plans for the future, should she manage to save the ranch, was to hire a truck to haul off all that junk. To think that someone might buy even one item as it was, broken, rusted and not very pretty, was a thrill she could never have anticipated.

Luke sat down at the kitchen table to use the wall phone next to it. He dialed a long-distance number and spoke to Maris. "Hope Jim's at home." While Jim's phone rang in his ear, he watched Maris puttering, apparently too antsy to stand still.

Then the phone was picked up. "Hello?"

"Jim? This is Luke Rivers. How are you?"

"Luke! Well, I'll be a son of a gun. Thought you dropped off the face of the earth. Where you been, boy?"

"It's a long story, Jim, and I'm using someone else's phone. What I called about is an old Corvette I ran across. Are you still collecting them?"

"Sure am. What'd you find, Luke?"

"It's a Sting Ray Coupe. Original paint with some rust in spots, four-speed transmission and black leather interior, also original. It needs work, but it's nothing you couldn't handle."

"Do you know what engine it's got?"

Luke could hear the excitement in Jim's voice. "No, I don't. Frankly I didn't even look at the engine, though I know it's got one. But I wouldn't know what I was looking at if I stared at it for three days. Anyway, I was wondering if you'd like to come to Whitehorn, Montana, and take a look at it?"

"Whitehorn, Montana, eh? Well, sure, why not? You might have stumbled across a real find, Luke. Who owns it?"

"The lady I'm breaking a herd of horses for. It's the No Bull Ranch, Jim, about thirty miles northeast of Whitehorn."

Maris's stomach was churning with excitement. From Luke's end of the conversation, his friend Jim was indeed interested in the Corvette.

But now they were chuckling over the name of her ranch. Maris shot Luke an exasperated look, wanting to say, "Get to the point. Pin him down about when he can come and see the Corvette." She said nothing, just stewed to herself and wiped the counters again, though they were already gleaming.

Luke put down the phone with a satisfied expression. "He'll be here within the week."

Maris's excitement totally eluded her control. "Oh, Luke, that's great! What if he buys it? How much do you think it's worth? To think it was sitting out there all this time and I never dreamed someone might buy it. Honestly, I feel so silly."

Luke got to his feet. "He hasn't bought it yet, Maris."

"But you think he might."

"I think there's a good chance, yes." He came around the table. "But I have no idea of the car's value, Maris. I have heard that some classic older cars bring high prices, but I don't think you should hang your hat on a large sum."

"Any sum looks good right now, Luke."

Luke was enjoying the spark of hope in her eyes and realizing an odd fact: it made him feel good to make Maris happy. His next thought wasn't nearly as high-minded, however. Recognizing desire streaking through his body, he drew a slow, uneven breath.

Maris blinked, suddenly aware that they were alone and that the kitchen was getting very dim, as she hadn't yet turned on any lights in the house. "Uh...maybe I'll go out and take a look at that Corvette myself." She started for the door, only to be stopped by a big hand on her arm. Her eyes lifted to Luke's, and what she saw caused that throbbing to begin again. "Please...don't," she whispered, wondering why in God's name her voice was deserting her at a time like this.

"Maris..." Luke took her by the shoulders and slowly brought her forward. She smelled wonderful, of soap and lotion and other feminine scents.

She couldn't move. In her mind's eye was a picture of Luke and Mother, the mare. Her own system was resisting common sense. His hands, his marvelous hands, were gently kneading her shoulders, and she knew he was going to kiss her.

He brought his face down to hers and very tenderly touched her lips with his. It felt so good and she didn't back away, so he did it again. Her hands rose to clasp his forearms, and when he looked at her, he saw the glaze of pleasure in her eyes.

That was all he needed to see. Almost roughly, he swept her into a full embrace and kissed her the way a man *should* kiss a woman, with passion and possession and a message of raw hunger. Maris's knees got as limp as last year's carrots. When had she last been kissed like this? When had she *ever* been kissed like this? Luke's lips molded hers to fit his, then urged hers open to take his tongue. It was hot and slick and bold as brass, delving into every nook and cranny of her mouth. A red haze was developing behind her closed eyelids, and the throbbing in her stomach was intensified further by the sensation of his strong arms around her, the length of his body pressing into hers, by his male scent and heat.

It was a lover's kiss, and it scared her. Her own response scared her. Breathing hard, she twisted her head to free her mouth. "Stop," she moaned.

"Maris, honey..." He didn't want to stop. Where that explosive passion had come from, he would never know, but Maris had suddenly become the most desirable woman he'd ever known.

"Please." Extricating herself from his arms, she took a backward step and then had to hang on to the back of a chair to remain upright and steady. "This isn't me, Luke. I don't do this sort of thing." Her voice was shaky and thin.

He looked at her strangely. "What do I say to that? You kissed me back, Maris."

"I know, but you took me by surprise."

Luke took a forward step. "What's wrong with you and me sharing a kiss?"

It was not a subject to debate with him, not when she still felt his kiss on her mouth and her legs would barely hold her up. "Intimacy is not a part of our arrangement," she croaked, trying to sound calm and in control and failing abysmally.

Luke looked at her for the longest time. "But what if intimacy is what we want?"

Her eyes jerked upward to see his. "Do you always get what you want?"

"No, but I always try. Don't you, Maris? Don't you at least try to get what you want? What you need?"

"That's enough." Her legs felt a little stronger, and she left the chair and began moving toward the door. "Don't make any more passes, Luke. I want and need those horses broken, a whole lot more than I want what you just offered."

"There's no reason why you can't have both," he said softly.

She paused at the door to look at him. "You're wrong. There is a reason, and it's very important to me. I never did and never will have an affair." She opened the door. "Especially with a man whom I know in advance is only going to be around for a few months." Showing him her back, she stepped outside, and an enormous surge of relief hit her, because Keith and Blackie were coming toward her and the house. Keith's presence would deter Luke's determination to persuade her into thinking his way.

"Where's Luke?" Keith called.

"Right here," Luke said in a voice that caused Maris's back to stiffen. Without even addressing her, he had let her know that he didn't agree with her attitude against kisses and affairs.

Luke walked past both her and Keith. "I'm going to bed. Good night."

Keith looked at Maris with a perplexed expression. "What's wrong with Luke?"

Maris took a breath and lied through her teeth. "I couldn't begin to guess. Call it a mood." She formed a smile for Keith. "I think I'll go to bed, too. Good night, Keith."

"Well, heck," Keith mumbled. "It's still light out and everyone's going to bed."

"If you turn on the TV, please keep the volume down. 'Night, Keith." Maris went back into the house and directly to her bedroom.

She wasn't over the shakes yet, but she was beginning to wonder if anything would ever be normal again until after Luke Rivers left the No Bull.

# Five

Luke waded through the weeds behind the barn, going from vehicle to vehicle to look them over, then inspected numerous electric and gasoline motors all but concealed by huge clumps of dandelions and overgrown wild grasses. He paused at the riding lawn mower and finally stopped his wandering near the row of old refrigerators, shaking his head in amazement, wondering why a man would collect and save so much junk. Maris had been right to ask if he'd known Ray at all; obviously he hadn't.

All morning while working with the horses, the junk strewn behind the barn had kept popping into his mind. What was junk to one person was pure gold to another. Take that Corvette, for example. Rusting away behind the barn it was worthless. But to Jim Humphrey the car was a collector's find. And if Jim found the car to his liking and bought it, it would no longer be worthless to Maris but cash in her pocket.

What if some of these other things could also be turned into cash? That was the question hounding Luke this morning, although the cold shoulder Maris had given him at breakfast was hardly an incentive to approaching her with any new ideas. He shouldn't have kissed her. Now she acted as though he was just lying in wait for another opportunity to grab her, which simply wasn't true. He understood the word *no* as well as Maris did and would abide by her wishes, even though he knew damned well that she had kissed him back and enjoyed it every bit as much as he had.

But...that was behind him. Behind *them*. Maris would soon realize it wasn't going to be repeated, and then she would relax around him again. In the meantime, he would act as though nothing had occurred in her kitchen last night, and he would begin by going up to the house right now and talking to her about the veritable gold mine in back of the barn. Starting on his way, Luke had to chuckle. "Gold mine" was a terrible exaggeration, when the truth was that she might pick up a few bucks by selling some of that junk. But his impression of her financial straits was that even a few bucks would be welcome.

Maris had told Keith to finish repairing the section of fence he'd been working on for several days now, so Luke hadn't seen the boy since breakfast. He hadn't seen Maris, either, but then, he'd been so engrossed in whatever horse he'd been working with in the corral, he hadn't been watching for her. She hadn't, however, come near the corral.

He strode across the compound from barn to house and rapped on the screen door, as the inner door was wide open. "Maris?"

Maris was in the kitchen, making sandwiches for lunch. She'd been out helping Keith with the fence repairs, and had returned to the house only a few minutes ago. Wiping her hands on a section of paper towel, she went to the screen door. "Lunch will be ready in a few minutes."

"Great, but that's not why I'm here. I need to talk to you about something."

"Oh. Well, come on in." Maris backed away from the door and returned to the counter, with its array of bread, cold meat and condiments. She had vowed to remain aloof of Luke's personal charms, but she had to allow communication on anything concerning the horses. "What is it?"

Luke was standing near the refrigerator, as that location provided a side view of what she was doing. "I just took another look at the stuff behind the barn and I think some of it could be sold."

Maris sliced a sandwich in half. "Other than the Corvette, that stuff is pure junk. Why would anyone want it?"

"Some of it could be fixed up, Maris. Cleaned up, at least. That riding mower is missing its battery and its tires are flat, but maybe those are the only things wrong with it. If we could get it in shape and slap a coat of paint on it . . ."

Maris turned. "Do you have the time to do it?" It wasn't said kindly. If they were still counting on that September 30 deadline, which she was wholeheartedly doing, then every minute of Luke's time was already scheduled.

Luke's face hardened. "I'll find the time. Keith could help and so could you."

"Me!" Maris emitted a sardonic laugh. "I'm hardly a mechanic. Besides, with tending the herd and keeping this place from falling apart, I've got enough to do."

"Well, you can damned well find the time to wield a paintbrush and use a little soap and water!"

"Don't you dare get angry with me because I didn't jump for joy at your suggestion!" Maris drew a calming breath. She didn't want to argue with Luke; they were skating on thin ice as it was. "I'm sorry. Let's not fight about something so silly. I appreciate your calling your friend about the Corvette but—"

Luke folded his arms and interrupted. "Maybe you're not as broke as you let on. Appears to me that a person who's as short of money as you've led me to believe would jump at the chance to make a few bucks."

Maris's eyes widened. "I have not misled you, and I'm not a liar. But trying to sell that junk would be a waste of time."

"Come out there with me."

"Why?"

"Maris, don't be so damned obstinate. I'm trying to help you out here."

Her mind was cluttered with problems, and Luke was one of them. Why, even now when he was angering her by pushing her into doing something she thought utterly senseless, was she so aware of his good looks? And remembering how she'd felt in his arms?

With her jaw clenched, she draped a clean towel over the food on the counter. "Fine," she snapped. "I'll go with you."

They made the trek in silence, but Maris's temper had cooled considerably by the time they had rounded the barn and reached the junkyard. Luke began talking. "There are—I counted them—fifteen motors of various sizes and types lying in these weeds. There are tools, electric saws, a lathe, woodworking equipment and on and on. You can see the old cars, trucks and tractors for yourself, and I have no intention of trying to put any of them in running order. Other than the riding lawn mower, which I think needs only minor repairs."

"There is also a room filled with junk," Maris said wearily, far from convinced that anything out here—other than the Corvette—was worth two cents.

"A room? Where?"

"Through that door."

It was just another door to get into the barn, Luke had figured. "Is it locked?"

"Is anything on the ranch locked?"

Shooting her an irate look—she sure wasn't being very cooperative—Luke made his way through the weeds to the door and pulled it open. He stepped in and then stared in utter amazement. Picture frames, paintings, old clocks, tables, chairs, bedsteads, boxes and boxes of hand tools, stacks of galvanized pails, golf clubs, skis, tennis rackets—he had never seen so much stuff crammed into one small room before. Everything was coated with a thick layer of dust, but it had been protected from the weather and he could see that the wood tables and chairs, for instance, weren't warped and misshapen.

"Maris," he said slowly. "You could hold a yard sale to end all yard sales."

Ray's obsession with junk had annoyed and irked Maris so intensely for so long that she found it difficult now to alter her attitude. "Who would want it?" she scoffed, looking directly at an ugly lamp without a shade. "Would you want that thing in your house?"

Luke followed the direction of her gaze and had to laugh. "No, I wouldn't want that thing in my house. But someone else might fall in love with it."

"Yeah, right," she drawled. But one of the old clocks had drawn her attention. It was a grimy, dull-black color, but it had an ivory face and had the configuration of an ancient Greek building. Winding her way through the litter, she reached the clock and touched it. Then she tried to pick it up, and found that she could hardly budge it. "This thing weighs a ton!" she exclaimed.

Luke came over to peer at it. "Looks like it's made out of marble."

Maris turned to survey the hundreds of objects crowded into the room. "Do you really think people would buy some of this junk? Wait! I know the person to ask, Winona Cobb. You had to pass her place on your way here, the Stop 'n' Swap? You must have seen it. Her front yard is littered with old sinks and hubcaps, and there are animals running everywhere. Winona is as eccentric as they come, but if anyone's an expert on junk around here, it's her.''

"I don't think you need advice from anyone about holding a yard sale, Maris. Haven't you ever stopped at a garage or yard sale and seen the kind of stuff people are selling?'' Luke gestured at the clutter. "You've got great junk, Maris.''

The remark tickled Maris's funny bone. "Great junk?'' she choked out as she started laughing.

Luke smiled broadly, enjoying the sight and sound of Maris laughing. When she had calmed down, he said, "Let's do it, Maris. Let's throw a yard sale that'll set Whitehorn back on its heels. You'll make a small fortune, I guarantee it.''

Maris was beginning to warm to the idea. "It would take a lot of work. Everything in here needs a good cleaning.''

"Keith and I could haul it outside and you could use the hose on most of it.''

"We'd have to set it up in the front yard.'' Maris laughed wryly. "The No Bull would look like Winona's place.''

"Only for a few days. Anything that doesn't sell we can haul to the dump.''

It was really beginning to sink in. What didn't sell would be hauled to the dump. She would be *rid* of it, once and for all.

"The big pieces out back couldn't be moved to the front yard, though,'' Luke told her. "But Keith and I could chop down the weeds and clean up the area so people could check out the items for sale.''

This time Maris was the one who folded her arms. "And who's going to be working with the horses while you're chopping weeds and hauling around furniture?''

"The horses come first,'' Luke said firmly. "Damn, Maris, I can do more than one thing at a time. Can't you? Can't anyone who really sets his mind to it?''

Maris's wheels were turning. A good two-thirds of the things in this room were light enough for her to carry outside for cleaning all by herself. Keith could chop down the weeds out back, and then she could put him to work helping her with the yard sale. Luke wouldn't have to do all that much on it and the horses wouldn't be neglected, which, of course, was a much more important undertaking than getting rid of this junk.

But the thought of the ranch being junk-free, finally, was elating. Someday she wanted white painted fencing around the close-in pastures instead of barbed wire, and someday she wanted every single building painted the same color. She'd been thinking—for a long time—of a soft blue-gray color with white trim.

"Someday" was still a long way off, but getting rid of this junk was an extremely satisfying first step to attaining her dream.

A smile lit her face. "You're absolutely right. I'll do it!"

"*We'll* do it."

Maris started out of the musty room. "Keith and I will do most of it. I want you to..."

Luke grabbed her arm, halting her flight. "Are you telling me to stay out of it?"

Surprised, she lifted her eyes to his. "It was your idea and I appreciate it, but you said yourself that the horses come first."

"And they will. But I can also help clean up this stuff."

Why was he so insistent on doing more than he'd bargained for? He was still holding her arm, they were still looking into each other's eyes, and it suddenly occurred to Maris to wonder if he wasn't doubling his work load because of her.

She flushed. What had happened in her kitchen last night was in Luke's eyes, and Lord help her, she wanted to move closer to him, to walk into his arms and have him hold her, and kiss her, and touch her.

Luke knew exactly what she was thinking. "There's something happening with us, Maris. We can pretend it isn't, we can act as though we're nothing more than boss and employee, but we both know that's not true."

She dampened her suddenly dry lips. "I...told you how I feel about an..." She avoided the word *affair.* "Don't push me into something that can only hurt me after you're gone. This has never happened to me before. I knew only one man, I've slept with only one man, and he was my husband. Do you think I could sleep with you and then forget it after you drive away?"

Her words, so candid, so frank, startled Luke. "Ray was the only man? Ever?"

Oh, dear God. How could she have said such a thing to him? Profoundly embarrassed, Maris glanced away.

Luke looked at her turned face with its high color for a moment, then released her arm. "I told myself I wasn't going to try anything else with you. I'm sorry. It won't happen again." It was a monumental effort to speak so calmly, when what he wanted to do was dust down one of those old tables and lay her on it. He could almost see himself peeling down her jeans and opening his own, almost *feel* himself inside of her, loving her, kissing her sensual mouth and beautiful throat. The intensity of his desire for Maris was overwhelming and impossible to comprehend.

They walked out of the room not looking at each other, both shaken, both trying very hard to appear nonchalant and undisturbed.

"Well," Maris said with false brightness, "I'd better get back to the house and finish up lunch. It'll be ready in about ten minutes. Keith is probably on his way in."

"Go ahead. I'll be up in a few minutes." As Maris disappeared around the corner of the barn, he mumbled, "Run away, little girl, and keep on running, 'cause the big bad wolf is right on your heels." Then his own words disgusted him, and he parked his hips against one of the old tractor wheels to berate himself.

But he was so hard he ached, and no amount of self-reproach was going to cool him off. Damn! Cursing under his breath, he hurried around to the front of the barn, went inside, took the stairs to the loft two at a time, threw off his clothes, gave his stubborn, erect member a poisonous look, turned the shower on to Cold and stepped under the icy spray.

Maris was becoming enthused about the yard sale idea. It would take at least two weeks to get everything ready, she figured. Along with cleaning each item, there were signs to make and distribute. Advertising the event in the newspaper was crucial to the success of the venture, but the ad shouldn't come out until the week just prior to the weekend of the sale. First things first, Maris thought determinedly, and the first chores, of course, were the sorting and cleaning.

That very afternoon she began by carrying out the stack of galvanized pails—three and four at a time—washed the dust out of them with the garden hose and turned them upside down to dry. During lunch she had told Keith of her plans, and he had immediately and eagerly offered to get involved. "Go back and finish the fence repairs," she had told him. "That job is nearly done and we have to keep our priorities in order. What Luke is doing comes before anything else. When he wants either of us to start riding those horses, that's what we'll do."

Luke had been rather grim lipped and silent throughout the meal. Not because of the horses and not because of the yard sale. But his own damned system was in some sort of rebellious mode and it was all because of Maris. He wasn't blaming her. It was himself, his own suddenly overactive libido that had him symbolically climbing the walls. He told himself to stop being such a damn fool. Women were a dime a dozen. He could walk into almost any tavern and find several of them sitting on bar stools or at tables with that expectant, inviting expression in their eyes. Of course, not every woman who went to a tavern without an escort was looking for a man. In his experience, however, the percentages were definitely in his favor.

But it wasn't a woman he hadn't even met yet that had his blood racing; it was Maris. Maris Wyler, rancher and the widow of his old pal Ray. Maris, with her sun-streaked hair and lean, sensual body. And Maris wasn't cooperating. She wanted to cooperate, he knew, or thought he knew. But Maris had high morals and strict standards, and she was right about him leaving the minute those horses were sold, so he couldn't blame her for saying no. Understanding Maris's attitude didn't alter his own, however.

After lunch, Luke had gone into the pasture and roped a nervous piebald gelding. He alternated further sessions with Mother and the other horses already in the training process with new trainees. The piebald wasn't being taken in by Luke's gift of apples, nor did he let Luke get close enough to rub him down with the feed sack.

The sun was high in the sky and hot. The piebald danced around the corral like a puppet on a string, and Luke patiently kept after him until his shirt was wet with sweat. Maris was hauling out straight-backed wooden chairs from the storage room, and she just happened to be setting one down on the grass, when she looked over to the corral and saw Luke tossing his shirt.

She stood up straighter and stared, drawing in a slow, uneven breath. With the leather gloves on his hands, his faded jeans, his boots and no shirt, he was the most gorgeous specimen of mankind she had ever seen. Intent on the piebald, Luke wasn't aware of Maris watching. He deftly roped the horse's back leg with one loop, then the animal's opposite front leg with another. The ropes were pulled taut and tied to posts in the corral fencing. Blowing and snorting, the piebald tossed his head in fury, but he was unable to rear or run, and Luke walked over to the water spigot at the trough and got himself a drink. That was when he spotted Maris.

In one smooth, fluid movement, he hopped over the corral fence and walked over to her. "That one's got a temper. He'll cool down after a while."

"You tied him down."

"Have to with some of them." Luke eyed the chairs. "Aren't these too heavy for you to be hauling around?"

Maris was trying not to look at his naked chest, but it wasn't possible to look at Luke at all without seeing it, especially when it was such a large chest. The impressive muscles of his shoulders, arms and chest rippled when he moved, and his skin was tan and looked as smooth as satin.

"They're not too heavy," Maris murmured, slightly breathlessly. "You're very good with a rope."

The left corner of Luke's lips turned up in an acknowledging half smile. "I've had a lot of experience. I wish you'd let me or Keith carry the heavy stuff."

"These chairs aren't too heavy for me. I'll let you know when something is. How long do you think it will take for that horse to calm down?"

Luke shrugged. "Not long. I'm going to put a saddle on Mother while I'm waiting."

"She's ready for riding?"

"No, but she's ready for a saddle. I'll leave it on her for two or three hours. She has to get used to the weight of a saddle on her back and the stirrups bumping her during movement."

Maris was beginning to understand that Luke had a pattern in his training of the horses. She smiled over it. "You work like an assembly line."

That little half grin flashed again. "Guess you could say that. I'm pretty satisfied with the way things are going. 'Course, I've saved the worst of the lot for last. When Mother's ready for riding it'll go a little easier. As I told you before, I intend to move Bozo and the other stallions out of the herd. They'll all be much calmer then."

"The stallions disrupt the others?" In spite of her determination to avoid looking directly at Luke's chest, she spotted a two-inch scar near his left nipple.

"The stallions are constantly aroused and keeping the herd, especially the mares, stirred up."

"Like when a bull is turned into the cows' pasture," Maris murmured absently, her thoughts on that scar.

"Did you used to have a bull?"

Putting Luke's manly chest with its two-inch scar out of her mind, Maris sighed. "He was sold with most of our other cattle. That's when Ray bought these horses."

Luke frowned. "Was he going to hire someone to do the breaking for him?"

She merely shook her head. "I don't know," she said, sounding a little broken herself. The subject was defeating, one of the trials she had lived through with Ray without ever understanding why he did what he did.

Bending over for the garden hose, she turned the spray on the chair. "Some of these things are going to need scrubbing with soap and water," she remarked. "Anything wood will have to have a coat of furniture polish, as well."

Luke was almost sorry he'd suggested the yard sale. Already he could tell that Maris was going to make too much of it. Everything for sale didn't have to look as though it had just come off of a showroom floor.

He watched her for a moment, then began walking off, heading for the barn for a rope and a saddle to take out to Mother's pasture. "See you later."

"Yeah, see you later," Maris said under her breath. But she looked up to get another glimpse of Luke's remarkable torso.

A small groan rose in her throat. No man should look the way he did without a shirt.

Maris was busily scrubbing a filthy table with a sponge and a bucket of warm, soapy water, when a car drove into the compound. A strange car. "Maybe that's your friend coming to see the Corvette," she called to Luke.

The roan in the corral was behaving much better than the piebald, and Luke had been rubbing the animal down with the blanket. He turned to see the car and then grinned when Jim Humphrey got out. "That's him," he called to Maris. "Come and meet him."

Maris dropped the sponge into the bucket and dried her hands on one of the old towels she'd brought out from the house, along with a basket of cleaning supplies.

The three of them met about midway between Jim's car and the corral. "Hey, Rivers, you look half-broken yourself," Jim exclaimed with a big grin. He glanced at Maris. "Hello, ma'am. Are you the reason this big galoot seems to be finally settling down?"

Maris's face turned beet-red. Luke quickly came to the rescue. "This lady is Maris Wyler, Jim, the owner of this place. I'm working for her."

Jim grabbed Maris's hand and energetically shook it. "Glad to meetcha, Maris. Then you must be the proud owner of that Corvette Luke called me about."

Despite Jim's hasty and certainly uncalled-for assessment of the situation, Maris couldn't dislike him. He was a jolly-looking man with a cherubic face and a constant smile. She couldn't help noticing the enormous diamond on his pinky ring, or his casual but unmistakably expensive clothing. Obviously, if Jim Humphrey liked the Corvette, he could afford to buy it.

"It's out behind the barn, Mr. Humphrey. Would you like to see it right away, or perhaps you'd rather come into the house and have something cold to drink first?"

"Corvette first, cold drink later," Jim boomed with a hearty laugh. "And for Pete's sake, call me 'Jim.'"

Maris smiled. "If you wish. Luke, would you show Jim the car? There's something I need to do in the house." It wasn't true. There was nothing she needed to do in the house, but she was suddenly nervous about the car, and Luke could probably handle it much better than she could.

The two men walked off, talking and laughing. Apparently they were old friends and glad to see each other. Maris did go into the house, first so she wouldn't look like a liar, and second because she was too flustered to return to her sponge and bucket of soapy water. Jittery, she moved from one window in the house to the next. What if Jim liked the car and actually bought it? How much would he pay for it? Would he make an immediate decision or ask for time to consider it?

Oh, damn, maybe she *should* have gone with them. At least then she would know what they were saying about the car.

To do something besides worry and fret, Maris made a pitcher of lemonade, using fresh lemons. It was almost an hour before she saw Luke and Jim coming around the barn, and by then she was totally frazzled. Springing to life, she fixed a tray with the pitcher of lemonade and three glasses containing ice cubes. Before the two men had reached the tiny patio at the back of the house, Maris had the tray sitting on the round table and she was smiling, as any sane and sensible person would be doing.

"Is that lemonade I see in that pitcher?" Jim asked jovially.

"It certainly is," Maris replied. She filled the three glasses and passed them around. They drank and looked at one another and smiled at one another and everything seemed just peachy. "Well," said Maris. "Would you like to sit down?"

"For a minute," Jim replied.

They all sat around the table. "Wonderful lemonade. It's not from a mix, I'll bet," Jim said.

"No, I used fresh lemons."

"I can always tell the difference," Jim said with unmistakable pride in his apparently trustworthy palate. "Well, young woman, I can tell you right now that I want that car. All we have to do now is settle on a price."

Relief washed through Maris, immediately followed by panic. "Uh...price, yes. Well..." She looked to Luke for help, but he was sipping his lemonade and ignoring her silent plea. To his way of thinking, it was Maris's car and she should do the dickering. Of course, if old Jim should offer too little for the 'Vette, he might step in and help Maris out.

"I'll tell you about your car, Maris," Jim said matter-of-factly. "The body can be repaired without too much expense, but Corvette wheels are costly and it has no tires. The standard engine in that model was a 300-bhp V8, but your 'Vette has the engine I'd hoped to see in it. It has the L-71 Tri-carb, which makes it a 435-bhp. Plus, it has the four-speed manual transmission. Put it all together, and we're talking power, young woman, power and speed."

Maris smiled weakly, grasping none of it. "I'm sure it would be a very pretty car... if repaired, of course."

"Pretty!" Jim guffawed so loudly, Maris jumped. "A Corvette is an object of rare beauty, Maris." He talked on and on, using phrases like "independent suspension" and "cubic inches" and then talking about wheelbase measurements and front/rear weight distribution.

Finally Jim ran down and stopped lauding the merits of his favorite automobile. His expression became serious. "The thing we don't know is how much work the engine needs, Maris. How long have you owned it?"

"Um... about two years."

"And it was running then?"

"Oh, no," Maris replied. "It never ran while we owned it. My husband traded—"

Luke hastily interrupted. "That's all beside the point, Jim. Maris never drove the car and I really don't think she knows very much about it. Isn't that true, Maris?"

"Very true." Thank God Luke had finally spoken. Why on earth had he been sitting there all this time without saying something?

"Well..." Jim looked off into the distance, apparently pondering the matter. "I'm prepared to pay three thousand for the car."

Maris's mouth dropped open. She had never even come near a figure that high. One thousand had been a hope, but certainly not three.

"It's worth more than that, Jim," Luke said with a male-to-male laugh. "You know it, I know it."

"Thirty-five hundred," Jim said, adding, "there could be damage to the undercarriage, Luke. Without putting it on a lift, there's no way of knowing."

"Five thousand," Luke said calmly.

"Five!" Jim laughed. "You're dreaming, Luke."

Luke sat there as cool as could be. "When that car is refurbished, it'll be worth twenty-five thousand, maybe more. That's something else we both know." It was a bluff. Luke knew that classic automobiles carried a high value, but he'd pulled that figure of twenty-five thousand out of the air.

"Yeah, but how much will it take to refurbish it? I'll go four thousand, and that's being damned generous, Luke."

"Forty-five hundred and we've got a deal," Luke returned.

Maris's startled gaze was going back and forth between the two men. They were actually thrilled to be sitting here dealing on the price of her car! She would have accepted the three thousand and been glad to take it. But she could see that Jim had *expected* some debate on the price and would probably have been disappointed not to get it.

Silently sighing, she sat back in her chair. Men and women were completely different creatures. Was it any wonder they didn't get along? Or that they rarely understood one another?

Jim stood up and offered his hand. "Deal!"

Luke nudged Maris. "He's talking to you, Maris."

"Oh!" Hastily she got to her feet and shook hands with Jim Humphrey. "Thank you." Forty-five hundred dollars for what she'd considered to be just another piece of junk behind the barn. She could hardly believe it.

# Six

That night before going to bed, Maris looked again at the five-hundred-dollar check Jim Humphrey had given her. "You'll get the balance when I pick up the car, Maris. Probably in a week or two."

So she still didn't have a large sum of money in her possession, but things were definitely looking up. If the yard sale was a success and then the horse auction, she could start running the ranch the way it used to function. From old accounting records and photograph albums, Maris had proof that the Circle W had once been a thriving, profitable operation. Her dreams went further than those old records and photos, though. It wasn't that she yearned for wealth, but she did want financial security. Living in beautiful surroundings would be wonderful, too. When she was married to Ray, she'd never known one minute to the next what to expect. She'd make plans for the ranch, only to have him pull the rug out from under her. Now that she was on her own and getting out of debt things would be different.

Maris put away the check, opened a window for fresh air, turned off the light and crawled into bed. Her body was tired. Other than sitting down for meals and to talk to Jim Humphrey, she had been on her feet and working at one job or another all day. She lay there thinking of all that was going on—the preparations for the yard sale, Luke's work with the horses, the unexpected windfall of Jim Humphrey buying that old Corvette.

A frown creased her forehead as a startling thought struck her: everything happening on the ranch was Luke's doing! Because of that IOU, Luke had come up with the idea of him breaking her horses and holding a big whoop-de-do—his word—auction; Luke was the one who'd recognized the value of the Corvette and then just happened to have a friend who collected older-model 'Vettes; and last, it was Luke who had suggested the yard sale.

Rather than feeling grateful that Luke had such a versatile imagination, Maris felt slightly wounded that every good idea to make money for the ranch had come from him. Where had *her* imagination been hiding? Why hadn't she seen the potential of Ray's junk?

Agitated and suddenly not tired at all, Maris threw back the blankets and got out of bed. Finding her robe and slippers without a light, she put them on and walked through the dark house to the kitchen, where she stood at the window and stared out at the compound to ponder Luke's involvement not only with the ranch but with her. The man had nothing of his own other than a pickup truck, and no one could ever accuse Luke Rivers of being dense or dull-witted. He recognized opportunity and didn't hesitate to act upon it, and wasn't a widow with a nice little ranch that could be a whole lot nicer a perfect opportunity for an unscrupulous man to better his lot in life?

A dull ache began in Maris's chest. Was that why he'd kissed her? Did he think her so lonely and vulnerable, so in need of a man, that she would be easy to woo into submission and ultimately some kind of partnership that would give him control of her ranch?

But he was looking forward to leaving at the end of September, a voice in Maris's head reminded. Anxious to return to rodeo.

Another voice argued, *That could all be an act to put you off guard.*

Was it an act? Was Luke unscrupulous? Was she a fool?

Her business arrangement with Luke regarding the horses didn't make her a fool, Maris decided. Neither did grasping his idea for the yard sale. And certainly she appreciated his assistance in selling the Corvette.

But most definitely there was some of the fool lurking within her when she admired, with weak knees and a palpitating heart, his physique without a shirt, or responded with soft, pliant lips to his kisses.

As she stared out into the darkness, her gaze lingered on the ground area lighted by the lamp at the top of a tall pole near the barn. Her chin lifted in a show of defiance, though there was no one to see it. There would be no more kisses between her and Luke, no more girlishly breathless glances at him while he worked with the horses. She would not be taken in by an unscrupulous man, however much he turned on the charm.

Maris narrowed her eyes. Someone—it had to be Luke, as Keith had gone to bed several hours ago—was down by the barn. She squinted to see what he was carrying and couldn't quite make it out. Why on earth was he still up, and what was he doing?

Without further speculation, Maris sped from the kitchen and through the door into the night. Her slippers fell softly on the grass of the backyard lawn and then on the hard-packed dirt between the lawn and barn. Luke had gone inside and turned on a light. She found him in the tack room.

Thinking that Maris had retired because of the dark house, he looked at her with surprise. "Anything wrong?"

Her gaze darted, as though searching for something out of place, or missing. "What are you doing out here so late?"

"Putting away the saddles I used on Mother and Zelda this afternoon. Why?"

His dedication annoyed her, probably because of her doubts about his scruples a few minutes ago. "You don't have to work all night, you know," she said tartly.

Luke held up a hand. "Wait a minute. You couldn't possibly be angry because I'm doing my job, so why don't you just come right out and say what's got your tail in a knot?"

Maris's head lifted until she was looking down her nose at him. "I don't think you need to use that tone of voice with me."

"You can use any uppity tone you please but I can't speak my mind? Forget that notion, Maris." He brushed past her. "It's late and I'm beat. Good night."

She stared, openmouthed because he would be so rude, as he headed for the tack room door, and felt fury solidifying in her belly. "Sometimes I think you forget which one of us *owns* this ranch and which one merely works on it." She hurled the words at his retreating back.

Luke came to an abrupt halt and then slowly turned around. "What's that supposed to mean? Why don't you cut the crap and tell me why you're out here at eleven o'clock at night trying to pick a fight?" He took a step toward her. "Is that what you want, Maris, a no-holds-barred fight? Maybe I've been doing something that's been rubbing you wrong. Or maybe I *haven't* been doing something you want done real bad."

She was suddenly wishing she hadn't come out here at all, let alone yelled at him. "I didn't mean to pick a fight," she said as haughtily as she could manage. "I saw you carrying something, and I merely wondered what you were doing out here so late."

"Yeah, right. When I told you what I was doing, what did you do?"

"I..." She tried hard to remember. "I didn't do anything!"

Luke took another forward step. "You told me in a smart-assed way that I didn't have to work all night. You were ticked when you walked in here, and since you were nice as pie during dinner, something happened to change your mood. What was it?"

The dark glower in Luke's eyes was intimidating. His unbuttoned shirt and beltless jeans were intimidating. Maris's eyes widened. "You were in bed and then remembered that you'd left the saddles on the horses!"

"So?"

"So, nothing. I'm sorry I bothered you." This time Maris brushed past him. He was only half-dressed, the same as her, even though her robe was ankle-length and tightly closed by a sash. Maybe she did want to pick a fight with him, but this was neither the time nor the place to do it.

Luke neatly hooked a finger into the sash at the back of her waist and yanked her backward. His arms closed around her. Maris gasped. "Just stop it! I didn't come out here for this!"

He was breathing into her hair, causing her scalp to tingle. "*I* think this is exactly what you came out here for. *I* think you were lying in your bed all alone and picturing me out here alone in my bed. It's a terrible waste, isn't it, you in one bed, me in another?" His voice had grown husky. "Damn, Maris, we could make some mighty sweet music together."

Her traitorous mind painted the image he'd suggested. Sweet music. Her eyes closed as the throbbing between her legs began again. Her aching breasts reminded her of the many unhappy, lonely nights she'd spent as a woman tied to a man who hadn't considered her pleasure since the first year of their marriage. The first few months, to be more accurate.

But what made Luke any different? Hadn't she and Lori, her best friend, talked endlessly about that very subject? And wasn't Lori's attitude virtually the same as her own—that a happy, romantic marriage was just a fruitless fantasy?

Besides, Luke wasn't offering marriage. He was offering her his bed and a night of sweet music.

She went limp and spoke listlessly. "Let go of me."

Her abrupt change of mood startled Luke into obeying. But he was breathing erratically and his body was uncomfortably geared up for that "sweet music."

"Go on. Get out of here," he said wearily. He couldn't resist a parting shot, however. As Maris hurried through the door, he yelled, "The next time you come looking for a fight— or something—in the middle of the night, count on getting it!"

Maris ran from the barn and kept on running all the way to the house.

"Keith, would you mind doing the grocery shopping for me this week? I don't want to stop working on the things for the yard sale." The telephone rang. Maris went to pick it up and said, "Hello, would you hold for a moment, please?" Then she held her hand over the phone's mouthpiece to finish up with Keith. "The grocery list and money are on the counter. Your paycheck is there, too."

Grinning, Keith walked over to the counter and gathered up the money, the grocery list and his paycheck. Earning his own money was the greatest feeling he'd ever had. "Thanks, Maris. See ya later." He went out the door whistling through his teeth.

Maris returned to her caller. "Sorry to keep you waiting."

"It's just me, Maris."

"Lori! Hi, how are you?" Maris sat down. "It's been ages since we talked."

"I'm fine . . . busy, as usual. How are you?"

Lori Parker Bains was a nurse and a midwife. She was an absolute doll with her gorgeous blond hair and big blue eyes, but her looks had never gone to her head and she had been

Maris's best friend since childhood. Lori had married her high school sweetheart, Travis Bains, but it hadn't lasted, so, in a way, she and Maris were in almost the same boat as far as their manless lives went.

Maris took a breath. "I've been busy, too. There's a lot going on right now."

"You needn't say another word. I've heard all about the hunk you've got working out there. The word around town is that he looks like Mel Gibson."

"The movie star? Good Lord, where did you hear that?"

"From the gals at the Hip Hop. Incidentally, John Tully is taking all the credit for sending him out to your place to ask for a job. Seems very proud of himself for having been so helpful."

Maris groaned. "Oh, God. Do you mean to tell me the whole town is talking about Luke working out here?"

"Afraid so, kiddo. Is it true? Does he look like Mel Gibson?"

"Of course he doesn't look like Mel Gibson. I've never heard of anything so ridiculous. He's nice-looking, but he's certainly not movie-star material." If she were Pinocchio, her nose would be four inches longer, Maris thought disgustedly. Luke might not look precisely like Mel Gibson, but he was every bit as handsome.

"Methinks the lady doth protest a little too much," Lori quipped in her ear with a laugh.

"Come and meet him for yourself," Maris retorted.

"At the very first opportunity, my friend."

They talked for about fifteen minutes, about other topics than Luke Rivers, then signed off with promises to see each other very soon.

Maris sat there more than a little disgruntled. Damned gossips. Why was everyone else's business so interesting to some people? Didn't they have enough to do keeping their own lives on course? Or were they so bored with their own routines and ruts that they became titillated over a widow hiring a man to break her horses? Of course, Luke really *was* unusually good-looking....

Slapping her palms on the table, Maris pushed herself to her feet. She was tired of the topic, and if one person—other than

Lori, of course—dared to mention Luke Rivers to her with a smug twinkle in his or her eye, she would let him have it with both barrels.

Luke was riding Mother. Maris stood with the soapy sponge in her hand and surprise on her face. He was in the secondary pasture, putting the mare through a variety of paces—a walk, a gallop, a trot. Mother tossed her head every so often, but obeyed Luke's commands. Dropping the sponge into the bucket of water, Maris deserted the old sideboard she'd been scrubbing down and hurried over to the fence to watch.

The grace and ease of Luke's performance awed Maris. He was a wonderful rider, using both the reins and his legs to guide the mare. Around and around the pasture they went, then, without warning, Luke would head the mare for the fence, draw back on the reins and call "Whoa!" The mare stopped, of course, not wanting to tangle with barbed wire. But Maris could see that the animal was learning what the word *whoa* meant.

Maris stayed at the fence for some time, but when she realized that Luke wasn't merely taking a short ride, she returned to the sideboard. Before reaching into the bucket for the sponge, she brushed back a stray lock of hair on her forehead with the back of her hand. At the same time she spotted an approaching vehicle. Smiling, she started walking to the parking area to greet Jessica Larson McCallum. Only last week Jessica had married Sterling McCallum, and if two people were ever more mismatched, Maris hadn't met them.

But the newly wed Jessica had a glow these days that was pure magic, which couldn't help denting Maris's theory that men and women simply were not compatible.

"Hello, Jessica," she called ahead.

"Maris, how are you?" Jessica called back while getting out of her pickup truck.

"It's nice seeing you. Come inside and we'll have a glass of iced tea."

"Thank you. I could use a cool drink."

Jessica was tall and slender and quite pretty. In sending her a sidelong glance on their way to the house, Maris decided that

Jessica was *very* pretty. Had falling in love added depth to her looks?

They entered the house through the kitchen door. "How is Sterling?" Maris asked.

"Wonderful, beautiful, loving, lovable..." Jessica stopped to laugh. "I could go on and on and bore you to tears."

"You're happy."

"Ecstatic, Maris. And baby Jennifer... well, words escape me when it comes to Jenny. But—" smiling teasingly, she pulled out her wallet "—I just happen to have a few pictures of her."

The baby had been left on the Kincaids' doorstep in April. No one could understand why they had been chosen, though everyone seemed to agree that boring, Milquetoast Dugin Kincaid was hardly the type of man to be roaming around the countryside, fathering children. Certainly Jeremiah Kincaid, Dugin's father, although still a vigorous man with an eye for pretty women, had been too old for those kinds of shenanigans. Of course, Maris thought, looks can be deceiving. It was more likely though that whoever left the baby chose the Kincaids simply because they were the wealthiest folks in town.

After the baby had gone into the social-services system Sterling McCallum had tried to find her mother, or anyone related for that matter, without success. Jessica, who was the head of social services, had gotten so involved with the child she'd arranged to become Jennifer's foster mother after marrying Sterling. Now, if everything worked out, Jessica, Sterling and Jennifer were going to be a happy family.

Looking at the photos, Maris's eyes filled with tears. She would never have such a beautiful little family, but maybe she could adopt a child on her own. Adoption was probably the *only* way she would ever have a baby of her own. "Oh, Jessica, she's the most beautiful baby I've ever seen," Maris said, all but bawling with emotion.

Jessica was blinking back a few tears of her own. "Sterling and I think so."

Maris handed back the wallet and went to the refrigerator for the pitcher of iced tea.

"How's Keith doing, Maris?"

Jessica was the social worker who had brought Keith to the Wyler ranch. Jessica had called soon after Ray had died and explained his situation, and Maris's heart had immediately gone out to the troubled, abused boy. She'd needed no time at all to consider helping Keith Colson; instead she'd told Jessica to bring him at once.

Maris brought the tea and two tumblers containing ice cubes to the table. "Keith is doing great, Jessica, and that's—" she grinned "—no bull." The two women laughed over Maris's little pun. "Seriously," Maris continued, seating herself at the table with Jessica, "he's a great kid." Her gaze met Jessica's. "I wish he were my son."

Jessica sighed softly. Maris had a good heart. Most people who suffered a sudden loss, as she had with Ray, wouldn't have been able to take a boy like Keith into their home and treat him so kindly.

"I know you're grieving, Maris, but time heals all sorrows. Most of us have lost someone important. It just takes time to get over it. Not that you'll ever forget Ray, but in time your pain will diminish."

"Grieving?" A moment of embarrassment pinkened Maris's cheeks. She liked Jessica, but didn't know her very well, certainly not the way she knew Lori, so there were some subjects she couldn't talk about with ease. And maybe she should be grieving. Maybe she should be wallowing in self-pity because her husband had died. "Uh . . . yes," she said lamely.

"Is Keith working somewhere on the ranch right now?" Jessica inquired. "I'd like to say hello."

Keith was a much more comfortable topic. "He went to town today." Maris smiled. "Armed with my grocery list for the week."

"And the cash to purchase the food?"

"I would trust Keith with anything on the ranch, Jessica." Maris leaned forward. "I would swear on a Bible that he will never get into trouble again."

"If that's true, it's your doing." Jessica reached out and touched Maris's hand. "Thank you. I just knew that all Keith needed was a chance, Maris. You've given it to him, and I truly believe that what goes around comes around. For your own kindness, you'll be rewarded in some way. You'll see." Jessica began gathering up her purse. "I'll be running along. Tell Keith hello for me. I'll drop in again when I'm out this way."

"Anytime, Jessica."

It wasn't until Maris was back outside and scrubbing the sideboard that she realized Jessica hadn't mentioned Luke. Apparently there were some people in the area who didn't listen to gossip, thank goodness.

While Keith carried in the groceries, Maris began putting them away. When everything was unloaded, Keith laid some money on the counter. "That's your change."

"Thanks, Keith." Placing canned goods on a shelf, Maris said, "Jessica stopped by to say hello." Instantly a wary glint appeared in Keith's eyes. "I told her you were doing great, so please don't worry about your future. You're welcome to stay here for as long as you want."

Keith looked down at his boots. "Uh...even after school starts?"

Maris went to the boy and took his hand. "Keith, I told you before that you can finish your schooling from here. Jessica told you the same thing. This is your home now." She smiled. "What on earth would I do without you? You're the only family I have."

Keith rarely mentioned his own family, especially his abusive father, and Maris never pushed him into talking about his past. But sometimes, like now, Keith's youthful dark eyes contained more pain than she cared to see in anyone's eyes.

"Enough of that," she said lightly, giving Keith's hand a playful shake. "I've got a new job for you. Luke has been riding Mother and Curly today. What I want you to do is to ignore everything else and help Luke with the horses."

"No kidding?" Keith's lapse into sadness completely vanished. "Can I start right now?" he asked eagerly.

Maris started putting food away again. "Go out and talk to Luke about it. I really haven't had the chance, what with one thing and another all day. But you heard him say those horses were going to need a lot of riding once he got them to a certain stage."

"Uh...Maris, I bought you a little gift."

Maris had noticed the bulge in his shirt pocket, but really hadn't given it any thought. Now Keith reached into the pocket and brought out a small object wrapped in pink tissue paper.

"It ain't much," he mumbled sheepishly, holding out the tiny package. "But it sort of reminded me of you...when I saw it."

With her heart melting, Maris accepted the package. So she wouldn't cry, she forced a little laugh. "They always say the best presents come in small packages." Gently she removed the tissue wrapping and saw a delicate, heart-shaped porcelain trinket. "Oh, it's beautiful, Keith."

"It's a little box," he explained. "The top comes off."

The "top" was decorated with miniature red roses and green leaves. Never had a gift touched Maris more. But why would this fragile, lovely little object remind Keith of her?

"The woman at the store told me that ladies keep things in little boxes like this." He frowned. "But it sure wouldn't hold anything very big, would it?"

It was already holding something for Maris that was more valuable than diamonds—Keith's affection. "I'll find something to put in it, never fear, and I intend keeping it on the top of my dresser so I can see it every day. Thank you." She gave him a quick kiss on the cheek and then saw the pleased surprise on his face. "I'll treasure it always. Run along now and talk to Luke."

The boy bounded from the house and let the screen door bang behind him. Maris smiled wistfully and looked at the tiny box in her hand. "It really is beautiful," she whispered. No one had ever given her anything quite like it before. She was not a porcelain-and-miniature-roses sort of woman.

At least she had never thought of herself that way.


Luke noticed Keith hanging on the corral fence. The horse he was working with at the present was a handsome animal. It had the configuration of a quarter horse with the distinct black-and-white spotted markings on its rump and loins of the Appaloosa. This was the first horse of Maris's herd that really excited Luke. He'd already named him Rocky, and he liked the way the animal moved, even though Rocky wasn't exactly receptive to Luke's advances.

Giving both Rocky and himself a breather, Luke walked over to the spigot, turned it on and splashed water over his head, arms and bare chest. "Hot today," he called to Keith.

"Yeah, real hot," Keith agreed.

After shaking the water out of his eyes, Luke ambled over to the fence. "So, how's it going in town?"

Keith shrugged. "Same as always."

"Do your friends live in town?"

"Uh . . . yeah, most of them." It was a tough question to answer, because his previous friends weren't going to be his friends when school started and he had to start mingling with his peers again. That was okay with him. He liked living like normal folks, and he wasn't going to screw up and do something to ruin what he had on the No Bull. Which meant finding new friends, kids who didn't get their kicks from stealing and vandalizing other people's property.

"Maris said I should talk to you about helping with the horses. She said you were riding Mother and Curly today. Are they ready for riding now, Luke?"

"Mother is. You can start riding her in the morning. I'll ride Curly a little more before turning him over to you." Luke grinned. "Glad to have you on the team, Keith, but I can almost guarantee you're going to get tired of riding before we're through with the herd."

"I won't, Luke. I know I won't." Keith gazed admiringly at the horse in the corral. "He's kind of special-looking, ain't he? How come he's got those spots on his rump?"

"Those spots are called a blanket, Keith. He's an Appaloosa, and someone bred him to get that exact effect in his coloring. Breeding Appaloosas isn't a simple matter. Mating an Appaloosa stud with an Appaloosa mare doesn't guarantee an Appaloosa foal."

"No kidding? That's kind of odd, ain't it?"

Luke ran his fingers through his wet hair, smoothing it back from his forehead. "It's just a trick of nature, I guess."

"Did you grow up on a ranch?"

Luke nodded. "In Texas."

Keith looked at the handsome animal standing on the other side of the corral. "You sure were lucky, Luke. I really like living on a ranch."

Luke was studying the boy. "Then you lived in town before this summer?"

"I've been here since May—just after Ray died."

"I see." There was a story behind Keith's connection to Maris and the ranch, Luke decided. For one thing, no one ever mentioned his family, or if he even had one. In fact, Maris had been very closemouthed about Keith right from the first.

"Are you related to Maris?" Luke quietly asked.

"No, but I wish I was. Hey, he's pawing the ground. Is he getting mad, Luke?"

Luke looked back at the Appaloosa and grinned. "He'd rather be out in the pasture. Well, I'd better get back to work. Me and Rocky are going to be friends, though he doesn't know it yet."

"You named him Rocky? Cool," Keith commented with an approving grin. "Is it okay if I stay out here and watch you work?"

"Yeah, it's fine. Just don't yell or make any sudden movements, okay? And keep Blackie on your side of the fence."

"Okay."

At supper that evening Keith talked on and on about Luke and Rocky. "You should've seen how Luke calmed him down, Maris. He rubbed him all over with an old sack, then with a blanket. Rocky loved it."

"I've seen the process," Maris said with a glance at Luke, who instantly sent her a grin that she saw as masculine smugness. Obviously he was basking in Keith's enthusiastic admiration and the whole situation worried her. Luke Rivers, after all, was not the best role model for a boy like Keith.

That was something she should have considered before this, she realized uneasily. Keith was all but bursting with elation because he was going to be helping Luke with the horses, and she couldn't very well reverse herself on that decision now.

She made another decision. After dinner was over she would talk to Luke and ask him to avoid telling Keith stories about his wild-and-woolly good times on the rodeo circuit. Maris actually shuddered at the thought of that sort of camaraderie developing between the two of them. She would be crushed if Keith followed in Ray's and Luke's footsteps, particularly since it would be her fault for exposing the boy to a man of Luke's feckless nature.

Immediately after dinner, she firmly resolved that whatever it took, she was going to talk to Luke alone. This was not going to be a conversation for Keith to overhear.

# Seven

"Luke, would you teach me how to use a rope the way you do?"

Still seated at the dinner table, though everyone had finished eating, Maris let her gaze drift from boy to man. Keith was no longer shy with Luke and was, in fact, developing a bad case of hero-worship. Maris opened her mouth to intervene, but Luke answered before she could suggest that learning to use a rope really wasn't a very high-priority item.

"Be glad to, Keith. How about a lesson right now?"

Keith's excitement had him up and heading for the door at once, and Maris's heart sank. Luke, grinning at the boy's enthusiasm, stood up to follow.

"Luke," Maris said in a low voice. "I need to talk to you."

Luke's entire expression changed, his face taking on a predatory cast. "Anytime, babe. Just say the word."

Maris's eyes flashed angrily. "I *said* talk!"

"Luke? Are you coming?" Keith called from just outside the door, obviously anxious to get started with his roping lesson.

"I'm coming." Almost lazily Luke moved around the table, stopping very close to Maris's chair to lean over and whisper, "What's it going to be this time, honey, another fight or something with a little spice to it?"

She lifted her eyes to send him a venomous look. "It's happens to be something very important, and I do not appreciate your crude jokes."

Laughing deep in his throat, Luke went through the back door to join Keith. Maris continued to sit at the table, while anger wreaked havoc on her nervous system. How dared he call her "babe" and "honey"? If only she didn't need his proficiency with the horses so badly. For a few seconds she indulged in a gratifying mental image of herself telling him what a careless, negligent, pleasure-seeking jerk he was, and then to get his gear together and get the hell off of her ranch.

Reality began overriding her anger. Luke wasn't careless or negligent when it came to the horses, and their training was moving along at a rapid pace. With Mother and Sugar and Zelda and all the other animals he'd been working with, he showed endless patience and an unquestionable expertise. She couldn't do something so stupid as to lose her temper and destroy the best thing she had going for the ranch, regardless of his insolent reminders that he would gladly take her to bed.

Besides, there'd been a teasing note in his whispery voice when he'd leaned over her. She probably presented a comical challenge to a man like him, which wasn't a particularly flattering idea to Maris. Yet what other amusement was there for Luke on the No Bull but to bait her and then watch her feathers ruffle? And dumb her, she bristled on cue. No wonder he'd walked out laughing.

The table full of dirty dishes suddenly seeped into her senses. Sighing dramatically, she got up to do the dishes.

But come hell or high water, embarrassment or even another argument, she was going to have that talk with Luke before she went to bed tonight. Keith had made remarkable headway since coming to the ranch, and Luke Rivers was not going to undermine that progress by painting outlandish scenes of romance and adventure on the rodeo circuit for the impressionable teenager.

Maris was just finishing up with the dishes, when the telephone rang. Wiping her hands on a dish towel, she picked up the phone. "No Bull Ranch. This is Maris."

"You're not really serious about changing the name of your ranch, are you, Maris?"

"It's already been done, Judd. Hi, how are you?"

"But I thought you were just kidding around with that new sign."

"The Circle W was the Wylers' ranch, Judd. The No Bull is mine."

"Now that doesn't make any sense at all, Maris, not when it's the same darned ranch."

"It's not 'the same darned ranch,' Judd, but it'll be a while before it's obvious to anyone but myself."

"Maris, are you all right?" She could hear concern in Judd's somber voice. "You're talking kind of funny. Is everything all right out there?"

Worrying Judd Hensley was the last thing she wanted to do. She was fond of him and appreciated his attention. "Judd, I'm fine and so is everything else."

"Well...the reason I called was to ask you out for supper on Friday night. Melissa's advertising an all-you-can-eat fish fry at the Hip Hop, and I thought you might enjoy it."

"I would, but..." Maris bit down on her bottom lip. With all that was going on right now, did she want to leave the ranch for an evening? "Judd... would you mind terribly if I begged off? I'm working very hard to get a yard sale organized, and frankly, I'm completely exhausted at the end of the day."

"A yard sale, you say? What're you planning to sell?"

"Every piece of junk on the place."

"Those things that Ray had stored out behind the barn?"

"Yes." Recently she'd been thinking of certain articles in the house that she'd be glad to see the last of, as well. Ray's gun collection for one. She hated guns, and there were eight rifles and almost as many handguns in a locked gun cabinet in her living room. Cabinet and all were going to be added to her growing list of sale items.

"Well...I'm disappointed about Friday night, but we'll do it another time. By the way, how's your hired man working out?"

"Luke is a wizard with horses, Judd. He's working out very well." Maris had been wondering if Judd would get around to mentioning Luke.

"Uh, Maris, I've been hearing some rumors about—"

"Don't say it, Judd," she interjected sharply. "I despise gossip, especially when it's totally groundless."

Judd was silent a moment. "Sorry I brought it up. I'll call again, or drop by, Maris."

"Do that, Judd."

After goodbyes, Maris put down the phone. So, even Judd had heard the gossip about Luke doing more than just working for her. Someone was mighty busy spreading lies, or perhaps no more than amused hints and sly innuendo. Maris had never been the subject of this sort of gossip before, and she didn't much care for the feeling it gave her.

But what could she do about it? It would die down after Luke left. Until then she would just have to grin and bear it.

Maris was becoming impatient. The sun had slipped down below the mountains, it was nearly dark and Luke and Keith were still tossing loops at fence posts. They were getting along famously, she saw from a window, talking and laughing together, whooping when Keith actually succeeded in roping a post. She didn't want to go out there with some heavy-handed comment about needing to speak to Luke in private, but it was getting late and she was not going to go to bed without having that crucial conversation with Luke.

From the window it appeared to Maris that Keith was having the time of his life, which raised some extremely disturbing ambiguities within her. She wanted Keith to have fun—he'd had little enough of that before coming to the ranch—but she didn't want him having fun with a man of Luke Rivers's ilk. Though she could tell they were talking at intervals, she couldn't make out their words, and what if Luke was boasting about wine, women and song on the rodeo circuit? Wouldn't tales of that sort influence a young man, maybe start him thinking that rodeo would be a great way to go?

With intense relief, she finally saw Keith handing his coiled rope to Luke and starting for the house. The yard light, which was on a sensor responsive to darkness, flashed on and provided enough light for Maris to see Luke going into the barn.

Keith came in through the kitchen door. "Hi." He went directly to the refrigerator and took out a gallon of milk. "Roping sure is fun, Maris. You should've come down and watched. Luke said I did real well for a beginner." After pouring himself a tall glass of milk, Keith grabbed a handful of cookies and sat at the table to eat his snack.

Maris leaned her hips against the sink counter. "You like Luke, don't you?"

"Yeah, he's an all-right guy."

"Does he talk very much about himself?"

Keith looked up. "Why would he do that? Don't you like him, Maris?"

She drew a slow and uneasy breath. "I like him just fine. I was just curious about...well, about what the two of you might have discussed."

Keith grinned. "We talked about roping. He's an expert, Maris. He can do all kinds of tricks with ropes."

"I'm sure he can."

Gulping the last of his milk, Keith got up and rinsed his glass at the sink, the way Maris had requested he do when he'd first come to the ranch. "I'm hitting the sack, Maris. Luke said I could start riding Mother first thing in the morning."

"Good night, Keith. See you in the morning." Maris wanted to kick herself. There was no way she could tell Keith that she'd changed her mind about him working with Luke and the horses, not when Keith's excitement was almost tangible.

Maris pushed away from the counter. That talk with Luke was imminent.

Luke had just stepped out of the shower, when he heard someone knocking on the door of his loft quarters. "Just a minute," he yelled from the tiny bathroom. Wrapping a towel around his hips, he crossed the living room and pulled open the door.

His near nudity shocked Maris into momentary speechlessness. Then she stammered, "Uh...put some clothes on. I'll wait out here." Shivering with an internal chill, she folded her arms around herself in the barren loft and tried not to listen to the sounds in Luke's room. His bare feet made a soft slapping noise on the wood floor. A door opened—the closet?—and then she heard the rustle of clothing. Her heart seemed to be beating unusually fast. Her mouth felt dry. She would have to ask him for a glass of water.

The look on Maris's face when he'd opened that door, wearing a towel, made Luke chuckle while he yanked on a pair of clean jeans. But he returned to her with a straight face. "Come on in. *Mi casa es su casa.*"

"Indeed it is." Maris swept past him into the room. Damn him! All he'd put on was jeans, and he hadn't even closed the button at his waist. She suspected that he already considered her a prude, so she wouldn't mention more clothing if her life depended on it.

"Have a seat," Luke drawled.

There were two places to sit in there, one straight-backed chair and the bed. Maris chose the chair. Luke sat on the edge of the bed, leaning forward with his forearms resting on his thighs. "Must be something mighty important eating at you to bring you into my lair," he said with deliberate and mocking somberness.

"I'm not here to bandy words with you, Luke, so please cut the macho lines, okay?"

He changed positions, leaning back on his elbows, half sitting, half reclining. His spread thighs seemed to be pointing directly at her, a flagrant display of manly assets that could only have been more clearly defined without the jeans.

Maris got up, moved the chair to another location—one without such an arresting view—and sat down again. "I want to talk to you about Keith."

"About Keith?" Luke's teasing came to an abrupt halt and he sat up. "What about Keith?"

Her mouth was dryer still. Telling, or even asking, Luke how to behave on any level wasn't a pleasant prospect. "Could I have a glass of water?"

He looked at her peculiarly, then pushed to his feet. "Yeah, sure." Disappearing into the bathroom for a moment, he returned with a paper cup of water.

"Thank you." Maris drank it down, every drop.

"What about Keith, Maris?" Luke repeated.

It couldn't be put off any longer. She lifted her chin. "I don't want you filling his head with romantic nonsense about rodeo life. It's *not* romantic, and it's not even very civilized, and . . ."

"Hold on a minute." Luke's expression had become as hard as granite. "In the first damned place, you don't know what you're talking about. How many rodeos did *you* compete in? How many did you even attend? But that's not the point. You have your opinion of rodeo and I have mine. What *is* the point is why you would think I would discuss it with Keith, and second, if it did happen to come up in conversation when we're together, what makes you think I would romanticize the subject? Rodeo is hard work and tough competition. Most of the men and women competing for the prize money love the sport and work damn hard to prove themselves. Where do you get the nerve to call it uncivilized, when you don't even understand it?"

Maris smirked. "I understand it perfectly."

"No, babe, you don't," Luke said sardonically. "You're against rodeo because Ray loved it, and that's the long and the short of it."

Maris leapt to her feet. "You smug bastard. Just a regular Mr. Know-it-all, aren't you? Well, let me tell you something. If Ray had stayed home and taken care of this ranch instead of traipsing all over the country to chase prize money—which he never won—and women—which I'm sure he found by the droves—this ranch wouldn't be nearly bankrupt. And you have the gall to stand there and tell me not to blame rodeo?"

"He wasn't gone all the time, Maris. What did he do when he was home? Even with rodeo a big part of his life, this ranch shouldn't be bankrupt."

It was the God's truth, the *stunning* truth, and Maris's fury wilted right before Luke's eyes.

"He drank," she said listlessly. "I ran the ranch, or tried to, and with him spending every cent coming in, I couldn't keep it afloat." Her eyes flashed with renewed anger at the pity she saw in Luke's. "None of that is any of your business. I will always despise rodeo and nothing you can say or do will ever change my mind. I meant what I said about Keith. He's a good kid and he's going to make something of himself. I don't want him influenced by a bunch of fairy tales about how wonderful bumming around the country to break his neck in some rodeo arena is."

Arguing with Maris over the pros and cons of rodeo life was a no-win proposition. Luke sucked in a long, slow breath. "Who is he, Maris? How come he's living here with you? Where's his own family?"

Maris hesitated. "If I tell you about his background, will you keep it to yourself? What I mean is, unless Keith himself mentions it, will you act as though you know nothing about it?"

"He's been in trouble with the law, hasn't he?" Luke said quietly.

"Do you promise?"

"Yes, I promise. I'll never mention it to Keith. What happened?"

Maris walked to a window and looked out at the black night. This side of the barn was opposite to the yard light, and there really was nothing to see, other than her own reflection in the windowpane.

"He lived with his father and grandmother. Terrance, his father, is an alcoholic. He beat not only Keith, but his own elderly mother. No one knew it. Keith started getting into trouble at school, then he got caught shoplifting. Sterling McCallum and Jessica got involved in the case. They suspected something terribly wrong in the Colson home, but Keith would never admit to anything. Finally, I guess he just couldn't take any more abuse. He got hold of an unloaded gun and tried to hold up Bill Murray's car lot. It was a cry for help. Every time he got in trouble, he eventually got sent back to his father. The poor kid decided that going to jail would be better than living with Terrance. It was Sterling and Jessica who saved him from juvenile detention. Sterling, actually. He called me and told me the story. I needed some help on the place—" Maris turned around to face Luke "—but that wasn't the reason I agreed to Keith's coming here. I can't bear the thought of youngsters being abused, and I wanted him to have a chance at a decent life. It's been working, Luke. You must be able to see for yourself what a great kid Keith is."

Forgetting everything but her vehement concern for Keith, Maris went to Luke and laid her hand on his arm. "I don't want him to become enchanted with some unstable vocation like rodeo. I want him to get an education and to do something with his life. He's so young—young enough to be my own son—and I've become very attached to him."

"He's what, sixteen? To be your son, you would have had to have him when you were a kid."

"I'm thirty-two, Luke." She was looking into his eyes. "That's not important. Keith's future is. Will you downplay your obsession with rodeo if he should ask about it? He likes you. He admires you. But I don't want him to be like you," she said, finishing in a tortured whisper.

Never had anyone said something that hurt Luke more than what Maris had just said: *I don't want him to be like you.*

He tried to put it out of his mind. "So where's Terrance Colson now?"

Suddenly realizing that she'd been hanging on to Luke's arm, Maris backed away from him. "He's in jail. Keith's grandmother moved away. I don't think there's any other family. Luke, will you cooperate with me on this?"

Without a dram of expression on his face, he nodded. "You have my word."

This time she didn't question the value of his word but believed him wholeheartedly. Something she'd said had reached him, thank God. "Many, many thanks," she said with all the gratitude she felt inside, making her voice slightly unsteady. "I won't forget this, Luke."

Luke ran all ten of his fingers through his damp hair. "I have a feeling that neither will I, Maris." *I don't want him to be like you.* "Would you like me to walk you to the house? It's awfully dark out tonight."

Maris shook her head. "Thanks, but I'm not afraid of the dark, and the yard's pretty well lit once I get beyond the barn. Good night, Luke."

She slipped out, closing the door behind her. He sank to the bed and sat there staring down at his own two bare feet. He was thirty-five years old and owned nothing but a six-year-old pickup truck and an IOU for three thousand bucks. A cynical smile tipped one corner of his lips. Maybe Maris wasn't wrong about rodeo, after all.

There was a bustle on the ranch in the ensuing days, which elated Maris. Keith and Luke worked nonstop with the horses, and often she heard their laughter ringing throughout the compound. She rode out every morning to tend the cattle, then spent the rest of the day on the yard sale. There were only a few more items left to clean and make ready.

During lunch one day she mentioned the weeds behind the barn. "They have to be chopped down," she said, looking at both Keith and Luke.

"We'll do it right after lunch," Luke assured her.

"Great. Thanks. I made up a bunch of posters announcing the sale, and I'm going to bring them into town this afternoon to display in store windows. I've also put an ad in the newspaper. I can hardly believe the sale is going to be this weekend."

She bit down on her lip, worried suddenly. "What if no one comes to it? What if no one cares that I'm having a yard sale?"

"They'll come," Luke said.

"They will, Maris," Keith earnestly agreed.

Of course people will come, Maris told herself repeatedly during the drive to town. She smiled grimly. Maybe some would come just to get a look at her hired man.

With her stack of posters, Maris started making the rounds of Whitehorn's commercial establishments. No one refused her request to exhibit her signs in their windows, and she got to talk to a lot of old friends, many of whom promised to come and see what she had for sale this weekend.

John Tully, the drugstore owner, beamed from ear to ear when she showed him the poster. "A yard sale, eh? Well, I could use a new yard. Maybe I'll buy yours." He laughed as though he'd just invented wit, and Maris, out of friendship, laughed with him at the tired old joke.

John put the poster in a prominent spot in his best window. "How's that?"

"That's great, John. Thanks. Well, I have a few more of these to distribute, so I'd better be running along."

John followed her to the door. "How's that fellow Rivers working out?"

"Just fine, John." Maris put her hand on the door to open it.

"I sent him out to your place, you know. We met in the Hip Hop one morning and he asked if I knew of any available jobs in the area. Naturally, the minute he said he wanted ranch work, I thought of you trying to run your place with just a boy for help."

"That was kind of you, John."

John kept smiling. "Guess it turned out better than I thought."

"Better how, John?"

"Well, with the two of you becoming . . . um . . . friends . . ."

Maris heaved a discouraged sigh. "Don't believe everything you hear, John. Incidentally, do you happen to recall who told you that Luke and I were becoming . . . um . . . friends?"

"Well, let me see, Maris." The druggist scratched his balding head. "Uh . . . seems like it was Lily Wheeler."

"Now, why doesn't that surprise me?" Maris drawled sarcastically. Before John Tully could come up with a reply, Maris was going out the door. "Bye, John. Thanks for the use of your window."

Lily Mae Wheeler. Maris fumed all the way back to the ranch. That woman would try the patience of a saint. She knew everything about everybody in town and within a fifty-mile radius thereafter, and if you happened to run into her on the street, you couldn't shut her up no matter what you did. Lily could talk faster than anyone Maris had ever known, and obviously the woman didn't need much oxygen, because she rarely ever slowed down for a breath of air.

But how on earth Lily Wheeler had gotten wind of Luke working on the No Bull, Maris would never know. But then, how did Lily get most of her information? The woman just naturally attracted news, even plain, everyday and rather dull news such as a stranger in town landing a job on a ranch thirty miles from town.

Judd should hire Lily to unearth the murderer of Floyd Oakley, Maris thought wryly. She must have plenty to say on *that* subject.

# Eight

Maris had advertised the yard sale to begin at nine in the morning and end at four in the afternoon. At ten minutes after eight on Saturday morning a car arrived. Maris was walking among her sale items, removing sheets that she'd been using to protect some of the better pieces from nighttime dampness, and she looked at the car with surprise.

Winona Cobb got out and called a cheery, "Hello, Maris."

Winona was at least seventy, but seemed to have more energy than people half her age. She was short and stout, a round little butterball of a woman with iron gray hair and a chipper smile. Today she was wearing a purple tunic and her usual jewelry—a large amethyst crystal pendant and assorted bracelets. Maris had always considered Winona to be a true eccentric. Along with the junk she collected, which she sold, swapped or merely stacked in untidy piles inside her small shop or in her front yard, she kept animals—dogs, cats, chickens and goats. And bees, lots of bees. She sold the honey they produced, and it was very good honey. Winona had a way with the insects and they never stung her—even though she never wore protective clothing. People called her a "bee charmer." But Maris wasn't especially fond of bees buzzing around her head and she never stopped at Winona's place anymore. Ray used to stop often. Ray had not only stopped, he had swapped and even bought. Winona was apt to recognize some of her own junk in today's sale, Maris thought with droll amusement.

Oh, yes, there was one more side to Winona Cobb, Maris recalled as she resigned herself to the woman jumping the gun on the opening of the sale and walked out to greet her: reputedly, Winona had psychic powers. Sometimes she had visions that came upon her like sort of a fit, or spell. Winona also told fortunes; if you asked nicely and she was in the mood, although Maris had never availed herself of Winona's services.

"Hello, Winona." She was already looking around, quite avidly, Maris noted.

"Where'd you get all this stuff?" Winona asked.

"From a room in the barn," Maris replied evenly.

Winona gave her a sharp-eyed, almost suspicious look. "How'd it get in the barn?"

Maris had to physically choke back laughter. "Ray put it there."

Winona grunted. "Never knew he had so much goods. How come you're selling it?" Her gaze landed on the old marble clock, which Luke had carried outside for Maris to clean, then carried it again when she asked him to place it on the sideboard. "What's that?"

"An antique clock. It's genuine black onyx, Winona, and the face is real gold and ivory." Those were facts, not fancy. The clock, once cleaned and quite beautiful, had raised Maris's curiosity enough that she had made a trip to Whitehorn's library to research old clocks. She had found a photograph in a book that depicted a clock very similar to hers. *Circa, late 1800s. Value, $400-$500.* The book was a year old, so it was quite likely that the value of her clock was even higher than quoted.

But this was only a yard sale, after all, and she had put a price of two hundred dollars on it.

Winona looked at the tag and sniffed. "No one's gonna give you two hundred for an old clock, Maris."

Maris smiled. "Then I'll keep it. I rather like it."

By eight-thirty, Winona had checked each and every item in Maris's yard, even the old trucks and cars behind the barn. "What about that Corvette?" she asked.

"It's sold, Winona. See the Sold sign on it?"

"Oh, yeah, I see it now." She turned to Maris. "Where's that hired hand I've heard so much about?"

Inwardly Maris stiffened; outwardly she smiled coolly. "He's here somewhere. Both he and Keith will be helping with the sale." Actually, what they were doing before the sale began was attempting to separate the stallions from the other horses still remaining in the main pasture.

Keith was riding Mother and Luke was riding Rocky. Both animals were reasonably well behaved now, and Luke had successfully roped the two younger stallions and led them to the cattle pasture, which was the most distant fenced field from the buildings.

Bozo, the big red stallion was a whole different ball game, however. Over and over again he cleverly dodged the rope and ran off kicking up his hind legs and snorting. "He's a sly devil," Luke called to Keith, though the comment was accompanied by a rather pleased smile. The stallion's spirit reminded him of Pancho's. No one but Luke had ever ridden Pancho, and Luke suspected that Bozo, too, would be a one-rider horse. Before he could even begin the training process, however, he had to catch him.

Winona's keen eyes caught sight of the two men on horseback, though the pasture was some distance from the barn. "What're they doing?" she asked Maris. "That smaller fellow is Keith Colson, isn't he?"

Before Maris could say more than "Yes," Winona was on her way to the pasture. Maris breathed an exasperated sigh. Obviously the woman was determined to get a closer look at Luke.

But what did it matter? Maris thought. She had nothing to hide. Luke was a hired hand and the twenty-five dollars she handed him at the end of each week was proof of their platonic relationship. He always looked at the money with sardonic amusement and he always pretended to not notice. But the cash he'd received thus far must all be in his wallet, as he hadn't left the ranch even once since he'd begun working with the horses.

Winona stopped at the fence; Maris did the same. "Keith looks well," the older woman commented. Her piercing gaze moved to Maris. "You like him, don't you?"

"Yes. Very much."

Winona looked off across the pasture again. "Terry Colson was born mean, you know. It wasn't just his drinking that caused him to beat his son and mother."

"You knew him?"

"I lived here all my life, Maris. I know everyone."

"Yes, I expect you do," Maris said with a smile.

"Except for that lanky fellow on the Appaloosa."

Maris was watching Luke, admitting to herself the splendid way he rode and looked, admiring even the hat on his head and the boots on his feet. Feeling Winona's eyes boring into her, a flush crept into her cheeks.

"You like him, too, don't you?" Winona said.

Maris's face got redder. "I . . . he . . ."

"Oh, for pity's sake, don't be embarrassed about it. Do you think anyone expects a young woman like yourself to live alone for the rest of her life?" Winona began walking off. "I've seen enough. Thanks for letting me look around."

Maris hurried to catch up. "Did you see anything you wanted to buy?"

"Nope. Just wanted to find out what it was you were selling." Winona climbed into her car. "Drop by and say hello sometime."

Maris nodded. "I will." She meant it. It wouldn't hurt her one darned bit to dodge the bees and the goats to say hello to a neighbor. "Bye, Winona."

In the pasture Luke admitted defeat with Bozo . . . for the time being. Coiling up his rope he spoke to Keith. "We'd better unsaddle now. It's almost nine."

They rode toward the gate. "Do you really think people will come to the sale?" Keith questioned.

"They'll come," Luke said confidently. He grinned at his younger companion. "We'll be ready for them, right?"

"Right," Keith agreed. He'd been assigned to handle the cash box, and was mighty proud about Maris's putting so much trust in him. He looked at Luke and couldn't imagine anything better than the two people he liked most becoming more than just friends. "Maris is real pretty, don't you think?"

Luke laughed. "Yeah, she is. What're trying to do, boy, match us up?"

Keith's face got red, but he grinned. "Seems like a good idea to me." Whooping then, he nudged Mother into a gallop.

As Luke kept Rocky at a walk, his laughter faded. Keith might think it was a good idea, and it set all right with him, too. But Maris was another story. Her opinion of rodeo riders sure wasn't one to encourage a man.

* * *

The number of people, who seemed to arrive in droves, stunned Maris. For hours she went from one group to another, discussing the various merchandise, and selling it!

Melissa Avery fell in love with the sideboard. "I have the perfect spot for it in the Hip Hop." She also bought most of the mismatched chairs and tables. "I'm planning on expanding the café," she told Maris.

John Tully bought the clock, after arguing Maris down to one hundred fifty dollars. A young couple purchased the bedstead and two dressers. A rancher bought the entire stack of galvanized pails and the riding lawn mower.

And so it went throughout the day. One man, who owned a gas station and dealt in used vehicles on the side, bought all the old, broken-down cars and trucks—other than the Corvette, of course—from behind the barn. After that transaction was made, Luke toted the miscellaneous motors around to the front of the building, as there was no longer a reason for him to hang around the larger equipment.

The hand tools went, the coat tree with the brass fittings, much of the glassware and, finally, one by one, Ray's gun collection.

By four Maris was exhausted. There were still some things unsold, and most of the larger items that were sold hadn't yet been picked up. But the cash box was overflowing, and when the last car drove off, Keith brought it to Maris with a totally amazed expression.

"There must be thousands of dollars in here, Maris."

Maris's weary spirit suddenly revived. "Let's count it." She and Keith started for the house. Maris stopped and turned. "You, too, Luke. Come on."

"No, you two go ahead. I'm going to take a shower."

Concealing her disappointment that he didn't want to be included in the most exciting part of the day, she nodded and proceeded to the house. She and Keith sat at the kitchen table.

"I don't believe this," she said while sorting the cash from the checks, then stacking the cash by denomination. "Keith, look. There are six one-hundred-dollar bills." They counted the cash and added up the checks, and Maris sat back, weak with incredulity. "Three thousand five hundred and sixty three dollars. And that's not counting the change." There was a small mountain of coins. "I'm looking at it with my own eyes and I still don't believe it."

Keith chuckled gleefully. "Hundreds of people came, Maris."

"Everyone from the whole area, I think."

"There's not much left out there for tomorrow."

"I know, but my signs said Saturday *and* Sunday, so we'll have to be here. Keith, this calls for a celebration." She picked up two of the twenties. "Would you do me a huge favor and go to town? I want three of the biggest, best steaks you can find. We'll cook them on the charcoal grill. How does that sound?"

Keith's eyes lit up. "Terrific! Sure, I'll go." He took the money from Maris's hand.

"And stop at the bakery and pick out something really special for dessert."

"A pie?"

"Or a cake or...whatever looks good to you. Okay?"

"Gotcha. I won't be long."

"Drive carefully," Maris called as Keith dashed out. She sat back again, sighing and shaking her head at the stacks of cash on the table. The sale was a lifesaver. She could catch up on the mortgage payments and certainly all the small bills that had been coming in the mail with Past Due stickers could be paid in full. Plus, she reminded herself, she would be receiving the balance due from Jim Humphrey on the sale of the Corvette. Oh, what a wonderful feeling it was to have the money to get herself back in the black.

Then she thought of Luke and that IOU. The means to pay him the full amount was sitting right in front of her. Her heart skipped a beat. If she paid him off, would he leave the ranch and her stranded with a herd of partially broken horses?

Oh, he wouldn't, she mentally argued. Surely he wouldn't.

But dared she take that risk? He had agreed to receiving payment from the sale of horses, and that was the arrangement she must hold him to.

Not nearly as excited as she'd been, Maris gathered up the money and brought it to her bedroom, where she put it in a shoe box in her closet. The coins remained on the table, and she returned to the kitchen to scoop them into a plastic bowl. Later, when she had the time, she would sort and count them. For now, she stuck the bowl in a cupboard.

Then she went outside to organize what items were left for tomorrow's sale. She was busily moving things around, when Luke walked up.

"Need some help?"

"Sure, thanks. I thought it would be best to close the gaps."

She was placing everything that wasn't already sold in one small area of the yard. Luke pitched in and the job was completed in about ten minutes. Maris stopped and looked thoughtfully at the goods. "There sure isn't much left."

"It was a success, all right." Luke had showered, shaved and put on clean jeans and shirt. The sale had been a success because they had worked their fannies off today. In fact, on this ranch they all worked their fannies off *every* day. He had never worked harder or put in longer hours in his life, and the funny thing, he realized while studying Maris studying the remnants of today's sale, was that he wasn't resentful, annoyed or unhappy about it. For some unimaginable reason he was unusually content, and Lord knows he'd never been content with ordinary labor. So... what was going on with him, pray tell?

"Well," Maris declared briskly, placing her hands on her hips to look at Luke. "You're all cleaned up and I'm a mess. I've got to do something about that. Listen, I sent Keith to town to buy some steaks. I think a little celebration is in order after today's big success, don't you?"

"Uh..." He'd been planning on going to town himself. For weeks now he hadn't even started his pickup, let alone gone anywhere. It was Saturday night and he'd been thinking of a few beers and maybe looking for a place with a live band. While showering, he'd toyed with the idea of asking Maris to go along, but had decided she would only say no. Now here she was, talking about a celebration dinner, and it wasn't as easy for him to say no as it was for her. "Sure, sounds great," he told her, thinking that he could go to town *after* dinner.

"Good. I'm going in now." Maris started away. "Oh. If you wouldn't mind digging out the barbecue grill—it's in the toolshed."

"Wouldn't mind at all. I'll get it."

"Thanks." He hadn't asked how much money she had taken in today, Maris thought gratefully as she went into the house and directly to her bedroom and bath to clean up. She paused at her closet to look over her modest wardrobe. Regardless of her fervent hope that Luke wouldn't suggest she pay him now instead of after the horse auction, she felt rather festive and didn't want merely to pull on a pair of clean jeans for the evening. Something pretty, she thought, while moving hangers around to check the garments. Something feminine. It had been ages since she'd bought any new clothes, but anything other than jeans would look new to Luke.

Frowning, she stopped to chide herself. She wasn't dressing up for Luke, was she? Did she want him to see her feminine side? Lord knows there'd been nothing feminine about her since he'd shown up.

Still, he'd kissed her. Maris's heart beat faster at the memory. He was a handsome, exciting, sexy man, whatever he did for a living or how short a time he'd be in the vicinity, and she was almost constantly aware of him. Common sense to the contrary, she was attracted to Luke and couldn't help believing that he was attracted to her.

But where could it go? Dismissing the whole discomfiting topic with a toss of her head, Maris pulled out a faded denim skirt and a yellow blouse. The outfit would satisfy her desire for something other than jeans, but it couldn't possibly give Luke any ideas about her "dressing up" for him.

They ate outside at Maris's small patio table. The food was great, the heat of the day had passed and the evening air was soft and silky. But all was not right. During the meal Maris had noticed that Keith seemed distracted and nervous, which wasn't like him. Upon returning from town with the steaks and a delicious-looking chocolate-and-raspberry torte, he had disappeared to shower and clean up. He'd returned to the kitchen wearing his best jeans and shirt and Maris had smiled teasingly. "My, you look handsome."

A slow flush had colored his cheeks, but he'd grinned and gone outside to sit with Luke, who was watching the steaks on the grill so Maris could finish the green salad she'd started earlier. Blackie, who was never very far away from Keith, lay nearby, her head on her front paws.

The food was wonderful, and they ate it with gusto and enjoyment. But Keith's unusual mood worried Maris. Since coming to the ranch, the boy had had his silent moments, which she'd considered only normal, given his background. But this was different. She wanted to ask if anything was wrong, but hesitated to do so in front of Luke, as it might embarrass Keith.

They were just finishing up with dessert, when Keith suddenly blurted, "Maris, could I use the truck tonight?"

Maris slowly put down her fork. This was a first, and obviously what had been on Keith's mind throughout the meal. She wanted to handle it sensibly. "To do what, Keith?"

His face was crimson and he was staring down at his plate. "I...asked a girl to see a movie with me tonight." He lifted his eyes. "She's a real nice girl, Maris. I...sort of liked her in school last year, but we never really spoke...very much. She was at the store when I was picking out the steaks. Anyway...we got to talking and I asked her to go to the movie with me, and she said yes."

An enormous relief flooded Maris's system. She'd been worried about dark, terrible things concerning Keith, not about something as innocent and natural as this. She glanced at Luke, who she could see was maintaining a completely impassive expression, though there was a spark of masculine amusement in his eyes. Maris looked at Keith again. Anxiety was written all over his handsome boy-man face. He'd gone way out on a limb, making a date with a girl, when he didn't know if he would have transportation. No wonder he'd been nervous.

"Yes," Maris said quietly. "You may use the truck, Keith."

He jumped to his feet, no boy-man now but all boy, excited and eager to be off. "Thanks, Maris. Thanks a lot. I have to go right now or I'll be late." He started away, then stopped. "I won't be home late. Um...no later than midnight, okay?"

Maris smiled. "Okay." Her gaze followed Keith to the truck, which was immediately started and then gone. Blackie whimpered. "It's all right, Blackie," Maris said soothingly. "Keith will be back."

"You're a nice woman, Maris," Luke said softly.

The comment startled her. "But who likes nice women, right?" she quipped as she took the steak bone from her plate and brought it to Blackie. The little dog instantly settled down with her treat.

"Nice men?" Luke drawled.

They were alone. With Keith gone, she and Luke were completely alone and the sun was going down. This, too, was a first. She could get very flustered right now, Maris realized. She could clear the table, and flutter from patio to kitchen and look very silly dashing about, simply because she was alone with a man who had kissed her and the sun was going down.

She took her chair again, calmly, coolly. "I'm not sure I've ever known any nice men."

"Present company excluded, of course."

That smooth-as-honey tone didn't fool Maris. Beneath it, he was laughing at her. But he was not going to rattle her, she vowed. "Our criteria for what constitutes 'nice' probably differs, don't you think?"

He shrugged, casually, adorably. Damn him, thought Maris, and damn myself, too. Why was she noticing every tiny detail of his appearance? The minute crinkles at the corners of his eyes, for instance. And the way his shoulders filled his white shirt.

"It appears to me that our criteria for anything differs," he replied. "'Course, that could be because you're female and I'm male. Men and women don't think alike."

"That should be my line," Maris said dryly.

He grinned. "Why's that?"

"Because it's something women know and men don't. Usually," she added. "How come you know it?"

"My mother told me," he said solemnly.

Maris stared, then laughed. "You're pulling my leg, right?"

"I never joke about my mother."

Was he yanking her chain, or what? "Is your mother living?"

"Alive and thriving in Texas."

"And your father?"

"He died ten years ago. Ma sold the ranch and moved to town. I see her about once a year." Behind the conversation Luke was thinking of his plans for the evening—heading for Whitehorn and a few beers. But this was an opportunity if he'd ever stumbled across one. Just once he'd like to see Maris Wy-

ler relaxed and enjoying herself. Maybe tonight was the night.
"What about your folks?" he questioned.

Maris sighed softly. "Gone, both of them. And I was an only
child. Do you have any brothers or sisters?"

Luke hooked his arm over the back corner of his chair.
"Nope. It's just me and Ma."

"If you see her only once a year, I hope you call her often,"
Maris said, then wished she hadn't. "Sorry. I'm sure you're not
looking for advice from me."

"It's okay. I know I don't call her enough."

"Feel free to use my phone, Luke. Anytime."

He nodded. "I'll take you up on that. Maybe tomorrow.
Maris, would you like to go somewhere?"

Her eyes widened. "Go where?"

"I don't know. For a ride, maybe?"

"Um..." Oh, Lord, what should she say? A ride in Luke's
truck was hardly a romantic outing, and yet, why had he suggested it?

"Hey, I've got a really great idea," Luke exclaimed. "You
haven't ridden any of the horses yet. How about us taking a ride
right now?"

"But it's getting dark." Despite her common-sense objec-
tion, the idea was appealing. "Which horse would I be riding?"

"Mother. I'll take Rocky."

He was fond of Rocky, Maris knew. Maybe the Appaloosa
would be the horse he picked to take with him when he left at
the end of September. Disturbed by that image, she became
very still.

"Come on, say you'll go," Luke said.

"I... have to clear the table and... and do the dishes."

Luke got up and began stacking plates. "Clearing away will
take three minutes. I'll help you with the dishes when we get
back."

Uneasily Maris pushed herself to her feet. "That wouldn't be
necessary, but Luke... I don't know. It's almost dark."

"A great time of day for a ride." He headed for the house
with most of the dirty dishes.

Maris gathered up the rest and followed. He was insisting and she really would like to do it. But was a moonlit ride on a velvety night a wise move for her to make with Luke?

Then she thought of the consequences of a firm refusal. Luke would either take that ride alone or go to his quarters in the loft of the barn. It was such a beautiful evening, and she would spend it in her kitchen, washing dishes, and then go to bed. With Keith gone, the house would be empty and lonely. Very, very lonely.

"All right," she said as she placed her load of dirty dishes in the sink on top of those that Luke had carried in. "Let's go."

Luke's pleased grin was a yard wide. "Great! Let's do it to it!"

Together they walked back outside, laughing at his silly remark. Maris closed the door behind them.

The moment Maris mounted the mare Luke realized she might have ridden quite a lot before, but she wasn't completely comfortable on a strange horse.

Maris's mind was elsewhere. "I should have changed into jeans," she said, arranging her skirt around her legs.

"You look great in a dress," Luke said quietly. He was standing next to Maris and the mare, making sure Maris was well seated, worrying some about her riding a strange, newly broken horse in the dark. He put the reins in her hands. "Hold them evenly, a little loosely. Mother responds well to a light touch."

"All right." Maris recognized the giddiness in her system. The moon was coming up, full and huge. Doing something like this, impulsive and unplanned, was completely alien to her present life-style. She had become rather staid, she knew, but there'd been a time when she had laughed easily and blossomed under a handsome man's attention. That was what she was feeling tonight, a blooming, an unusual radiance, and more than a little daring. Maybe her rare mood was because her financial worries were easing, or because the moon was full and bright.

Then again, it could be because of being alone with Luke.

"Are you set?" he asked. "Do you feel comfortable in the saddle?"

"I'm fine." She laughed for no reason, merely because it felt good to laugh. "Come on. Get on Rocky and let's go."

Frowning slightly, Luke left her side to mount the Appaloosa. "Maybe we should just ride around the pasture."

"No way," Maris exclaimed. She was ready for adventure and picturing the miles of open land beyond the fences. "The night is heavenly. Let's ride and ride and ride," she said with a dreamy sigh.

Luke's pulse rate took a noticeable jump in speed. Maris was beautiful in the moonlight, and her mood was one he'd never witnessed before. The husky tone of her voice and her carefree gestures told him that anything could happen tonight.

Anything.

# Nine

The landscape was beautifully eerie in the moonlight. Trees and bushes, sparse in number, cast long, dark shadows upon grass and ground that appeared silvery and spectral. The air was still and unusually warm for a Montana night.

Luke tended the gates and they left the fences behind and headed into open country. Blackie was following, staying about ten feet behind. Maris looked back at the dog. "With Keith gone, Blackie has apparently attached herself to us," she remarked to Luke.

Luke glanced back. "Seems so." His gaze lingered on Maris. "How're you doing?"

"Luke Rivers, are you worried about Mother or me?" she asked teasingly.

"Mother can take care of herself."

"And I can't?"

"You're not used to riding a strange horse."

"Well, I like riding and I'm doing just fine. And I rode plenty of strange horses before Ray traded them for that Corvette." Maris wished she hadn't mentioned Ray. She didn't want to talk about Ray tonight, but with Luke's next words, she knew they were going to.

"Did Ray ever ride with you?"

"Occasionally. But Ray was usually busy with one thing or another."

There was a trace of bitterness in Maris's voice, which piqued Luke's curiosity. "Where'd you two meet? I know Ray grew up right here, but what about you? Have you always lived in the Whitehorn area?"

Maris took a breath, not completely comfortable with Luke's questions. "I came here as…a bride. I grew up in another small town, Demming, Montana. Have you heard of it?"

"Can't say that I have. So you met Ray in Demming?"

"No, in Bozeman. I was in college ..." She sensed Luke's sudden, sharp look. "In my final year. I was planning to teach at the elementary level." She had met Ray Wyler through friends, and had fallen so hard her teaching plans had almost immediately taken second place.

Luke was frowning, all but scowling, recalling his own lack of education. He'd been so enthralled with rodeo that he'd barely made it through high school. His folks had wanted him to attend Texas A&M and had offered to pay for everything— tuition, housing, books, even spending money—and he'd refused and gone off to join the rodeo circuit, leaving behind his high school diploma and the ashes of his parents' hopes.

For the first time ever he doubted his wisdom in that decision, wondering, in fact, if there'd been any wisdom involved. He could have gotten an education, *then* roamed the globe, chasing rodeo, if that was what he still wanted. But today, tonight, riding along with Maris Wyler, he would be able to say, "My school was Texas A&M." It would surprise and maybe please her. Instead he had nothing to say on the subject of education.

His voice became a little gruffer. "You met Ray in Bozeman, married him and moved to the ranch. Did all of that take place in rapid succession?"

Maris was looking straight ahead. "We got married the day after I received my diploma."

Luke uneasily shifted his weight in the saddle. "You must've loved him."

"It was a long time ago, Luke. Let's talk about something else." She had loved Ray madly, and had come to the ranch brimming with starry-eyed dreams for their future. Remembering their first happy weeks together, their first months, was painful, and she didn't want to dwell on that or what had come after.

"But you did love him," Luke persisted, not ready to drop the subject.

Maris drew in and then released a long breath, finally allowing a terse "Yes."

"What happened?"

"What makes you think something happened?"

"Maris, I was with the two of you in Casper, remember?"
There was no love between them that night in Casper, Luke
would swear. A man who loved his wife—and he'd been around
plenty of guys who did—didn't play around with other women
right in front of her. Ray had been a total jerk that night, a
drunken, loudmouth fool who hadn't seemed to care one
damned bit that Maris was sitting at a table and seeing everything he did.

"I really don't want to remember that night. It's no kindness to remind me of it, Luke."

"It proved that something happened to kill the feelings the
two of you had for each other when you got married," Luke
said stubbornly.

Maris shot him a fierce look. "Which really isn't any of your
business, is it?"

"Technically, no. But I have this great big lump of curiosity
in my gut, Maris." He nudged Rocky a little closer to Maris's
horse. "Tell me about it. Please."

Maris gave a short, bitter laugh. "Tell you about my marriage just to satisfy your curiosity? Really, Luke—"

He broke in, brusquely. "You have to know why I'm curious." Just then Blackie darted in front of Mother's front
hooves. The mare spooked and reared. Maris let out a yelp of
confusion. Luke could see her losing the reins and falling
backward. He leaned far to the right, snaked out an arm and
caught her by the waist. "Hang on to me," he yelled. Maris
clutched at his shirt with one hand and the other went up
around his neck. It happened so fast. One second she was
peacefully riding Mother, the next she was draped across Luke's
lap and the mare was hightailing it for parts unknown.

Luke pulled Rocky to an abrupt halt. "Are you all right?"

"Just shaken up," Maris said hoarsely. "What happened?"

"Blackie ran under Mother's hooves. Scared her."

Maris shivered. "Not as much as she scared me." Luke was
holding the reins with one hand and Maris with the other. His
solid body and arms felt like sanctuary, and asking to be put
down on the ground never entered her mind. "Thanks," she
whispered raggedly. "You're very quick."

"Quick in some things, slow in others," he said with his lips
sunk into her hair, which had the most arousing scent he'd ever

encountered. His reply was a reference to his dull-witted refusal to go to college when he'd had the chance, though it was also a hint of how he would like to make love to her. "You're not comfortable," he said huskily. "Put your left leg over the saddle horn. We'll head back."

"Maybe I should ride behind you." It was a sensible suggestion, arising from the recognition of the intimacy of their embrace. It *was* an embrace, make no mistake. His body cradled hers, and with her legs separated by the saddle horn she felt extremely vulnerable.

"Are you afraid of me, Maris?"

"No, of course not, but . . ."

Luke's lips thinned slightly. "Maybe you should be. We're getting closer to making love every hour that we spend together, and you have to know it as well as I do." He clucked his tongue and got Rocky moving. "Say something, Maris."

Her heart was beating like a jackhammer. "I . . . I'm not sure what to say. Do you really believe that?"

"Wholeheartedly," Luke said, grim lipped.

"Have I said or done anything to give you that idea?"

"Yeah, you have. You've smelled sweet and looked beautiful. You've smiled and worked hard and treated Keith kindly. You've cooked my meals and washed my clothes. You've worried in front of me and worried even harder when you thought no one was looking. You don't have the remotest understanding of how pretty you are, and you'll turn sometimes, unexpectedly, and dazzle me with the beauty of your face and smile. And when I kissed you, you kissed me back. Yeah, you've said and done a lot to give me that idea."

Maris gulped and whispered, "Not intentionally, Luke."

"You've watched me working with the horses, Maris."

"Only because I was interested in your methods."

"You do most of your watching when I'm working without a shirt." He transferred the reins from his right hand to his left, which was the arm supporting her back. Then he stopped Rocky and tipped Maris's chin with his fingertips to look into her eyes. "I want you, lady, and you want me."

She couldn't move, merely sat there in his arms, on his lap, absorbing his maleness and declaration of intent. "I don't know how to deal with you, Luke," she whispered.

"Yes, you do." His mouth brushed hers once, gently, then settled into a serious kiss. She felt hunger in that kiss, from him and within herself. Her own happiness, for which she had once held such high hopes, was only an old memory and seemed so far away as to have involved a woman other than herself. This was real and happening now. A man's strong arms around her. His mouth moving on hers, molding it, urging it to open for his tongue. His scent, the feel of him.

Luke lifted his head. "See? You know exactly how to deal with me." Before she could even think of a reply, let alone say it, he kissed her again. Somewhere within the maelstrom of wildly beating hearts, which she could hear, and labored breathing, another unique and sensual sound, and kisses, another and another, she was vaguely aware of Rocky moving, heading for home.

Regardless of the solidity and strength of the man holding her, Maris was becoming too dizzy to put much trust in her perch. She clutched at Luke's arm and turned her head to break their kiss. "Please . . . let me get down. I have to get down, Luke."

He readily grasped why she had made the request. Making love on the back of a moving horse was utterly ludicrous. Especially when the horse had been completely green no more than two weeks ago and still wasn't all that certain about people climbing all over his back. Rocky was skittish and prancing sideways instead of honing in on a straight line for the ranch.

"Whoa," Luke commanded the horse while pulling on the reins. "We'll both get down and walk back. It's not that far. I'm going to dismount first so I can help you down. Hang on to the saddle horn for a second." Swinging his left leg over the horse's rump, Luke slid to the ground. Because he wasn't completely positive of Rocky's reaction to all of this unfamiliar maneuvering, Luke tied the reins around a small tree before assisting Maris.

He returned to Rocky's right side, reached up and laid his hands on Maris's waist. "Put your hands on my shoulders," he instructed.

She obeyed and he lifted her down from the saddle. Only he didn't immediately set her feet on the ground. Instead, he brought her up against himself and let her slide down very slowly. A small gasp escaped Maris. The friction of clothing against clothing and body against body created a rippling thrill that took her breath.

The "Don't, Luke" she whispered came from her sane and sensible side; something else inside of her prevented her from physically moving away from him. The reactions of her own body to Luke Rivers were startling, and yet she understood them. She had lived without a man's love and affection for so long that her system was bound to respond to so much male chemistry, wise or not.

"Maris," he whispered, drawing her closer still, seeking her lips. His kiss was hot and heavy, and she found herself leaning into him and kissing him in the same hungrily demanding way. His hands moved on her back, from shoulders to hips and up again. Her breasts were chafed, almost harshly, by the pressure of his chest, and there was no ignoring the power of his arousal moving suggestively against her abdomen.

She knew she should break this up and didn't seem to have the strength to do it. Maybe the full moon was making her a little crazy, she thought. Certainly kissing a rootless man and reveling in the delectable sensations dancing and darting within her own body was an extreme departure from her usual behavior.

But it felt so good and she felt so alive, so *glad* to be alive, and she raised on tiptoes to nestle against him. Luke's response was a deep-throated growl of pleasure. He pulled the bottom of her blouse from the waistband of her skirt and growled again when his hands glided over the smooth, hot skin of her back. A deft flicking of his fingers unhooked her bra, then he stepped away from her only enough to permit his hand to squeeze between them.

His hand on her bare breast brought a gasp from Maris, but the small sound neither intruded upon nor hindered their feverish kisses. It had never been like this for Maris before, where everything within her burned with sensation and yearning. Even during the early months of her marriage, when she had doted on Ray and responded to him in bed, she had never felt so overwhelmed by desire.

But it wasn't right. She shouldn't be standing in the middle of a dark field under a full moon and making love with Luke Rivers. Yet even knowing with every certainty that she was inviting future heartache, she couldn't leave his arms. Couldn't resist one more kiss. Couldn't stop his exploration of her body.

Instead she moaned while he caressed her breasts and aroused her nipples into hard peaks, and then let him unbutton her blouse so he could bend his head and lavish kisses to each sensitized crest. He gently tugged one into his mouth and sucked. Her fingers curled into his hair while her mind spun dizzily. "Luke . . . oh, Luke," she whispered raggedly.

Straightening his back, he brought her close again and mated their mouths for a long kiss that had her clinging to his shirt for support. Lost in sexual turmoil, Maris only vaguely registered her skirt being drawn up. He caught the elastic top of her panties and slid them down her thighs, and then his hand was seeking her most private spot. She jumped when he found it.

"Relax, honey," Luke whispered thickly, though he suspected neither of them would relax again until they had finished what they'd started tonight. No, that was wrong. The excitement between them had begun long before tonight. Their first kiss might have been the beginning, or maybe it went clear back to the day he'd come to the Wyler ranch looking for Ray to collect on that IOU.

When it began was immaterial. They were together now, single-minded and focused on the grand finale. Kissing her sensual mouth, his hand lingered between her legs. Her every reaction raised his own blood pressure another notch. Then he whispered, "Now, Maris, right now, right here." He unzipped his jeans.

Her body was in flames and caught in a whirlpool of intense longing. But the sound of his zipper created a chink in her dazed mind. "Wait . . . Luke . . . wait," she stammered huskily.

He lifted his head and looked at her. "Wait for what, honey?"

"I . . . please . . . this isn't right."

He snorted out a brief, disbelieving laugh. "What isn't right?"

"You . . . and me. Like this." Her whole body felt damp and prickly. Her clothing was half on, half off. His hand was still between her legs, and some erotic portion of herself that she hadn't even known existed was in control of her physical side. Her brain, however, was objecting, albeit dimly and rather ineffectively, to such audacious behavior.

Luke brought his hands up to cup her face. He gazed into her eyes. "We're adults and unattached, both of us, and we're doing nothing wrong."

She was embarrassed by the turn of her thoughts, but couldn't stop herself from expressing them. "But... you only want me for tonight."

Luke went very still. "Meaning?"

"You have to know that I don't... What I mean is..."

"Do you want me for more than tonight? And please don't deny the wanting. I can feel it, Maris. I can see it on your face."

"In other words," she said in an agonized whisper, "you would consent to an affair with me while you're here."

"Consent?" Luke emitted a short, clipped laugh. "Hell, yes, I'd consent. Why wouldn't I?" His eyes narrowed on her face again. "Why wouldn't you?"

"Is it really that simple for you?"

"It's not simple at all." As if to prove it, he took possession of her mouth in a kiss that wasn't even slightly simple. Within it emotions flowed back and forth between them, sizzling emotions, complex emotions. Maris's entire life didn't exactly shoot through her mind, but she was suddenly bombarded with a hundred fleeting glimpses of herself before meeting Ray and after meeting Ray. Influencing every image was her present loneliness, which was probably the only reason she was in Luke's arms this very minute. At least he wasn't devising lies about being in love with her, or making false promises not to leave her in September.

She wasn't in love with him, either, she remembered, and maybe it was time to stop being so rigid and straitlaced. Accept him as he is, a voice said in her head. He's handsome and sexy and just possibly the kind of man you need right now. You certainly aren't looking for another husband, are you?

Indeed she was not. The mere thought of legally tying herself to another man put a bad taste in her mouth. Being independent had many more pluses than minuses. Sure she had her moments of loneliness, but Luke was more than willing to remedy that particular affliction, and so what if it was only a temporary cure?

She wrapped her arms around his waist and snuggled against his hard body. Breathlessly she whispered, "Forget everything I just said, Luke. I don't want to talk at all, not about anything."

Holding her, Luke frowned in surprise and then smiled, just a little; he didn't want to talk, either. Maris's cheek was against his chest and she could hear the hard, fast beat of his heart. "We won't talk," she whispered. Talking would change everything. As a logical thinker, she looked for logic in moods, attitudes and actions. There was no logic in tonight's activities and talking would only confuse her.

She tipped her head back and Luke promptly kissed her upturned lips. In seconds she felt as though there had been no interruption, no doubts at all. She wanted Luke simply because he was a powerfully attractive, sexy man, and because she desperately needed closeness and intimacy with another human being. It had never happened to her before, but she was no longer questioning its logic.

"Luke," she whispered, and started unbuttoning his shirt. The shadowy planes of his muscular chest were finally hers to explore, and she ran her hands over his smooth, taut skin and into the triangular patch of hair between his nipples. "You're a dangerously handsome man." Her voice was low and not very steady.

Luke laughed softly, deep in his throat. "Are you calling me dangerous because I make you feel like a woman? That's not danger, Maris. This is the way it should be between a man and a woman, exciting, thrilling, erotic." He covered her hands with his own and pressed her palms to his chest. "I like you touching me." He paused, then added, "I like everything about you."

Her eyes lifted to lock with his. "You do?"

Without warning, Luke moved away from her. "I do." Taking off his shirt he spread it out on the grass. On his knees, he looked at her. "Give me your skirt and blouse."

He was making them a bed, Maris realized. Mesmerized by him, the beautiful night and her own aching body, she stepped out of her skirt and handed it to him. Her fingers undid the few remaining buttons of her blouse he hadn't already opened, and she slid the garment from her shoulders and dropped it near the makeshift bed. Luke stopped to look at her in the moonlight. "Damn, you're beautiful," he said hoarsely. "Come here."

Maris sank to her knees on her own skirt. Luke finished removing her bra, and she felt the burn of his hot gaze on her bare breasts. Then he yanked off his boots and socks, and slithered out of his jeans and undershorts. She stared and stared, entranced by the utter beauty of his maleness.

But he was doing the same with her, drinking in the sight of her body without clothes. They sat there looking at each other—then, quite suddenly, it wasn't enough to merely look.

Luke pulled her down, placing her on her back. His kisses started out tender and gentle, but quickly became rough and hungry. He took a breath of air deep into his lungs and told himself to take it easy. At this rate, things would be over almost before they'd begun, and that wouldn't be fair to Maris. There were all kinds of women in the world, he'd discovered through the years. Some deserved teeth-gritting patience from a man, some didn't. Maris was in the first category. In fact, Maris Wyler was in a class all her own. He had never—never—felt this way about any other woman.

Frowning slightly, he lifted his head to see her face. Her eyes, even though dusky with shadows, held a dreamy cast. She touched his cheek. "What is it, Luke?"

He had no glib reply, no immediate answer of any sort. Recognizing special feelings for a woman was foreign to his experience. "Um...nothing important," he mumbled, deliberately blocking out everything but the woman beneath him. She was beautiful in the moonlight, beautiful and sensual and eager to make love. Why in hell was he wasting time?

His kisses began at her forehead and moved slowly down to her nose, her lips, her throat. Her hands moved over him, lingering on the muscles of his back, then sliding down to his hips. "Touch me all over," he whispered. "I want to feel your hands on me."

The images behind Maris's closed eyes were of Luke working in the corral without a shirt, his sweaty skin glistening in the sun, the leather gloves on his hands, the snug fit of his jeans. Those mental pictures were as arousing as having Luke naked in her arms. In one tiny corner of her mind lurked the knowledge that she would regret this tomorrow. But tomorrow seemed so far away. For once in her life she was going to live for the moment.

Luke's mouth glided down to her breasts, where he gave each perfect mound equal attention. "Sweet . . . so sweet," he whispered.

"It . . . it's torment," Maris moaned as he gently sucked on her nipple.

"Do you want me to stop?"

"No . . . no. I couldn't bear it if you stopped now."

"Then it's good torment."

"Yes, oh, yes."

Luke's hand slid down to the soft hair at the base of her belly, and then farther, deep into the secrets of her body. "Is this good torment, too?"

Maris groaned. "You know it is." She couldn't lie still. Her hips arched upward. "Luke . . . please . . ."

He knew what she was asking for in that husky, ragged tone, but he also knew that once he entered her he wouldn't last very long. "Easy, honey," he whispered, and lay down beside her. Nimbly he adjusted her position, placing her head in the crook of his left arm so he could kiss her mouth while he made sure she reached the pinnacle with his right hand.

Writhing beneath the incredible stroking of his fingers, Maris felt a gathering in her lower abdomen, the beginning of the end, a radiating pleasure. "Luke . . . oh, Luke."

"Go with it, honey," he whispered. "Don't fight it."

She could do nothing *but* go with it. The spiraling thrills were consuming her, so strong and overpowering she could barely breathe and had to tear her mouth from Luke's to gasp for air. Then, moaning, she buried her face in the curve of his neck and shoulder and savored the delicious sensations rippling throughout her body.

Luke held her for a few minutes, giving her time to come down from that awesome peak. But he knew that too much time would completely deplete her desire, so at a huge release of breath from Maris, he moved on top of her. Watching her face, he slowly slid into her. Her lips parted. There was a look of bewitchment in her eyes. Luke couldn't know it, Maris realized, but never had she felt so wanton before, so completely submerged in lovemaking.

Her hips lifted to meet his first thrust. Taking his face between her hands, she brought his head down for a breathy, passionate kiss. "You are an amazing lover," she whispered.

Her words sent Luke's spirit soaring. An amazing lover. Yeah, by damn, he was.

But so was she. "Maris . . . Maris . . ."

They were kissing again, their bodies moving together in perfect harmony. He slid his hands under her hips. "Put your legs around me," he whispered thickly.

She did it, and then things got really wild. A red haze of pure lust burned behind Luke's eyes. He couldn't slow himself down any longer, and his thrusts into her velvety heat became faster, harder, deeper.

"Making love to you is like riding the tail of a comet," he whispered hoarsely.

"For me, too, Luke," she gasped. Without intent, her fingernails dug into his back. "Don't stop. Please don't stop."

"No way, baby. I couldn't stop now even if I wanted to. Even if *you* wanted me to."

Maris's moans turned to whimpers, and her whimpers became cries. "Luke . . . Luke . . . *Luke!*"

He went over the edge himself. "Maris . . ." He wanted to say more, but he was suddenly too weak to do more than collapse upon her.

It seemed an eternity before either was able to move. Maris lay under him with her eyes closed and listened to her own heart returning to its normal beat. Her skin was damp with perspiration—so was Luke's—and suddenly the night air didn't feel as warm as it had.

As she opened her eyes and felt the weight of Luke's limp body clamping her to the ground, her system went into shock. Had she lost her mind tonight? She stared at the full moon and blamed it for her aberration. It was a common belief that people behaved peculiarly when the moon was full, but making love on the ground with a man who would never commit himself to anything or anyone—other than rodeo—was insane, not peculiar. Especially when they had used no protection.

"Oh, God," she moaned.

Alarmed at the agony in her voice, Luke raised up. "What?"

"Let me up."

"Honey, what's wrong?"

"You need to ask? Luke, we didn't use any protection." She pushed on him. "Let me up."

"Well...sure...but..." Luke moved to the ground, but he caught her hand before she could leap up and dash away. "Tell me you're not sorry about this."

Maris jerked her hand out of his. "If I did it would be a lie." She grabbed a corner of her skirt and yanked. "Please get off my clothes."

He got to his feet. "Maris..."

"I can't talk now." Hastily gathering her clothing, she looked around the dark landscape and spotted a large bush. While Luke watched, confused and a little queasy over her attitude, Maris disappeared behind the bush.

With a distinct lack of enthusiasm, he found his own clothes and began dressing.

He was standing next to Rocky when Maris reappeared. "The last thing I expected was immediate regret," he said gloomily. "Why do you feel that way, Maris?"

She stopped. "Something happened to me tonight, Luke. I don't know what it was—"

"How about needing a man?" he interjected cruelly.

She flinched, but forced herself to stand there. "I'm not blaming you."

"You're not. Well, for some damned reason that doesn't make me feel a whole lot better. If you're not blaming me, then you're blaming yourself, and that's just plain idiotic. Needing sex is as natural as needing food and water. Are you ashamed of being human?"

"Having sex is not the same thing as sitting down to a meal, so that argument leaves me cold. I'm walking back to the ranch. Alone. You ride Rocky home. I need to think."

The ice in her voice unnerved and angered Luke. "Lady, you are one mixed-up human being. Ten minutes ago you couldn't get enough of me and now you hate my guts."

Maris's jaw dropped. "I don't hate you! Why would you say such a thing? I...I'm confused. Can't you understand that?

I've never done anything like...like what I did tonight in all my life.''

"Why didn't you think about that *before* we made love?" Luke put the question harshly. Maris's attitude hurt. Maybe she was confused, but so was he. He didn't want her talking this way, acting this way. While making love he'd had visions of...visions of... Well, they weren't clear, but for a fact they had included Maris.

Maris looked at him for a long moment. Then she lifted her chin. "I should have. Good night. I'm going home." Turning, she started walking.

"Maris!" She kept going. "You can ride behind me." She kept going. "Damn you," he shouted, and then wondered in the echo of his own anger if he wasn't damning himself.

# Ten

Maris had a hard time falling asleep that night. Again and again she got up to prowl around the house and question her behavior with Luke. Taking momentary pleasure while ignoring the aftermath was so unlike her that the episode was deeply unsettling.

The only time she made sure she was in her room was when Keith came home. With her lights off she listened to the boy's stealthy movements in the house, obviously an attempt not to wake her. It was a few minutes before midnight, exactly as he had promised. Her heart melted just a little for Keith. He was a dear and she loved him as a woman must love her own son.

Then she remembered how careless she and Luke had been tonight and that she could be pregnant this very minute.

A sudden abandoned joy leapt through her body. A baby. Maris had been sitting on the edge of the bed and she got up to pace, curling her arms around herself. What if it was true? What if Luke had made her pregnant tonight?

She stopped pacing to calculate dates, then frowned at the result. Her most fertile time wouldn't be for another day or two. This was something she understood very well. Before learning of Ray's vasectomy she had faithfully kept track of her monthly cycle, steadfast in her hope of becoming pregnant. The habit had stayed with her, albeit absentmindedly and without cause, but she was always able to pinpoint which stage her body was undergoing.

Disappointment created a furrow between her eyes. It was highly unlikely she had conceived tonight. If she and Luke had made love—by mere coincidence, of course—when her cycle was at its peak, she could have had the child she'd always yearned for.

Her mouth was suddenly cotton dry as a shocking idea struck her: seducing Luke at the right time to conceive. Luke would never know, she told herself. He was leaving right after the horse auction, and she couldn't imagine a reason why he would ever return to Whitehorn. Ray's death hadn't been that long ago. She could tell everyone the baby was Ray's. She had heard of ten- and eleven-month babies, and often, she had also heard, a first baby came late.

Oh, my God, she thought frantically. Could she actually do something so deceitful?

But Luke was probably her one and only opportunity to have a child with no one being the wiser. And it wasn't as if he would care, even if by some improbable chance he should figure out her scheme. He was a drifter, a man who by his own admission visited his mother only once a year. He had no ties and obviously wanted none. He would undoubtedly be surprised if she instigated further lovemaking, but why would he question her motives? He would believe, as he had tonight, that she merely needed a man.

Trembling, Maris crawled into bed and pulled the covers up to her chin. Her eyes were wide and staring. *Could she do it?* Could she deliberately trick Luke into thinking she wanted his body once or twice more merely because she was lonely? This was Saturday night, or rather, a very early Sunday morning. Monday or Tuesday would be her fertile period. But how would she accomplish it? With Keith on the place, how could she spend time alone with Luke?

Her morals battled with her intense desire to have a baby. Again she relived that awful moment when Ray had told her about his vasectomy. He had cheated her out of something that was only every woman's right—the right to bear children. *Life* had cheated her, Maris decided bitterly. If Luke was the kind of man who needed a family she wouldn't even consider doing something so underhanded. But he was a loner, a man who actually worked at remaining rootless and unencumbered. Aside from that one personality flaw he was a perfect candidate to father a child, physically strong and healthy, reasonably intelligent and ambitious in his own way.

By morning Maris had decided that yes, she could do it, and then no, she couldn't, so many times, she got up bleary eyed and depressed. She made pancakes for breakfast, then took a cup of coffee to her bedroom while Luke and Keith ate. The thought of food made her stomach roll, though the coffee tasted good. The truth was that she didn't want to look Luke in the eye this morning. She didn't want to see what had happened between them on his face, and she was sure there would be some sort of reminder in his expression.

Groaning because there was no way to avoid him once the yard sale began, Maris got ready for the day. Her skin was pale, she saw in the bathroom mirror, and she applied some blusher to her cheeks and lipstick to her lips.

When she finally braved the kitchen again, Luke and Keith were gone. A glance out the window told her where they were: working with a horse in the corral. Maris sighed. Luke was the most constant, the hardest-working man she'd ever known. Compared to Ray's lackadaisical interest in any aspect of the ranch, Luke was a saint.

Standing at the window and squinting to watch the two men and the horse within the corral, Maris knew that she couldn't delude and manipulate Luke into giving her a baby. How could she have even thought of something so dishonest and conniving? Some of the tension drained from her system. Feeling better at having ultimately made a sane and sensible decision, she tackled the breakfast dishes. When the kitchen was tidy, she went outside to await any visitors to her yard sale, though she really didn't expect a repeat of yesterday's onslaught.

The first car that arrived was familiar. Smiling, Maris walked out to greet Lori Parker Bains. "Lori, hi." She gave her friend a hug. "Gosh, it's good to see you."

Lori was carrying a small box. "I made a batch of fudge last night. I brought you some."

"Homemade fudge? I haven't made fudge in years. Thanks."

Lori frowned. "Maris, are you feeling well? You look a little peaked."

And that was when the first lie came out of Maris's mouth, without warning, without intent. "I...I've been a little queasy in the morning for the past few weeks." Maris could hardly believe she'd said that, and to her best friend, to boot. She felt embarrassed, and her face burned.

"Every morning?" Lori asked with a serious edge to her voice. "Maris, queasiness in the morning is a symptom of pregnancy. Do you suppose . . . ?"

Maris felt about two inches high. Lori was the one person in Whitehorn who knew how much Maris had always wanted a child. However, Lori was a nurse and a midwife, and if anyone had the training and talent to see through Maris's lie, it was her.

"I doubt it very much," Maris said firmly, wishing to God she hadn't told that abominable lie. *Why* had she lied? Hadn't she decided not more than a half hour ago in the kitchen that she wasn't going to trick Luke into anything?

"Beside a queasy stomach, how else have you been feeling? Are your breasts tender?"

Maris's breasts were very tender this morning, but only because of the extremely ardent attention Luke had given them last night. "Uh, sort of," she mumbled.

Lori was beaming. "And what about getting up in the night? Are you using the commode a little more than usual?"

"No." She absolutely could not tell one more lie to her best friend. "It's nothing, Lori, really. Just forget I said anything, okay?"

"Forget it? Maris, if you are pregnant it's very important to begin prenatal care as early as possible. Your baby will benefit by it and so will you."

Maris felt as though her stomach had dropped somewhere down by her knees. Never had she rued an impulse more than she did this one. "It's nothing, Lori. I swear it." She forced a bright smile. "Did you come to look over my sale items? There isn't much left. It was a little crazy here yesterday and most of the good stuff was sold."

Lori was not distracted by Maris's change of subject. "Promise me one thing, at least. If you don't want to see a doctor right away, buy one of those home pregnancy tests." She named a brand. "It's really quite reliable, Maris."

Buy a home pregnancy test in Whitehorn's one drugstore? Maris's heart sank. John Tully would have a field day spreading that news around town.

"I'll think about it."

"Maris, you have to do more than think about it," Lori said in her most professional voice. "Look, I know what you're thinking. There's only one place in Whitehorn that carries that product, and you would just as soon keep your condition private until you know for sure. How about if I buy the test and bring it by sometime tomorrow?"

"That...would be nice," Maris said weakly. Out of the corner of her eye she spotted Luke walking across the yard, which presented a golden opportunity to desert the topic of pregnancy. "There's Luke Rivers. Would you like to meet him?"

Lori turned to see Maris's hired man. "Wow," she whispered. "Maris, he's gorgeous. I would love to meet him."

"Luke," Maris called. When he looked her way, she beckoned him with her hand.

He began ambling toward the two women. Earlier this morning Maris hadn't even looked at him, and he had to question why she was friendly again.

"Hi," he said when he'd reached Maris and her companion.

"Lori Bains, Luke Rivers."

Smiling, Lori offered her hand. "Nice meeting you, Luke. I've been hearing your name quite a lot around town."

"Is that right?" Luke shook Lori's hand and grinned. "Why would anyone be mentioning my name?"

Lori shrugged prettily and Maris felt an uncharacteristic pang of envy. She could never look the way Lori did, not if she spent the rest of her life trying every cosmetic on the market and even resorting to plastic surgery. Lori's blond hair challenged the sun's bright light, and Lori's smile could grace a toothpaste ad.

"Well, you're new to the area, for one thing," Lori replied. "And you're single and good-looking." She smiled teasingly. "People just like to talk, Luke, especially in a small town."

"Guess that's true." Luke thought that Lori was one of the prettiest women he'd ever seen. She was also very friendly and, he suspected, a warm and compassionate person.

But it was Maris who was making his skin tingle, not Lori Bains. He gave Maris a melting look. "How are you this morning?"

Maris turned three shades of red. "Fine...just fine." As she had feared, every detail of last night's misadventure was in his eyes. "Uh, Lori wanted to meet you."

His gaze returned to Ms. Bains. "Well, it was good meeting you, Lori. I'm sure we'll see each other again before I leave."

"Oh? How long will you be here?"

"Until the end of September." Luke looked at Maris. "That's still our agreement, isn't it?"

"Yes," Maris said quietly, wondering why he would ask her that. Nothing they had said last night or at any other time could possibly be construed as a deviation of their agreement.

"Well, I'd better get back to work." Nodding at Lori, he walked away.

Both women watched him for a few moments. Lori spoke first. "Luke is in love with you, Maris."

Maris's eyes widened in shock. "Don't be silly! Luke can hardly wait to get out of here."

"Do you mean to tell me that you don't feel something from him?" Lori looked exceedingly doubtful. "Hasn't he said or done anything to let you know he's interested? He is, Maris, believe me. I saw the way he looked at you."

"Your imagination is running wild, Lori. He didn't look at me any differently than he looked at you."

"Hogwash. Well, I can't make you like him, but I do. Not for any romantic reason," Lori added. "But he seems like a darned nice guy to me."

Maris was more depressed than ever. Not only had she told that abysmal lie to her best friend about feeling queasy every morning—apparently to pave the way, she thought disgustedly, just in case she changed her mind again about using Luke—she'd felt the heat of Luke's gaze and knew that he was thinking of further intimacy between them.

But as for him being in love with her, that was utterly ridiculous. She was glad to see another car arriving. "Look around if you want, Lori. I'll go say hello to the Jensons."

Sheriff Judd Hensley drove in around two that afternoon. He was out of uniform and in his own car, obviously enjoying a day off. There were so few things left to sell that Luke and Keith had gone back to work with the horses and Maris was tending the sale by herself.

Judd walked up. "Hello, Maris."

"Hello, Judd."

Judd was looking around. "Appears that I should have come by yesterday. I heard that people were buying your stuff like crazy. Seems to be the truth."

"The sale was a huge success," Maris agreed. "I never dreamed so many people would show up. As you can see, there are only a few odds and ends left."

Judd's steady gaze rested on her. "How are you doing?"

"Just fine, Judd. Please don't worry about me."

Judd jerked his head toward the corral. "I see you've still got Luke Rivers working for you."

"And doing a very good job," Maris replied evenly. She drummed up a smile. "The next event for the No Bull Ranch is going to be a horse auction at the end of September. I'll be putting out signs and notices in the newspaper to advertise the sale in a few weeks."

"An auction, eh? Sounds like a good idea, Maris." Judd paused briefly. "What happens after that?"

Maris drew a breath. "Then Luke will be leaving and I'll be back in the cattle business."

"He'll be leaving?"

"He's only here to break my horses, Judd. I told you that."

"Yeah, guess you did." Judd paused. "How about having supper out with me tonight?"

Supper out with anyone was the last thing Maris wanted for tonight, but maybe spending time with another man besides Luke would put her back on course. "Sure, why not?"

Judd shaped one of his rare smiles. "I'll pick you up around six, all right?"

"I'll be ready."

After Judd left, Maris went to the patio and sat down. She'd hardly had a chance to catch her breath yesterday, but people had merely dribbled in today. Judd could very well be her last customer, she decided, and then turned her thoughts to what she could prepare for Keith's and Luke's supper.

She bit down on her lip, suspecting that Luke wasn't going to like her going out with Judd tonight. But last night's foolishness didn't give Luke any say in what she did or did not do. Last night had been a mistake. What in God's name had caused her to behave so brazenly? Loneliness was no excuse for completely losing herself in a man's arms.

Then, sitting there in the quiet, she thought again of a baby, and of the names she had chosen shortly after her wedding day. Her first son would have been named Robert Ray Wyler, after his father. Her first daughter would have been named Samantha Ray Wyler, also after her father. It would be wise, of course, to keep the "Ray" in either name, should she become pregnant.

Maris shuddered. Why was she still thinking that way? She wasn't going to do it, so why couldn't she eradicate the idea from her mind?

Blackie wandered over and lay down beside Maris's chair. "Blackie, my friend," she said quietly. "A dog's life is very simple compared to a human's. Be glad you're a scruffy little mutt, okay?" Patting Blackie's head, Maris got to her feet and started for the house.

Luke saw Maris going in. "Just keep him moving in a circle like you're doing, Keith." The bay gelding was on a long lead, and Luke had shown Keith how to swing a rope with one hand while hanging on to the lead with the other. It was another step in the training process, teaching the horse to obey a human's commands and not to fear a rope. "I'm going up to the house to talk to Maris about something. I won't be long." Taking hold of a corral post Luke vaulted over the fence.

"Sure thing," Keith agreed. "I'll keep him moving."

Luke jogged to the house and walked in. "Maris?"

She was in the kitchen, putting together a casserole of rice, vegetables and chicken, which would be baking in a slow oven until suppertime. Luke's coming in without Keith put her on guard. "What is it?"

"I think we should talk about last night."

Maris turned her back on him, giving the casserole her full attention. "There's nothing to talk about."

"Nothing?" Luke went to stand beside her at the counter and crooked his head around to see her face. "You're calling what happened last night nothing?"

"No, it's just that I don't see any good reason to talk about it."

"You don't. Well, supposing I do?"

"Don't pressure me, Luke."

"Stop puttering and look at me."

"I'm not puttering. I'm making dinner. Yours and Keith's. I won't be here."

Luke narrowed his eyes on her. "Where will you be?"

"I'm having dinner with Judd."

The bottom fell out of Luke's stomach. "You're going out with Judd? Why?"

Maris sent him a quick, nervous glance. "Because he asked me. He's a good friend, Luke."

"How good a friend, Maris?" Luke's voice was lethally quiet.

"Not the way you're thinking. He's a *friend*. Do you understand the definition of the word?"

"Don't patronize me, Maris. I might not have gone to college like you did, but I'm not stupid."

She realized that she had hurt him, and she turned to face him. "I never meant to imply you were. But last night shouldn't have happened." Oh, Lord, he was handsome. Just looking at him made her spine tingle. He was sweaty and smelled musky and male. His heavy dark hair was damp and drooping down his forehead. There was a fierce, defensive pride in his eyes. "I'm sorry," she whispered, deeply shaken by what she was feeling for him. "It just . . . shouldn't have happened."

Luke kept looking at her. His past relationships had been sweet but brief and he'd never wanted them any other way. Maris was different. He was different because of her. He didn't want her going out with Judd Hensley or any other man.

But nothing came out of his mouth.

"Luke? Do you understand?"

He nodded. "Yeah, I understand." Whirling, he strode from the kitchen, gave the screen door an unnecessarily hefty shove, causing it to bang loudly behind him, and headed for the corral.

Clenching her hand into a fist, Maris brought it up to press against her lips. Which one of them was hurting more, she wondered with tears dribbling down her cheeks, her or Luke?

A second later she wiped them away with a kitchen towel. Another car was arriving. Pasting a smile on her face, she went outside. Her smile became genuine when she saw Jessica. "Hi."

"Hi, Maris." Jessica got out and opened the back door of her car. "I have Jennifer with me." Jessica began unbuckling the safety straps of the baby's car seat as she thought to herself. She missed her truck, but having the car was much more practical with Jennifer.

Maris felt a burst of joy at sight of the baby. "Oh, Jessica, she's so beautiful."

"Yes, isn't she?" Jessica said proudly. Lifting the sleeping child from the car seat, Jessica held her daughter so Maris could look at her. "She's so special to Sterling and me, Maris."

"That's how it should be with a baby," Maris said softly, her gaze riveted on the child's adorable little face.

Jessica spotted Luke and Keith in the corral. "I need to speak to Keith, Maris." She smiled. "Would you like to hold Jennifer while I do it?"

"I'd love to hold her." Jessica passed the baby to Maris's arms. "Oh, she's wonderful," she whispered emotionally. "I'll sit on the patio with her."

"I shouldn't be very long with Keith," Jessica said, then started walking toward the corral.

Maris resumed her chair on the patio and stared in awe at the sleeping child on her lap. She touched Jennifer's tiny fingers and then undid the lower portion of her lightweight cotton blanket to look at her little feet. The baby's warmth and powdery scent penetrated Maris's clothing and skin to wind around her soul.

She wanted a baby of her own. Every cell of her body ached from the wanting, and it wasn't wrong, she told herself. Wanting a child was natural and right. She wasn't warped or crazy to yearn for motherhood. Nature intended for the female of every species to procreate.

Luke looked up to see a woman standing at the corral fence. "Hi," he called.

"Hello."

Keith turned. "Mrs. McCallum!"

"Hello, Keith. Could you leave your work for a few minutes to talk to me?"

Keith's face was red, but he remembered his manners. "Mrs. McCallum, this is Luke Rivers."

Luke nodded a greeting. "Nice meeting you, ma'am. Keith, you go on and talk to Mrs. McCallum."

Keith considered vaulting the corral fence the way Luke did, but he figured he'd better try it for the first time when no one was around, and he went through the gate. "Anything wrong, Mrs. McCallum?"

Jessica began walking, leading him away from the corral. "I'm not here to deliver bad news, Keith," she said calmly. "At least, I don't consider my message bad news. You'll have to make up your own mind on that score." They stopped under a large elm tree. She looked Keith in the eye. "Keith, your father would like you to visit him." There was a sudden sharp withdrawal in the boy's eyes. "You don't have to do it. You never have to see him again if you don't want to. But you should know what's been happening with him in prison. He has joined Alcoholics Anonymous and has voluntarily requested emotional therapy. The prison psychologist sent me a report that indicates definite progress in Terrance's attitude and outlook."

Jessica touched Keith's arm. "I'm not advising you one way or the other on this, Keith. I'm merely passing on Terrance's request." The boy was silent for so long, looking off into the distance, that Jessica spoke again. "You don't have to make up your mind this minute, Keith. Maybe you'd like to think about it for a while."

"Why does he want to see me?"

Jessica looked at the boy. "I don't know. Perhaps he's thinking about making amends. You're his only child and he's getting old, Keith. Without alcohol pickling his brain, maybe he's sorry for what he did to you."

"He'll start drinking again when he gets out of jail," Keith mumbled.

"That's possible. It's also possible that he will never touch liquor again." Again Jessica touched Keith's arm. "It's your decision, Keith. No one can make it for you, nor should they. I'm going now. Call me after you've given it some thought."

Jessica began walking toward the patio. "Mrs. McCallum?" Keith called.

"Yes?" Jessica stopped and turned.

"Uh . . . I'll go and see him. Can I go tomorrow?"

"If I can arrange for your transportation that soon, I don't see why not. I'll call you as soon as I know, all right?"

Keith nodded. "Thanks."

Jessica smiled. "You're quite welcome. Incidentally, you seem to enjoy working with horses."

"Luke's teaching me a lot."

"I'm pleased to hear it. Goodbye for now, Keith."

"Bye."

Jessica continued on to Maris's patio. "Well, are you tired of holding Jennifer?"

Maris lifted her eyes to baby Jennifer's mother. "I could never get tired of holding a baby, Jessica. I'm not completely certain—I haven't seen a doctor yet—but I think . . . I think I might be pregnant." Maris licked her suddenly dry lips. "Please don't mention it to anyone. I don't want it to get around until I know for sure."

Jessica's eyes misted over. "Oh, Maris, how wonderful for you. Don't worry, I won't say a word to anyone."

Maris remained on the patio after Jessica had driven away, though she had turned her chair to face the corral and Luke. Her arms still felt the imprint of baby Jennifer's firm little body and there was a lingering scent of baby powder on her clothes. Her face bore a look of determination, even though her stomach roiled with guilt. She was going to get pregnant, and that man out there in the corral was going to be the baby's father.

*That* decision was final.

# Eleven

Maris tried very hard to be an attentive dinner companion to Judd that evening, but her mind was at the ranch with Luke and not on the busy Hip Hop Café or the excellent stir-fry dish she had ordered.

"Something's bothering you, Maris," Judd said after he'd had to repeat himself several times to get a response from her. "Would you like to talk about it?"

"I'm sorry, Judd." Reaching across the table, Maris patted his hand. "I don't know where my mind is these days."

"You're not over Ray's death yet," Judd said with a somber expression. He was also thinking of himself, of the death of his son and of his divorce. It had been seven years and he still wasn't over those two tragic events. Maris was a courageous woman, but Ray's death had to have hit her hard. "How could you be?" Judd stated logically. "It's only been a few months."

Two and a half months to be exact, Maris thought. Who would be stupid enough to believe she'd been pregnant when Ray died?

But who, Maris decided next, would be rude enough to mention dates to her face? There would be talk, of course, and more than likely Luke's name would come up. *He lived on the ranch with Maris for several months, you know. If you ask me, Luke Rivers is the father of that baby.*

It wouldn't matter, Maris thought with sudden fierce resolve. She would have her baby, and the gossips could speculate from then until doomsday and they would never know for sure.

"I'm pretty much over Ray's death," she told Judd, speaking calmly and certainly honestly. There'd been a time when losing Ray would have nearly killed her, but those days were long gone and she didn't like thinking about them.

It was getting dark when they left the Hip Hop. "How about a drive somewhere?" Judd asked. "You don't have to hurry home, do you?"

"No, I suppose not." Maris hoped her reluctance didn't show. After they were in Judd's car and driving along, she thought about Judd's invitation that afternoon and why she'd felt so obliged to accept. He'd been kind and considerate since the night he had come to the ranch to tell her about Ray's death. She recalled every word:

*"Judd!" Maris had answered the doorbell, and was surprised to see the sheriff on her front porch. It was late, or early, depending on one's point of view: 2:30 a.m.*

*"May I come in?"*

*"Well... yes, of course." Nervous suddenly, Maris pinched the lapels of her robe together. The sheriff didn't make calls in the middle of the night without cause and Ray wasn't home yet. Silently she led Judd to her living room.*

*"Sit down, Maris," he said gently.*

*She sank to the sofa. "Something happened to Ray, didn't it? Is he all right?"*

*Judd sat next to her, compassion in his dark eyes. "Ray's dead, Maris."*

*Shock bolted through her system, all but immobilizing her. "Dead?"*

*Judd reached for her hand. "It was a highway accident. He drove into a cement pier at an underpass."*

*Maris swallowed because her throat felt so tight and sticky. "Was anyone else hurt?"*

*"No one. He was alone and no other vehicles were involved."*

*Maris leveled a demanding look on the sheriff. "Tell me the truth. Was he drunk?"*

*"I don't have the coroner's report yet, but I was there and my own opinion is that yes, he was very drunk."*

*"Dead drunk," Maris said with intense bitterness. It was a macabre pun and not funny. Tugging her hand out of Judd's, she raised it and her other to cover her face. Her eyes burned, but there were no tears. Her heart ached for Ray's wasted life, but there was no real sorrow. It was as though she had known for a long time that something like this was going to happen.*

*She felt Judd's hand on her shoulder. "Maris, is there any-one you would like me to call to come out here and be with you?"*

*She dropped her hands and spoke dully. "I'll be all right, Judd."*

Ever since, Judd had checked on her regularly. He wasn't really courting her, she felt, nor did she think that he was fall-ing in love with her. She turned her head to look at him. It was too bad they *weren't* falling in love. Judd was steady as a rock, and wasn't that the very quality she would hope for in a man, should she ever marry again? Instead, she was getting much too involved with Luke, who was a lot more like Ray than Judd could ever be.

Judd realized he was being stared at and sent her a glance. "What?"

Maris smiled. "I was just thinking. You're a nice man, Judd."

He chuckled cynically. "Not everyone would agree with you on that point."

"Maybe not, but it's still the truth." Judd took his duties as sheriff very seriously, and there were people in the area—es-pecially those of Terrance Colson's ilk—who had nothing good to say about Judd.

But Maris saw beneath his reticent, stern exterior. He was a proud, solitary man and she suspected that he viewed her as bearing the same traits. Judd's own marriage had ended in di-vorce after he and his wife had lost their eight-year-old son in a tragic accident. Judd was no stranger to loss or loneliness. Maris *was* lonely, too, but her loneliness hadn't begun with Ray's demise. Only one person, Lori Bains, knew that Maris's unhappiness had started within the first six months of her marriage.

Maris sighed. Everyone had to live with his or her own past, but the water under her bridge was murky and dark with shat-tered dreams and ideals. It was up to her to bring some sun-shine into her life; she was the only one who could do it.

Judd drove out to the Laughing Horse Indian Reservation, turned around and took some side roads back to town. They talked about impersonal topics, the library's current fund drive to increase its reference material, the new houses being con-

structed on the outskirts of Whitehorn and local politics. Maris
had held up her end of the conversation, but she was glad to see
the lights of Whitehorn. It surprised her when Judd drove past
the turn onto Highway 17, which led to her ranch.

He sent her a small smile. "Let's have some dessert before
calling it a night."

What could she do but agree? "All right."

Judd stopped at a fast-food restaurant that featured ice-
cream specialties. "A banana split sounds about right to me,"
he commented as they got out of the car.

Maris ordered a chocolate soda and Judd ordered a banana
split with extra caramel sauce. The rich desserts were delivered
to their table. Judd picked up his spoon and began eating. After a few bites he said, rather casually, "Maris, I hope you
know I would never deliberately say anything to you that would
hurt your feelings."

She gave him a questioning look. "Yes, I know. What's on
your mind, Judd?"

Judd spooned another bite of ice cream and banana into his
mouth, chewed briefly and swallowed before answering.
"There's talk around town about you and Luke Rivers."

Maris sat back. "That's not news, Judd. I would have been
a lot more surprised to hear you say that no one ever mentions
it."

"Well, for my part, I'll be glad to see the last of Rivers."

"Why is that?"

"Just a feeling that he could be trouble, Maris."

Instantly defensive, Maris leaned forward. "Let me tell you
about Luke Rivers, Judd. He's up before dawn every morning
and only stops working for meals. He hasn't taken any time off
since the day he started working for me. If Ray had possessed
even one-tenth of Luke's drive, our ranch would have pros-
pered. Luke is kind to Keith and..."

"Kind to you?" Judd said softly.

Maris drew a breath. "We get along, but there's nothing..." The lie got stuck in her throat. "I despise gossip, and
I'm surprised you're listening to it."

"If there's no truth to it, it shouldn't bother you."

"You must believe it or you wouldn't have mentioned it."

"That's not true, Maris. I only wanted you to know about it."

"So I could do what, Judd? Get all fired up and kick Luke off the ranch?" Disgustedly Maris pushed aside her unfinished soda. "I'm not going to tell him to leave. I need him to break those horses and he's doing a darned good job of it. If the lily-white citizens of Whitehorn weren't talking about me, they'd be talking about someone else. Maybe I'm doing someone I don't even know a big favor."

"Don't be bitter, Maris."

She laughed and it was indeed a bitter sound. "May we go now? I'm tired and would like to go home."

Judd tried to make amends during the drive from town to Maris's ranch. She replied to everything he said, but her tone of voice remained unrelentingly cool. Finally Judd came right out and apologized. "I'm sorry I even brought it up, Maris."

"So am I, Judd," she said wearily. No one could possibly grasp her situation. If she explained everything from her current financial picture to the sham her marriage really had been, they would understand, but even when things had been unbearable with Ray she'd kept her private life private. Occasionally she had unloaded on Lori, but even Lori didn't know it all.

Other than one small light illuminating the kitchen window, the ranch was dark when they arrived. Obviously Keith and Luke had gone to bed, which she'd expected, as it was after ten. Judd walked her to the back door. "We're still friends, aren't we, Maris?"

"Yes, we're still friends, Judd. I hope we always will be. Thank you for dinner. Good night."

"Good night. I'll drop by in a few days."

"Do that."

Judd walked off. Instead of going in, Maris stood with her hand on the doorknob and listened to his car driving away. She glanced behind her to the dark barn and thought of Luke in bed, undoubtedly sound asleep. There were faint noises in the night—the movements of the horses, the chirps of crickets in the grass, the rustling of leaves in a nearby tree.

She didn't want to go in to her lonely bed. Her heart began fluttering wildly, because what she wanted to do was brazen and brash. But, standing there in the dark, she knew she was going to do it.

Feeling breathless and keyed up, she went to her car for the flashlight she kept under the seat. Getting to the barn in the dark wouldn't be a problem, but once inside the pitch-black structure she would need a light. She left her purse in the car, then sped across the compound to the barn. Quietly opening one of its smaller doors, she stepped inside. The inky blackness was as she'd anticipated and she switched on the flashlight.

For a moment her courage deserted her, and she shook in her shoes while pondering how much she had changed since meeting Luke. Until Luke, Ray had been her one and only lover. Her high school and college boyfriends had never moved her enough to get past her strict morality. Ray had sweet-talked her into bed on their third date, but only because she had been so in love with him. She had been a stupid, gullible, naive girl to fall for Ray's line of patter, although even now, in retrospect, she believed that he had loved her for a while. Their problems had begun when she'd happily settled into marriage and he couldn't. Settling into anything for any length of time just wasn't in his nature, she had ultimately learned.

A creaking noise in the old barn startled Maris back into the present. Nervously she shone the flashlight on the ladder to the loft. She wasn't here only because she wanted a baby, she realized. Luke had brought an excitement into her life she couldn't have imagined before experiencing it. His leaving in September was going to create a void that would take a lot of time to accept, but until then he was here and why should she deny herself the pleasure of being in his arms?

Quietly she crept up the ladder, then tiptoed across the wood floor to the door of the loft bedroom with her heart beating like a tom-tom. Maris slowly turned the knob and pushed the door open. Even without the flashlight she could make out Luke's form in bed. He was on his left side, facing the window, which put his back to the door and her. His even, shallow breathing told her he was deep in sleep, and she wondered if she should just walk around the bed and awaken him, or if there was a better way.

That "better way" took shape in her mind. Before she could lose her nerve she laid the flashlight on a chair and started undressing. She did it quickly, piling her things on top of the flashlight and leaving her shoes on the floor. Naked and barefoot, she moved silently to the bed, cautiously lifted the blankets and then very slowly sat down. Her weight jiggled the bed slightly, but Luke never moved. Taking a very deep but very quiet breath, Maris stretched out and drew the blankets over herself.

Then she lay there with her heart pounding. It was a large bed and Luke was several feet away. She could probably stay here all night without his knowing it until he woke up in the morning.

But she hadn't taken this daring, brazen step just to sleep on one side of the bed while Luke slept on the other. She began inching over, thinking that it was a wonder the hammering of her heart didn't awaken Luke, as loud as it was in her own ears. The closer she got to him the more she felt his radiating warmth. It was what she needed, his heat, his passion.

She took the final slide and lay against his back, realizing with mounting excitement that he slept in the nude. Swallowing the choking sensation in her throat, she turned to her side and slid her arm across his waist, nestling her body against his. Her insides began the meltdown she had known would happen, and she started pressing kisses to his back and shoulders while the hand that was over him began caressing his chest and belly. He made an odd little sound, but Maris could tell he hadn't yet awakened.

Her hand went lower, and when she was holding his manhood and it was getting hard and full in her grasp, she could no longer breathe silently. His hips began moving, thrusting himself against her hand, and his breathing wasn't even and shallow as it had been before.

He came awake suddenly, startling Maris, raising up and turning over to pin her to the bed. He said nothing, but he found her lips in the dark and kissed her roughly, almost savagely. There were no other preliminaries before he kneed her legs apart and thrust into her, hard and fiercely. It was wild and crazy and the most erotic experience of Maris's life. She writhed beneath him, moaning and whimpering, urging him on, arching to meet his tempestuous lunges.

Then the feverish pleasure began for Maris, the delicious spasms in her lower belly. She cried out. "Luke...Luke..." He finished only seconds later and collapsed upon her, weak and drained.

She lay with her eyes closed. It had happened so fast. Never could she have visualized her body performing with such haste.

Luke lifted his head and uttered one harsh word: "Why?"

Nervous suddenly, Maris swallowed. "Dare I be flip and ask why not?"

"You refused to talk about us today, then you come crawling into my bed tonight. Tell me why, Maris."

He wasn't speaking kindly. There was anger in his voice, and resentment. "You liked it, didn't you?" she said.

"Hell, yes, I liked it. Any man would like it, but I still want to know why." Luke was trying to make out her features in the dark. "What happened? Did your boyfriend get you all worked up and then leave you hanging?"

Maris gasped. "I told you Judd and I were only friends. Why won't you believe that?"

"Because it sounds like a damned fairy tale," Luke muttered, moving to the side of the bed to sit up. He grabbed a handful of tissues from the box on the nightstand and tossed them to Maris. "You're a sexy woman, and maybe I can't see old Judd keeping his pants zipped for a whole evening with you."

"For your information, Judd has never even tried to kiss me!"

"Then maybe he doesn't like women." Moving quickly, Luke lay on top of her again, surprising Maris to a startled gasp.

"That is a reprehensible remark and this is a ridiculous conversation. Get off of me so I can get up."

Luke studied her shadowed face. "No, I don't think so. You started this, baby, but I'm going to finish it."

"You already finished it!"

He chuckled softly, deep in his throat. "That was only round one, Maris. Round two is just coming up."

She could feel what was "coming up," quite distinctly. "Luke, it's getting very late. I...I could come back tomorrow night." And the night after that, as well, she thought. Three nights in a row during her fertile time would almost guarantee pregnancy.

And then an awful thought struck her. Luke was very careless about using protection. Maybe he, too, had had a vasectomy! Her body went limp. That was it, she thought morosely, the reason he made love without protection.

"Wonderful idea," he whispered, bringing his mouth down to hers. "Tomorrow night and every night after that."

Until you leave, Maris thought dully. Damn! She'd been naive again, gullible, dreaming her own silly little dreams, just as she'd done with Ray.

But then Luke's kisses began seeping into her senses. He had the most incredible mouth, with lips that were both soft and firm, and a unique way of angling his head for a perfect union. The taste of him had her head spinning. His weight merely snuggled the configuration of his body into hers, and in mere seconds she was kissing him back and straining against his feverish skin with her hands locked together behind his head.

They kissed and cuddled and touched each other. Luke's hands were everywhere, caressing her breasts, her thighs, her belly. She ran her fingertips over his muscular build, absorbing and reveling in his maleness. A disturbing thought crept through the pink haze of desire clouding her mind: she cared for him, maybe even loved him. No, no, a voice in her head cried. That wasn't supposed to happen. She wasn't ready to fall in love, and certainly not with a man of Luke's transitory nature. Yet, spellbound by their intimacy, she couldn't force herself to break away from his arms, his kisses, his hard, sexy body.

A second shock followed on the heels of that one. Luke abruptly raised his head and huskily whispered, "I've been really lax about protection, Maris. We don't want you getting pregnant, do we? We won't take any more chances. Don't move, honey. Let me get something out of my wallet. I'll only be a second."

The bed was so large that he had to break all contact with her to reach his wallet on the nightstand. Sudden shock had Maris stiff and chilled. He *hadn't* had a vasectomy. He was perfectly capable of making her pregnant, but now he was going to eliminate that possibility by using a condom. And fool that she was, she was falling in love with him, while to him she was merely a convenient and very easy lover!

Seared with humiliation, she scooted to the edge of the bed and got off of it. Luke turned. "What are you doing?"

Maris stumbled to where she'd left her clothes and began feeling around for her underwear. "I . . . I have to go."

Frowning, Luke snapped on the bedside lamp, nearly blinding Maris for a minute. Blinking against the sudden infusion of light, she turned her back, quickly drew on her panties and reached for her bra. She could feel Luke's stare and sensed his perplexity.

"Maris . . ." There was a note of confusion in his voice. "I don't get it. What happened?"

"Nothing happened, except I realized just how late it really is," she lied. This whole affair—the most appropriate name for their relationship—needed rethinking. She wasn't going to get pregnant if he used protection, but what bothered her more was recognizing how emotionally involved she was becoming with Luke. He was going to leave at the end of September, and if she continued sleeping with him, making love with him, she was going to be in for some heavy-duty heartache.

Luke got up and yanked on a pair of jeans. "If this doesn't take the damned cake, nothing does," he muttered angrily.

Maris was hurrying into her dress, her blue-and-white checked shirtwaist that she'd worn for her dinner date with Judd. "You have no right to be angry with me," she told Luke. "Nor any reason."

"Lady, I didn't come sneaking into your bed. You came to me!" He rounded the foot of the bed and stopped right in front of Maris. "Just what the hell is going on with you? You want me, you don't want me. How do you think that makes me feel?"

"Blame it on hormones," Maris mumbled, making sure her dress was buttoned and tidy.

"Extremely changeable hormones, apparently," Luke said dryly. "Where do we go from here, Maris?"

She looked at him with a raised eyebrow. "Where do we go? Where do you want us to go, Luke?"

"Well, I sure didn't want everything to just stop cold like it did."

"An evasive answer, if I ever heard one." Buckling her belt around her waist was her final step in dressing, other than slipping into her shoes.

"Maris, you're a hell of a lot more evasive than I could ever be," Luke said darkly.

She couldn't rebut such a blatant truth. Luke had promised her nothing and she was fully cognizant of his obsession with rodeo and his plans to return to the circuit as soon as possible. As for her role in this fiasco, she had been plotting and praying for pregnancy, using him and his body to accomplish her goal.

The whole damned plot was backfiring, which was probably no more than she deserved. Regardless, falling in love seemed to be an awfully high price to pay for a few days of fantasy.

Well, that was over. Any more fooling around with Luke would cause her nothing but future misery. Already just thinking of the day that he would drive away created an ache she damn well didn't need.

Seeing that she was ready to go, Luke moved closer and put his hands on her shoulders to probe the depths of her eyes. "Be honest with me, Maris. Please. Tell me what you're thinking, what you're feeling."

She certainly couldn't tell him that she was falling in love with him, nor could she confess her foolish hopes of becoming pregnant.

Her gaze remained steady, though her knees were shaking. "You're good in bed. I like making love with you."

A bleakness entered Luke's eyes. "And that's it, all of it."

"What else could there be?" That peculiar, slightly hurt look in his eyes made Maris's blood run faster. "Is there more for you?"

He took a breath, releasing it slowly. He would never beg a woman, not for anything. "No."

Maris's spurt of hope died. "That's what I thought." She picked up the flashlight. "Good night."

"Want me to walk you to the house?"

"Please don't. If Keith should happen to wake up when I go in, I'd rather he not see us together."

"Maris, he's not a child. Don't you think he knows what goes on between men and women?"

"That's beside the point. I want Keith's respect."

"You have Keith's respect. Why would him adding up two and two about us change that?"

Maris went to the door. "I won't take that risk. Good night, Luke."

Luke followed her down the ladder, then stood at the door of the barn and watched her winding her way to the house. She was the confusingest woman he'd ever known, the most stubborn, the most irritating.

The most exciting. "Damn," he muttered with his lips in a thin, grim line. If she liked him in bed so much, why had she suddenly turned off on him?

Maris stole into the house on tiptoes. She almost turned off the kitchen light without looking around, but fortunately she saw the piece of paper taped to the refrigerator just as she reached for the light switch.

Walking over to it, she pulled it loose. It was a note from Keith:

Maris,
I'm going to see my dad tomorrow. Mrs. McCallum arranged for someone to pick me up at five in the morning. I'll probably be gone all day. See you when I get back, unless you're up in the morning before I leave.

Keith

Maris had mixed feelings about Keith visiting his father, but it wasn't her place to judge.

Sighing heavily, she turned off the light and made her way to her bedroom in the dark. Nothing was ever easy or simple, not one blasted thing.

# Twelve

Maris made sure she was up, dressed and ready to say a few words to Keith before he left the next morning. "How did this happen, Keith?" she asked gently.

Keith explained Jessica's message, adding, "Mrs. McCallum said I didn't have to go, but . . ." The boy looked down at the floor for a moment, then lifted his gaze to Maris's. There was maturity in his eyes and a strength that Maris hadn't seen before. "It's something I have to do, Maris."

She couldn't doubt his sincerity, or the gravity of his decision. "I understand, and I'd like to say how very proud I am of you." Unable to resist the impulse, Maris put her arms around Keith and hugged him. To her surprise, he returned the hug without embarrassment. It was a lovely moment for Maris, and she had to blink back tears.

A car horn honked outside. Immediately she put on a bright smile. "That must be your ride. Take care, Keith."

"I will. See you tonight. Tell Luke . . . tell 'im I'm sorry about not being here today to help with the horses."

"He'll understand."

After Keith had gone Maris put on a pot of coffee. She didn't expect Luke to walk in quite this early, but he was suddenly filling her kitchen. "Good morning," she said calmly, though her pulse did a great deal of fluttering.

"'Morning. Where'd Keith go so early?"

"To visit his father." Maris related the facts behind Keith's departure. "He said to tell you he was sorry about not being here to help you today."

"He's a nice kid." Luke looked at the gurgling coffeepot. "Not quite ready yet?"

"In a few minutes. I'll make breakfast while it's brewing."

Luke took his place at the table, not to rush Maris with breakfast but because he wanted to watch her, and the chairs around the table were the only things to sit on. After several silent minutes he said, "Guess we're going to be alone on the place today."

Maris concentrated on her pancake batter rather than look at him. "I can deal with that."

"But maybe I can't."

Maris's heart skipped a beat. "You have work to do and so do I. Keith being away should make no difference to our day."

"Is he going to be gone all day?"

"I . . . don't know," she said.

"And you talk about me being evasive," Luke said with a snort of derision.

Maris turned to face him. "Last night you asked me for honesty, so here it is. I'm getting in too deep with you, and if we don't stop . . . uh, sleeping together, it's going to hurt like hell when you leave."

His gaze remained steady. "And you didn't think about that before coming to my room last night?"

A flush heated Maris's cheeks. Her confession could only go so far. Mentioning her hope of getting pregnant would shock him and humiliate herself. "Obviously not," she replied, turning back to the counter.

She was right, Luke was thinking with a frown of personal discomfort. This thing with Maris wasn't one of those brief and expendable affairs that dotted his past. Its differences weren't readily grasped or understood, but they bothered Luke all the same. Maris bothered him. This ranch bothered him. Everything going on these days bothered him. He watched broodingly while she poured pancake batter onto the hot griddle. It would be best for both of them if he left now, before, as she'd said, they got in too deep.

"Maris, would you rather I left right away?" he asked.

Her back was to him and she bit down hard on her bottom lip. Instead of suggesting he *never* left, he had immediately come up with leaving sooner than planned. Hurt over his insensitivity, she said rather caustically, "You're thinking I have the money to pay that IOU, aren't you?"

"No, that is not what I was thinking. But I guess it's true, isn't it?"

Maris scooped up some pancakes with a spatula and dropped them on a plate, which she brought to the table and set down in front of him. She spoke without friendliness or warmth. "We have a business agreement, Luke. If you left now, I'd be stuck with a herd of half-broken horses."

"I think Keith could finish the job. They wouldn't be ready for sale by the end of September, but he knows what to do now. I'm only mentioning it for your benefit. If you don't want me around anymore, you have the means to send me packing. And don't forget that Jim Humphrey will be showing up with the balance due on the Corvette."

"He seems to be taking his own sweet time about it."

"Jim's rarely in a hurry. He'll be around one of these days."

The thought of Luke loading his pickup with his gear and driving away today made Maris feel a little sick. She wasn't ready for that yet. Beside, maybe Keith could finish breaking the horses and maybe he couldn't. Certainly the process would take him much longer than it would Luke, especially after school started and Keith was busy with his studies.

Maris brought two cups of coffee to the table, gave one to Luke and sat down with the other. "I don't want you leaving until after the horse auction," she said with a granitelike look over the rim of her cup. "That doesn't mean we have to...to..."

"Just say it, for hell's sake," Luke said with a flash of anger. "We made love, and don't get all surprised and shook if we do it again." He hadn't even started eating, and he leaned forward, ignoring the plate of food between his elbows. "Do *you* know what makes one woman special to a man? I sure as hell don't, but I do know this—I want you all the time and that's never happened to me before. Last night makes me think you're going through some of the same damned misery. Tell me I'm wrong."

She took a breath. "You're wrong."

Luke's expression could have curdled milk. "I guess that's clear enough." He got to his feet. "I'm going to work."

"What about breakfast? You didn't eat anything."

"I'm not hungry." He strode from the kitchen and out the door, every line of his body exuding fury and frustration. Maris sat looking down at the table, undergoing some of that "damned misery" Luke had mentioned. Maybe it was masculine logic for him to say he wanted her and almost at the same time suggest leaving today instead of after the horses were broken, but it was pure gibberish to her. Maybe because she was falling for the big jerk. Falling too hard, too fast. This was the last possible scenario she could have dreamed up while making that deal with Luke.

It occurred to Maris while she was taking care of chores around the ranch and avoiding the corral that morning that she hated worrying about what Luke really thought of her. In the first place she already knew how he felt. She'd been available and willing, and he was male. End of subject.

But deep within her the subject was far from exhausted. She had crossed a line with Luke that had always been inviolate, and why had she been so responsive to him when other men—Judd, for one—simply hadn't interested her beyond friendship? Even before Ray's death and she had been alone so much there had been opportunities for sexual adventures with other men, and she had always repelled any and all advances. It was as though she had lost some sense of herself where Luke was concerned, which was a mystifying deviation from personal standards and ethics that she didn't find particularly comforting.

Then there was that foolishness about hoping to get pregnant and passing the child off as Ray's. Maris knew she had behaved stupidly with Ray many times. In retrospect, what good had come out of her turning a blind eye to his faithlessness, his lack of respect for her and his own roots, his dishonesty, and his out and out laziness? Rather than fight with him about a problem—he'd been extremely adroit at sidestepping an ordinary discussion hinting at any flaw or fault in his behavior—Maris had simply buried her pain and kept her mouth shut.

But thinking she could use Luke to get pregnant with no one catching on really was the most absurd idea of her life, far surpassing any mistakes she had made with Ray. Obviously the day that Luke finally left the No Bull, Maris Wyler would be much better off.

The stickler in that conclusion was Maris's own emotions. Never before had she felt what she did in Luke's arms. Just looking at him across the compound sent feverish tingles through her body. Wishing he were a different kind of man, one who was looking for solidity and stability, was wasted energy. He was addicted to rodeo, and to living a transient, disorderly life. No woman would change him, she was certain, especially a plain countrywoman like herself.

When Luke didn't come in for lunch, Maris brought some sandwiches and a thermos of lemonade out to the corral. "I know you're angry with me, but you have to eat." He was shirtless again, and his bronzed skin gleamed with perspiration. Maris tried not to notice.

He took the food from her hands. "Thanks. And I'm not angry, Maris—I'm confused. I guess I don't understand you. Maybe what's really got me confused is that I don't usually try to understand women." He held her gaze. "Does that make any sense to you?"

"Uh . . . no. I mean, should it?"

Releasing a long breath of resignation, Luke looked off into the distance. "Probably not. It's just that..." His voice trailed off. "Forget it. Do you want one of these sandwiches?"

"I already ate, thanks." Maris looked beyond Luke into the corral and saw the snow-white mare he'd been working with. "She's a pretty horse, isn't she?"

"I've been calling her Snowflake."

"It suits her. I like it. Is she taking to the training?"

"Pretty well. She definitely has spirit."

"You know," Maris said speculatively, "I'd kind of like to keep one or two of the horses for myself."

"Snowflake might be a good candidate. We'll see how she turns out. Maris..." Luke had just swallowed a big bite of sandwich and was washing it down with a drink of lemonade. He wiped his mouth. "I've been wondering again where Ray might have bought these horses. They're not just common broncs. Oh, a few of them are, but most have great conformation, indicating good bloodlines. Do you realize that if you could prove ancestry on some of these animals that their value could easily double or triple?"

Maris's eyes widened. "How would I prove ancestry?"

"By finding out who owned the horses before Ray bought them. You said a trucking firm handled their delivery. You must have been given something, a receipt, a manifest, bills of sale, something, from the truckers."

A frown creased Maris's forehead. "Ray took delivery. As a matter of fact, I wasn't here that day. I had gone to Billings for something—a dental appointment, I think."

"But there must be some paperwork somewhere, Maris. I think you should take a look around the house and try to find it."

Slowly Maris nodded. "And then what?"

"If you can find out who owned these horses before Ray bought them, we'll go and talk to the person and ask him or her about the animals' history. Might get some real good information."

Maris frowned slightly. "I should have thought of doing that before this."

"You've had a lot on your mind," Luke reminded her.

"Yes, but..." Breathing a sigh, Maris questioned her ability to run the ranch, which she'd never done before. Raising animals had been brand-new to her when she'd married Ray and come here, but when it became apparent—very quickly— that Ray had very little interest in operating the place as it should be operated, she had gradually assumed his duties and responsibilities, until she had ended up running the whole show. Obviously she still didn't see every opportunity and grasp every subtlety of profitable ranching. Surprising to realize was that Luke did. He'd immediately seen dollar signs in Ray's old junk and had suggested the yard sale. It was Luke's doing that had sold the Corvette, and now he'd come up with this, an idea that just might increase the value of the horses.

Her voice was rather disapproving when she spoke. "You'd make a good rancher."

Luke looked at her with a restrained, unreadable expression, though without question he'd grasped Maris's reproachful tone. "It must be in the genes."

Resenting his overly casual, cavalier reply, Maris couldn't stop herself from expressing her opinion. "You're wasting your life in rodeo. You're talented with animals and have a natural instinct for business. There isn't anything you couldn't do if you put your mind to it. Certainly you're the hardest-working man I've ever met, and—''

"That's enough, Maris,'' Luke broke in. He'd been having some of the same thoughts that Maris had just put into words, but his mind wasn't made up yet, not about anything, and whatever decision he arrived at concerning his future, he was the one who had to make it. He handed her the empty thermos. "Thanks for lunch. I'm going back to work.''

Walking to the house, Maris alternated between anger over Luke's wasting his talents and regret that she'd been so quick to tell him so. She didn't even speak to Keith in that censuring tone, believing that everyone should have the freedom and space to choose his own path in life. But Keith was sixteen years old and had plenty of time to make those choices, where Luke was old enough that he should already have done so.

*He has done so,* a voice in Maris's head said loud and clear. Indeed he'd chosen his path years ago, and why would he veer from it now?

Sighing despondently, Maris went into the house. Like it or not, sensible or not, she had feelings for Luke Rivers that she wished she could eliminate with a toss of her head, or something equally as mundane. In the depths of her soul, she knew it wasn't going to happen.

One of the bedrooms in Maris's house never had contained a bed from the time she'd moved in. Ray had used it as a combination storage room and office, haphazard as his record keeping had been, and though Maris had gone through some of the boxes and thrown out things she considered useless— even while Ray was alive—the room still couldn't be considered well organized. It was, in fact, the only room in the house that Maris didn't keep neat and clean at all times. It was where her Christmas decorations were stored, for one thing, and numerous other cartons containing seldom-used items.

There was also a desk—a huge old thing with a dozen drawers—and two file cabinets. Maris was digging through the drawers, looking for some scrap of paper from that trucking company, when she suddenly sat back, impatient and unsettled with herself and everything else going on at the present. In fact, what she really was, she thought unhappily, was depressed—depressed because she'd gone to Luke's bed last night, and because he was outside and she couldn't stop thinking of him. Her future was so miserably uncertain, which added to her depression, and the thought of going through all of the boxes and files in this room made her want to bawl, another indication of the depression gripping her.

Knowing that if she sat there much longer she'd fall apart completely, she got up and left the room, closing the door behind her. She'd look for those papers, but not today. What she needed right now, desperately, was to go somewhere, to get away from the ranch and Luke and responsibility, if only for an afternoon.

After changing from her jeans and T-shirt to a pair of white slacks and a green blouse, she quickly applied a little makeup and ran a brush through her hair. Grabbing her purse, she dashed from the house and out to her pickup.

Luke saw her leaving and stood in the corral with a scowl on his face. In his mind's eye he saw her meeting Judd Hensley again.

But last night she'd come from Hensley to him, which had to mean something. Maris wasn't the kind of woman to keep two men on the string, so it was doubtful that she'd be meeting the sheriff again today. Luke had no prior experience with jealousy, yet he recognized the condition in his body and didn't like it.

Sighing heavily, once again admitting utter confusion, he returned to work.


The simple act of driving away from the ranch gave Maris's spirit a decided lift. She loved this wide open country, she loved its distant mountains and enormous sky. The air was so clean and clear it seemed to sparkle.

Maris switched on the radio and drove with the window open, enjoying the music and the warm breezes tossing her hair around. Though she'd left without a destination in mind, she automatically headed for Whitehorn. Everyone that she might want to see was at work, which was probably best, she thought, as she really wasn't fit company in her present mood, though unquestionably she felt much better than she had a half-hour ago.

Still, she didn't feel like talking, answering questions, or pretending that everything was wonderful, which would certainly be the case should she run into any of her friends. Other than Lori, that is. With Lori she could be honest and herself.

Except, Maris remembered with a pang of genuine remorse, she had deliberately lied to Lori about the possibility of her being pregnant. It was Luke's fault, she thought with an angry twist to her lips. Everything happening lately was Luke's fault. Damn Ray for borrowing money from Luke and not paying it back! Without that IOU, Luke never would have come to the ranch. She would never have made love with him, or never gotten that stupid idea about having his baby, or...

Cynically Maris shook her head. Everything wasn't Luke's fault—it was Ray's! God, she was going off the deep end, looking for someone, anyone, to blame for her own sins. What she should be doing is giving thanks that Luke *had* come along. Without his help, she'd have been in such terrible financial condition by now that she might have already lost the ranch.

Reaching the outskirts of Whitehorn, Maris slowed the pickup to the speed limit and slowly cruised Center Avenue. On impulse she made a right turn on Kinsey Way and pulled into the movie theater's parking lot, which was all but vacant, as the theater didn't have matinees during the week.

Leaving the truck, Maris began walking. Again she had no destination in mind, but it was pleasant strolling along and peering at the courthouse, the mayor's office and into the windows of Whitehorn's few shops that sold clothing. It was long past the lunch hour, so as Maris approached the Hip Hop Café, she figured the odds were in her favor for not running into anyone she knew.

She went in and was glad to see only a few patrons, none of whom she recognized.

"Hi," a waitress called. "Sit wherever you'd like, ma'am. As you can see, this isn't exactly the rush hour."

"Thanks," Maris called back, and chose a table in the far corner. She ordered a piece of apple pie and a cup of coffee from the friendly waitress. The pie was delicious, and Maris was thoroughly enjoying it, when the café's door opened and a woman came in. Maris had met Mary Jo Kincaid one time, but she doubted that Mary Jo even remembered the introduction, so it was quite a shock to see the woman suddenly spotting her and then walking over to her table showing a warm and friendly smile.

"Maris, how are you?" Mary Jo asked in her sweet way.

"Just fine, Mary Jo. How are you?"

"It just wouldn't be possible for me to be any better, Maris. I'm so very, very happy married to Dugan. You were at our wedding, weren't you?"

Maris's heart sank with undeserved embarrassment. Didn't the woman know whom she'd invited to her own wedding? "No," she said simply, hoping Mary Jo would realize her own faux pas and drop the subject.

"Oh, that's too bad. It was quite an affair," Mary Jo said in a way that implied that Maris had deliberately missed Whitehorn's event of the year. Maris frowned slightly but her own good nature prevented her from correcting Mary Jo's mistaken impression.

The woman was hovering, obviously hoping for an invitation to join her, Maris realized uneasily. "Uh...would you like to sit down?"

"I would indeed. Thank you." Mary Jo pulled out a chair and gracefully sank onto it, laying her expensive-looking handbag on a corner of the table. "My, this is nice. I was hoping someone would be here that I know." She looked up at the waitress, who had just appeared. "Oh, there you are. I'll have a small bowl of sugar-free gelatin and a pot of herbal tea, please."

Maris searched her brain for something to talk about, recalling the little she knew about Mary Jo. Apparently she had suddenly turned up one day in Whitehorn and established herself by landing a job in the children's library. It wasn't long before she began dating Dugin Kincaid and then, rather quickly, they had gotten married. It was two months before their wedding that baby Jennifer had been left at the Kincaid ranch. And yes, Maris remembered now, someone had been murdered at the ranch on their wedding. Judd had told her about it, a man by the name of Floyd Oakley.

As if guessing Maris's thoughts, Mary Jo said, "Well, even if you didn't attend the wedding, I'm sure you heard about the unfortunate...incident. You know, that fellow that was found

murdered on our property? Fred something-or-other I think
was his name...."

"Floyd Oakley, you mean?" Maris corrected her.

"Yes, that was it. Poor Mr. Oakley. Never even got his share
of all that free champagne, I imagine," Mary Jo said, looking
a bit embarrassed to be smiling at her own joke.

"Well, it must have been awful for you, having to deal with
such a horrible situation on your wedding day."

Mary Jo lowered her gaze to examine her manicured nails
and thick, diamond-studded wedding band. "Oh, you know
what they say, the show must go on." She gave a brave little
laugh. "I tried my best to keep a smile on my face, for Dugin
and his daddy's sake. Even though I was quite shaken up," she
admitted in a low, serious tone.

"I can imagine," Maris replied, though she guessed that it
took quite a bit—maybe even more than a murder on her wedding day?—to shake up this lady.

"Dugin was wonderful. He's just my tower of strength,"
Mary Jo added sweetly.

"Dugin is a very...kind man," Maris said, searching for a
reply that would be both tactful and still basically truthful.

Having known Dugin for years, she sincerely found it hard
to imagine him *anybody's* tower of strength. He was known to
be spoiled, weak-willed and totally dominated by his father,
Jeremiah. Dugin's older brother, Wade, had been Jeremiah's
favorite. But Wade had died years ago, in Vietnam. It was said
that Jeremiah would have much preferred mourning Dugin, if
the tough old cowboy had been offered the choice. But maybe
that bit of gossip wasn't entirely fair to Jeremiah. Maris had
always known him to be a fair man, if a bit hard at times.

Mary Jo certainly didn't share the popular opinion of Dugin,
though. It was newly wed enthusiasm that had clouded her vision, Maris thought and on those grounds she could be ex-
empt from having a rational perspective. After all, it had taken
her quite a long time to see Ray clearly, and even then it had
taken her longer to fall out of love with him. She wondered if
Mary Jo was indeed in love with Dugin, or just in love with his
money.

"I certainly admire you, Maris," Mary Jo said suddenly.

"You do?"

"You, a widow, running a ranch all on your own." Mary Jo shook her head. "In my book, *that* takes courage and a tremendous amount of strength. Both physical and emotional, I mean."

Maris took a sip of her coffee. "It's just my life. I really don't think of it as being superwoman or anything like that," she said with a smile.

The waitress arrived with Mary Jo's order and Maris thought it a good moment to excuse herself. "Speaking of the ranch, I'd better be heading back. Nice talking with you, Mary Jo," Maris said, getting up from the table.

"Nice visiting with you, Maris. Let me know the next time you're coming into town. Maybe we can have lunch."

"Well, my visits are usually in sort of a rush. Just running in for supplies or some other emergency. But maybe we'll bump into each other again sometime," Maris replied. She picked up her purse and left a dollar and some change near her plate for a tip. "So long, Mary Jo."

"Bye, Maris." Mary Jo looked up at her with a warm smile.

Maris left the table feeling a little sorry for Mary Jo and a little guilty at brushing off her offer to get better acquainted. It wasn't easy to be new in a town like Whitehorn, where most people knew each other for years. She had once been in the same position herself. But Maris didn't have much time for socializing, and Mary Jo just wasn't her type. In fact, there was something about the woman that made her downright uncomfortable, Maris decided.

Mary Jo watched as Maris paid her check at the cash register and left the café. Then her eyes fell on the money next to the empty coffee cup. Her fingers virtually tingled, instinctively about to reach for it. She made a little fist instead, then took a spoonful of her diet gelatin.

Mary Jo laughed to herself. It was hard sometimes to remember that she was now the wife of the richest man in town and hardly in need of stealing a tip from a poor little waitress. But grabbing for that loose cash came just as automatically to her poor old body as breathing. And she always did have a light hand. Light as a feather, Floyd used to say. But old Floyd had always taken too much credit for her success. Sure, he'd taught her some of the finer points. But she'd been basically a self-taught operator when they'd met. Plying her trade as a truck-stop hooker, she'd quickly learned how to double her profits by cleaning out a john's wallet right under the poor guy's nose—or some other unsuspecting part of his anatomy.

The trick was not to get caught. If you got caught, you had to pay. Painfully, too. It hadn't taken her long to learn that rule either. And she'd never forget it.

But no telling how far you could go if you *didn't* get caught, Mary Jo reminded herself as she sipped the last of her tea. Her diamond wedding band sparkled in the late afternoon light, catching her gaze. She held out her hand, admiring it. How far she had come. Floyd had been impressed. And to think this was only the start. Just the first step in her plan.

The waitress came by just then, interrupting her thoughts. "Anything else today, ma'am?"

"Just the check, please," Mary Jo said.

The waitress totaled the order and tore it off her pad. "Would you like me to take that up to the cashier for you?"

Mary Jo glanced at the amount and nodded. The check came to a little under three dollars. She took out her wallet; the smallest bill she had was a ten. She pulled it out and handed it to the girl with her check.

"Here you go. And you keep the change, honey," she said generously.

The waitress stared down at the money a moment, then back at Mary Jo. "Gee, thanks. Thanks a lot."

"That's all right." Mary Jo closed her purse with a loud snap and got up from the table. "It's my pleasure, honestly," she added with a charming smile.


Luke was still working, Maris saw when she drove into the ranch compound and parked the truck. She sat there a moment, thinking about her next move with Luke. After last night was it any wonder he'd expected more from her this morning than the cool reserve she'd shown him? Then there was that lecture she'd laid on him, which had been rude and presumptuous. Her next move with Luke should be an apology.

Getting out of the pickup, Maris headed for the corral. Luke saw her coming and went over to the spigot to splash water over his sweaty face and chest. He was drying off with a towel when Maris walked up to the fence.

She got right to the point. "I owe you an apology. We both know how we each feel about rodeo versus ranching, so there's no point in my constantly haranguing you about the choices you've made in your life. I'm sorry."

"Well, now, I sure didn't expect to hear that from you," Luke said calmly. "But I appreciate it. Thanks."

"You're welcome." She looked at the horse he'd been working with, a black gelding with a white blaze on its forehead. One by one he was making his way through the herd, but he had to be getting tired of the same routine, over and over. "You must have the patience of Job," she told him. "Doing virtually the same thing every day. Isn't it starting to wear thin?"

He looped the towel he was holding around his neck and walked over to the fence where Maris was standing. "I guess I do have patience, Maris. And it doesn't stop with the horses, either."

"Meaning?" Her heart was suddenly beating harder. Looking into his shimmering blue eyes was definitely raising her blood pressure.

He suddenly became bold and brash and gave her an impudent grin. "How about the two of us taking a shower together? You can wash my back and I'll wash yours."

Maris gulped. "You never give up, do you?"

"Not when a woman crawls into bed with me all of her own volition. Maris, we're good together." His eyes narrowed slightly. "I wonder if you realize just *how* good. If I asked about your previous sex life, would you give me a straight answer?"

"If I asked about yours, would you give *me* a straight answer?" she retorted.

He thought a moment. "Yes. Do you want to hear about it?"

"Every detail?"

"If that's what you want, yes."

Maris scoffed. "I don't believe you."

"Try me."

She took a breath. "No, I don't think so." Turning, she walked away, heading for the house.

"Someday we'll talk about it, Maris," Luke called. "You'll see."

"Maybe when hell freezes over," she called back over her shoulder.

# Thirteen

Keith got back late that night. Maris awakened when he came in, but though she was curious—and a little worried—about his day, she remained in bed. Keith would tell her what he wanted her to know in the morning, she decided, and if he told her nothing at all, she wouldn't push him. Seeing his father in jail had to have been a traumatic experience, but it wasn't her place either to sympathize or offer guidance. That was for Jessica McCallum to do.

Once awake, however, Maris didn't immediately fall back asleep. Keith went directly to his room, and in a very few minutes the house was silent again. As Maris stared into the dark, the day flicked through her mind.

Sighing, Maris turned on her side to face the window. Was she falling in love with Luke? Was she really so stupid as to fall for another man who couldn't stay in one place for more than a few weeks without getting antsy? Hadn't she vowed several years back that if she ever found herself single again for whatever reason, she would never get married again?

Maris's lip curled wryly. Luke had hardly proposed marriage, so that line of thought was a little ridiculous. But a relationship went either forward or backward, and "forward" to Maris meant marriage. What it might mean to Luke was a complete mystery, other than lots of hot sex and then a cheery "So long, babe. See you one of these days."

"God," Maris moaned aloud. Her agony was all her own fault. She should have set Luke straight the night they took that horseback ride. Instead she'd gotten all female and giddy and responded to him as though he were her only hope for life itself. Then there was that business of her going to his room and getting into his bed. How could she have done something so moronic? Small wonder that Luke had seen today as another opportunity. If she had agreed, he probably would have kept her in bed all day.

That thought brought Maris's body temperature to a fever pitch. She moaned again. Wanting Luke was becoming a painful, miserably uncomfortable habit, particularly when her sane and sensible side refused to comply.

Would September ever arrive? Nothing would be normal again until Luke Rivers left for good, she thought for perhaps the hundredth time in the past few weeks.

Keith was unusually subdued during breakfast the following morning. Maris smiled across the table at him and he managed a thin smile in return. But he wasn't offering information about yesterday and she couldn't bring herself to ask. He ate quickly and, grabbing his hat from the wall hook near the back door, started out. "I'll be at the corral, Luke."

Luke nodded. "I'll be there in a few minutes, Keith." When Keith was gone, Luke looked at Maris. "Do you think he's all right?"

"I think that yesterday was difficult for him."

"Everyone has problems." Luke took a swallow of coffee. "Keith, you, me, everyone."

"What problems do you have?" Maris sounded skeptical.

"You don't think I have any?"

Maris was silent a moment. "Yes, I think you have problems, though I doubt very much that our opinions would coincide on what they are."

Luke surprised Maris by grinning. "You tell me yours and I'll tell you mine."

"You're teasing," she said shortly, getting up to begin clearing the table.

"I'll be serious if you will," Luke responded quietly, all signs of levity gone from his voice.

Maris turned, one eyebrow cocked. "Fine. How about if you go first?"

"Me first? Well . . . I think I'd rather have you go first."

"That's just about what I figured you'd say." She hadn't believed for a second that he would really talk about himself. Not about anything truly private, such as feelings, at any rate.

Luke finished off his coffee and got to his feet. Maris was heading for the sink with a stack of dishes and didn't see him walk around the table and come up behind her. But no sooner had she deposited the dishes in the sink than his hands were on her upper arms, drawing her back against his chest. "You look mighty pretty this morning," he said huskily, breathing into her hair.

"Luke, don't. Please don't." Her voice had instantly and foolishly become hoarse. "Keith is right outside."

"Keith is down by the corral. In fact..." Luke peered around her and out the window. "I can see him from here. He's sitting on the top rail of the corral fence with his hind side to the house." Forgetting the window, Luke lifted the back of Maris' hair and pressed his lips to her neck.

The thrills began compounding in Maris's body. "You're making me angry," she whispered.

"Yeah, I can tell," he murmured, nuzzling her neck and the side of her face. His hand crept around her waist to the front of her jeans, which he deftly unsnapped and unzipped. Then that wily hand slid down into her clothing, under her jeans, under her panties, and stopped right where he wanted it to be.

"Luke, no!" Maris grabbed at his hand.

"Tell me it doesn't feel good," he whispered. Her gripping his hand through her jeans and panties was no deterrent to the movement of his fingers. She could feel him rubbing his aroused manhood against her behind, and the whole thing was so erotic she couldn't find her voice to speak.

Instead she moaned, softly and deep in her throat. His fingers were pure magic, opening her, stroking her most sensitive spot. "You're hot and wet," he whispered. "I'm burning up. Let's go to your room for a few minutes. That's all it would take, honey, just a few beautiful minutes."

A wildness swept through her. Not only was she on fire with sexual need, there was a very good chance that Luke was too worked up to remember protection.

"Do it here," she said thickly.

"What?"

Ignoring his surprise, Maris turned quickly and opened the buckle on his belt. Excitement whipped through Luke with the impact of a tornado. He yanked down her jeans and his own.

Then he lifted her to sit on the counter and buried himself inside of her hot, velvety depths. She was utterly swamped with overwhelming desire. Her fingers ran through Luke's hair and gripped his broad shoulders.

As Luke had predicted, it took only a few beautiful minutes. Dazed and dizzy, clinging to her lover, Maris moaned as the rapturous spasms began. Luke's cry of release was seconds behind her own.

Panting and disheveled, Luke brought her head to his chest. "Maris...damn. You're really something."

She jerked her head away to look outside and make sure Keith hadn't suddenly decided to come to the house. And then, without warning, she burst into tears.

"Hey, hey, what's this?" Luke put his arms around her.

To her complete humiliation, she couldn't stop crying and instead sobbed uncontrollably into his shirt.

"Maris...honey...what's wrong? Why are you crying?"

"It's perfectly obvious, isn't it? I...I'm totally disgusting!"

"You're what?" Luke pushed her away to see her tear-streaked face. "Listen, *I* might be a little disgusting, and sure as grass is green a whole lot of other folks are definitely in that category. But not you, Maris, not you. Why would you say such a thing? Why would you even think it?"

"After what I just did, you have to ask?" She could hardly force herself to look at him.

"Making love makes you disgusting?" It was written all over Luke's face what he thought of that sentiment. "Are you deliberately looking for a guilt trip, or does it just come natural to you?" He gave her shoulders a gentle shake. "Maris, you're only human, the same as everyone else. Why are you so hard on yourself?"

Being assigned the same slot as "everyone else" didn't elevate Maris's flagging spirit, not when Luke's life revolved around men like Ray and easy women. Maris's shoulders slumped. That's what she had become, easy pickings. All Luke had to do was put his hands on her and she melted into a chunk of mindless desire. Emotionally she was a mess, and the urge to cry about it was again filling her eyes with salty tears.

"I'm not being hard on myself," she said, her voice cracking. "But there is such a thing as common decency, you know." Pushing on Luke's chest, she forced him to step back. "You've got work to do. Keith is waiting."

"Now you're mad at me," Luke observed grimly.

She had slid off the counter and was scrambling to straighten her clothes. "At you, at myself, at the whole damned world!"

"That's silly, Maris."

"So I'm silly. Sue me!" Maris started from the kitchen. "Go to work, Luke."

He walked out of the house, scowling and shaking his head. Why in hell did he keep going back for more of Maris's illogical, inconsistent, irrational behavior? What made her so appealing he couldn't keep his hands off her? She was pretty, sure, but so were a million other women.

Enough was enough. The next time he got that itch around Maris, he would ignore it if it killed him. And that was a promise.

Luke put Keith to riding the horses in the secondary pasture, those that had already gone through the training process. Recalling how Blackie had spooked Mother the night Maris had been riding the mare, Luke cautioned Keith to keep a sharp eye out for anything that might alarm his mount. "Ride each one for about an hour," Luke instructed. "Make sure they're responding to your commands."

Luke's own plan for the day was another go at Bozo, the big red stallion. Riding Rocky, he roped the stallion and led the balky animal into the corral. Once he was freed within the enclosure Bozo's eyes contained a feral gleam, and anytime Luke tried to approach him, Bozo would swivel around and kick at him with his hind feet. After a good hour of trying to coax the stallion into calming down, Luke admitted defeat. There was only one way to break Bozo, and that was to ride the buck out of him. After this morning Luke was in the proper frame of mind to take on a bucking bronc. Determinedly he set about doing so.

First he called Keith from the pasture. "I need your help with this brute." Luke roped Bozo from two directions, tying the ends of the taut ropes to opposite sections of corral fencing, virtually immobilizing the large animal. With murder in his eye, Bozo squealed, tossed his head, swished his tail and kicked out his hooves, but that was all he could do.

Taking up a saddle, watchful of those flying hooves, Luke threw it over the stallion's back.

Keith's eyes were as big as saucers. "What're you doing, Luke?"

"I'm gonna ride the ornery out of this stallion," Luke replied grimly. Bozo was prancing and doing his best to get rid of the burden on his back, but Luke managed to connect and tighten the cinch belt. It took some time, but he finally forced the bit into Bozo's mouth. "Here's where you come in, Keith. Once I'm in the saddle and give you the word, cut those ropes loose."

"Cut 'em, as in using a knife?"

"Right."

Keith grinned with sudden excitement. This was going to be some show. "I'll wait for your word."

Luke smoothed the leather gloves on his hands, then moved quickly, leaping onto the saddle without using the stirrup. Bozo went crazy. Luke twisted the reins around his left hand. "Cut 'im loose!" he yelled to Keith.

Unfettered and enraged, the stallion threw himself around and around in a tight circle. Luke hung on. Bozo arched his back and went straight up in the air, coming down hard on all four feet, jarring Luke so hard his teeth hurt. Bozo fishtailed, bucked, squealed and reared, but Luke held on.

"Holy smoke," Keith mumbled in awe.

Alerted and alarmed by the noise coming from the corral, Maris came running up. "What's going on?"

"Luke's riding the ornery out of Bozo," Keith explained. "I've never seen anything like it, Maris."

Maris was staring at Luke and Bozo. *She'd* seen similar displays before, at various rodeos. Only rodeo broncs were usually goaded into anger and Bozo was crazed with genuine fury. "My God," she whispered. One mistake and Luke would be mashed potatoes. "You damned fool," she mumbled. Her heart was in her throat, beating hard and fast.

Keith was practically turning inside out with excitement. "Look at Luke go," he cried.

Maris was looking and the sight within the corral made her knees weak from fear. Bozo threw himself into the fence; Luke drew up his leg just in time to avoid it being crushed by a post. The stallion went airborne again, a mighty leap that put space in between Luke's seat and the saddle. Coming down was another jarring blow. Gritting his teeth, he pulled the reins tighter, sawing the bit against Bozo's tender mouth.

The battle between horse and man went on and on. Maris found herself holding her breath one minute and gasping for oxygen the next.

"Bozo's getting winded," Keith exclaimed.

"So is Luke," Maris retorted. "This really ticks me off."

Keith sent her a look. "How come?"

"I'm not paying Luke enough money to get himself killed," she snapped.

"Heck, he isn't gonna get killed, Maris," Keith said with every confidence. "He's the best rider there ever was. Yee-hah!" Keith yelled as Luke survived another bout of fishtailing from Bozo. "Ride 'im, Luke! Show 'im how it's done!"

Then, suddenly, it was over. His massive chest heaving from exhaustion, Bozo stopped dead in his tracks. Luke took a long breath, then leaned forward and stroked the stallion's neck. "Atta boy, Bozo. Good boy." He nudged the horse with his knees. "Take a few steps, boy." The stallion obeyed. Luke walked him around the corral, then called "Whoa" and pulled gently on the reins. Bozo stopped.

Luke looked over to grin at Keith and saw Maris. She wasn't smiling. "Uh...were you watching?" Without answering, she whirled and walked off. Luke's gaze met Keith's. "She didn't like it, huh?"

"She said she wasn't paying you enough money to get yourself killed," Keith confided.

Luke turned his head to watch Maris stomping off across the compound. Something within him sighed. "She was already mad at me, so I guess one more reason doesn't matter."

Keith looked curious. "How come she's mad at you?"

"Uh . . . it was something that happened this morning." But while Luke was walking Bozo around the corral, he knew that wasn't the whole truth. Maris was either hot for his body or hot under the collar *because* of him. How could a mere man figure out that one?

Maris was determined to find that bill of lading, or whatever document Ray had been given when the horses were delivered. There had to be something, she knew, but where had Ray put it? Surely he wouldn't have thrown it away, not when he'd never thrown anything out in his entire life.

It was late that afternoon when she finally found a sheaf of papers at the very bottom of a cardboard box without any sort of label. Other than those important documents, the box contained an assortment of magazines and pamphlets related to the breeding and raising of quarter horses. Quickly Maris thumbed through the papers and nodded with satisfaction. The name of the trucking firm was there, as well as bills of sale for the ninety-three horses, all signed by a Katherine Willoughby with a rural Wyoming address.

"Great," Maris declared aloud. Now she could contact Ms. Willoughby and find out if there were any existing records of ancestry on the horses she'd sold Ray.

Bending over the corral spigot, Luke splashed water on his face and naked chest. He straightened and gave his head a shake to get the wet hair out of his eyes. Keith had shed his shirt, too, and when Luke moved aside, he wet himself down the same way Luke had.

"It's gonna rain, Luke." Keith looked up at the sky. "Not too many clouds yet, but the humidity is really climbing."

"Feels like it," Luke agreed. The summer heat had become oppressive this afternoon. He'd sweated more today than anytime since starting this job. So had Keith. Luke grinned at the boy. "Water's dripping off the end of your nose, kid."

"Yours, too," Keith retorted. "Hey, Luke, I've never seen anything like that ride you took on Bozo today. Do you think I'll ever be as good as you are with horses?"

Maris's cutting words on that subject were suddenly in Luke's mind: *I don't want Keith giving up everything else for rodeo, Luke. I don't want him to be like you.*

Luke walked over to pick up the feed sacks and blankets he used on the horses, which had been dropped on the ground in a heap. He began draping them over the corral fence. "Well, that depends," he said calmly. "First, I suppose, you have to decide if that's what you want to do with your life. Got any plans?"

"Plans? Like what kind of work I want to do after high school, you mean?"

"Yeah, plans like that. Only don't rule out college without some really serious thought. I did, and the older I get the sorrier I am that I stopped my education with a high school diploma."

Keith smirked openly. "How in heck would I ever go to college? That takes money, Luke."

Luke swung another blanket over the corral fence. "It sure does, but I've heard there are scholarships available to good students. Have you ever looked into it?"

"I've heard some talk about scholarships and loans, but my grades were never that good."

"You're a bright kid. Shouldn't be too tough to change that pattern," Luke commented. He stopped with his hands on his hips. "I'm not preaching, Keith. I'm not even advising. I just don't like the idea of you or any other kid in high school selling himself short. You can do or be anything you want. If breaking horses for a living suits you, then fine. Be the best damned handler you can be. But if in the back of your mind are some dreams that you're afraid wouldn't stand a snowball's chance in hell of coming true because you don't have the bucks, then don't settle for common labor. Go after that education, like I wish I'd done."

Rubbing the back of his neck, Luke gave a wry little laugh. "Guess I *am* preaching. Sorry. I'm the last guy who should be dishing out sermons." He walked across the corral to where he'd hung his shirt on a post.

Keith followed, his youthful forehead furrowed by a frown. "Luke, do you have a dad?"

"My dad's dead, Keith. My mother's living, though. Down in Texas."

"I'm just the opposite. My mom ran off when I was just a little kid, and I think she's dead, but my dad is . . . alive."

Luke guessed what was coming and decided to play dumb about Keith's background. "Is that so? Then this is just a summer job you have here with Maris, I guess."

"Uh . . . not exactly. Didn't she tell you about me?"

"Maris doesn't tell me much of anything about anyone, Keith."

"Oh. I thought you two were getting along pretty good. Guess not. I forgot you said she was mad at you."

Luke hung his shirt around his neck. "She'll get over it." He paused and looked toward the house. "Or maybe she won't," he said softly, more to himself than to Keith. "Anyway, what would she be telling me about you, if she were so inclined?" Keith's troubled expression hit Luke hard. The boy was hurting. "What is it, Keith?" he asked gently.

"My...my dad's in jail," the boy blurted out. "That's where I went yesterday, to see him. He...he wants me to live with him again when he gets out in a few months. Luke, can people change? I mean, can they do terrible things and then change and be different? He said he's changed. He said he stopped drinking and that he'd never hit me again. He made a bunch of promises and he...he cried. I never saw him cry before." Keith stared down at the ground. "I didn't know what to tell him."

Luke's suddenly livid brain lined up a whole slew of curses. Whether or not it was his place to give advice to Keith, he was going to do it on this subject. "Tell him to prove his promises, Keith. Tell him you're staying here until he does. Give him a year. If he doesn't drink for a year after he gets out of jail, then you might think about living with him again. That's what I'd do, and I wouldn't feel guilty about it, either."

Keith stood there staring into Luke's hard blue eyes for the longest time. Then the boy nodded. "Thanks, Luke. I think that's what I needed to hear."

"Feel free to come to me anytime you need to talk, Keith. I don't have the smarts to answer every question you might think up, but I'll try to be honest with my answers, okay?"

Keith smiled shyly. "Okay."

"Let's get back to work. I want you to take Snowflake for a ride around the pasture."

"Snowflake it is!" Keith exclaimed, heading for the saddle he would use on the white mare. Lifting the saddle, he stopped for a parting shot. "Whatever else I might do to earn a living, Luke, I'd still like to be a good enough rider someday to stay on a bronc the way you did with Bozo today."

Luke laughed. "Sure, kid, anything you say. Now, go catch Snowflake and give her a good workout."

Supper was a quiet affair that night. Maris had decided to locate Katherine Willoughby without Luke's help, maybe just to prove that she didn't need him making *every* decision concerning the ranch, so she ate with very few comments. Keith seemed engrossed in his own thoughts, mulling over Luke's advice, which seemed sounder the more he thought about it. And Luke was silent because he wasn't feeling particularly friendly toward Maris and didn't give a damn if she knew it. She was the only woman he'd ever known who could turn him inside out with a word, a look, a gesture, and he wasn't overly pleased about it.

About three-quarters of the way through the meal Maris caught on to Luke's sour mood. Her chin lifted as she sent him a defiant look. He sent one right back to her, even more defiant than hers had been. They glared at each other until Maris began feeling foolish and broke the staredown by looking at Keith. "More potatoes, Keith?"

"No, thanks. I'm getting stuffed."

"More potatoes, Luke?" she asked sweetly.

"No, thanks." Luke got up and took his plate to the sink. "Good night." He walked out.

Maris felt awful. She had pushed him too far this morning and he wasn't going to let her forget it. Uneasily she picked at the food on her plate until Keith was through eating. He, too, took his plate to the sink and said good-night, and all within the space of five minutes she found herself alone at the table, alone in the kitchen.

She was still sitting there fifteen minutes later, pondering and ruing her many mistakes with Luke, when she heard his pickup start up and drive away. She jumped to her feet and ran to a front window, to see the truck disappearing in a cloud of dust, heading for the highway. Her stomach suddenly tied itself into a painful knot. Where was he going? And to do what?

Those questions and a few others were still with her when she went to bed at ten o'clock and Luke hadn't yet returned. What's more, she had called information for Katherine Willoughby's telephone number and learned that there was no phone, either listed or unlisted, in that name at the Wyoming address written on those bills of sale. "Is there a phone at that address in someone else's name?" she had questioned the operator.

"I'm sorry, but I do not have that information, ma'am."

"Is there anyone in your company who does?"

"You might try calling the business office in the morning, ma'am."

"Thank you, I will." Utterly depressed, Maris put down the phone. That Wyoming address was hundreds of miles away, but if there was no way to reach Katherine Willoughby by telephone, how else could she talk to her but to make that long drive?

# Fourteen

After leaving the No Bull, Luke merely drove around for a while, taking roads he hadn't been on before to see where they might lead. His curiosity about the unexplored country of the area was weak, however, and it soon petered out to indifference. When that low hit him, he drove on into Whitehorn and parked his truck on the street in front of the Sundowner Saloon. The exterior of the building was old brick, unplaned weathered boards and darkly tinted windows. The place appeared to Luke's eyes to be a neighborhood bar, which seemed appropriate for his state of mind, as he wasn't looking for excitement, loud music or crowds. Opening the heavy wood door, he stepped inside and looked around.

Three men sat at the bar, two together, one at the far end by himself. A table was occupied by a group of three, one man and two women. Along the wall opposite of the bar was a row of booths, and the one way back in the corner was occupied by a man and a woman. Country music, notably muted, came from the jukebox and a big-screen TV over the bar was tuned—with the sound all but turned off—to a baseball game that no one seemed to be watching. The place was quiet, dimly lit, and everyone appeared to be minding their own business. Luke went on in and slid onto a bar stool, putting space between himself and the other men at the bar.

A short, chubby, male barkeep slapped down a paper napkin in front of Luke. "What'll it be, friend?"

"A glass of beer."

The drink was placed on the napkin. Luke laid down one of the twenties in his wallet and the barkeep rang up the sale and delivered Luke's change, placing it next to the napkin.

"Raining out there yet?" the man asked.

"Not yet." Picking up his glass of beer, Luke took a swallow, then deliberately turned his head to avoid eye contact with the barkeep. He wasn't here for conversation and wanted the man to know it. The bartender moved down the bar to the lone patron at the far end.

Staring into his glass of beer, Luke broodingly watched the tiny bubbles rising to the top of the amber liquid. Nothing felt right. His life was out of sync. Loose ends were developing by leaps and bounds and he didn't like the feeling. He thought of Keith and the advice he'd given the boy, which he probably shouldn't have done. On the other hand, he'd only told Keith how he felt, and that shouldn't be a crime. At least he had tried to encourage the teenager toward further education, which should please Maris if she ever heard about it.

He sipped his beer and scowled over Maris's image in his mind. She was not the type of woman he was normally drawn to. Maris was one of those strong-willed women who would have outfitted her own wagon in the old days and made the trek west, fighting off bachelors and would-be Lotharios every step of the way. Still, she took life much too seriously one minute and then became all woman in his arms the next. Her mood swings were impossible to understand for a simple country boy like himself, which raised some mighty disturbing questions. Why did he care? Why did he care that she made love with him willingly, eagerly, then turned on him as though he had held her down and ripped off her clothes by force? Why couldn't he simply enjoy her friendly moods and ignore the others? After all, it wasn't as though he were attempting to forge some sort of permanent bond between them.

In the background of Luke's troubled thoughts he could hear the conversations of the other patrons. The two guys sitting together on his right were talking about fishing. At the table with the man and two women mixed topics were being discussed, though right at the moment the young women were discussing childbirth, while the man sat there beaming, obviously thrilled with the subject. Those three were a convivial group.

It was the couple sitting in the corner booth who began sounding a warning bell in Luke's system. Although they weren't screaming at each other or even speaking overly loud, they were fighting. Arguing intensely and trying to keep it quiet. He glanced over his shoulder at the duo and saw a woman of about forty, with bleached hair and layers of makeup, and a man maybe a little younger, wearing a cowboy hat and a fierce expression. With the music and the other talk in the room, Luke could make out only bits and pieces of their animosity.

"You did it. Why don't you stop denying it?" the woman hissed.

The man's head was turned toward her, and Luke couldn't make out his reply, though from the set of his jaw he was angry through and through.

The saloon door opened and two men walked in. "Hey, Pete," one called to the bartender. "Bring us a beer." They sat in a booth.

Pete delivered the drinks and stood by the booth to chat about the impending rain. "Been a long dry spell" was Pete's opinion. The two men agreed that the area needed a good drenching.

Luke took another swallow from his glass and tried to relax, though the tension in his body felt like a fixed condition. He was normally a pretty loose guy, so it wasn't at all difficult to blame Maris for feeling as though his backbone had turned to granite. He wouldn't have to put up with her on-again off-again attitudes for much longer, he reminded himself. September first was just around the corner. In a few more weeks he'd have his money, a new horse and be gone.

For some reason that thought was no longer satisfying. Monotonous long drives between rodeo sites and strange motel rooms had lost their appeal. Not that those aspects of his chosen vocation ever had been all that appealing, but neither had they really bothered him before. Picturing himself wandering from rodeo to rodeo until he was too old to compete created what felt like a lead weight in his gut. Did he have Maris to thank for that aberration, too?

Thin-lipped with annoyance, he picked up his glass for another sip of beer. Pete was behind the bar again, delivering drinks to the two fishermen. A sharp crack rang out, followed immediately by a wail from the woman in the corner booth. Startled, Luke swiveled on his stool to see the man from the booth getting up and heading for the door. The woman was

crying, holding her face. Luke's eyes narrowed. That bastard
had hit her!

He got off the stool, strode toward the man and tapped him
on the shoulder just as he reached the door.

The guy turned, snarling. "Whadya want?"

Luke's expression was as cold and forbidding as a glacier. "I
don't know the circumstances and I ain't asking, but hitting a
woman for *any* reason makes a man lower than pond scum,
mister."

"Are you calling me pond scum?"

Luke could hear the woman sobbing in the corner booth. The
two women from the table had gone over to her. "I think I said
*lower* than pond scum," Luke replied in a lethal tone. He sort
of expected what happened next: the guy threw a punch.

A feeling of elation rushed through Luke as he sidestepped
the blow. "I'd be a little careful if I were you," he warned.
"Beating up women is more your style than fighting with a
man, isn't it?"

"You son of a bitch!" the man screamed, and jerked out his
arm again, clipping Luke on the jaw. Luke backed up a step,
then rushed the guy with a flurry of punches that targeted his
face and gut.

The men in the place jumped to their feet. Pete reached for
the phone and dialed the sheriff's office. The guy came at Luke
again. More punches were thrown. Luke's lip was cut and
bleeding. The guy's nose was gushing blood. People were
shouting. A couple of the men tried to break up the fight, but
one was in the wrong place at the wrong time and received a
blow from Luke that had been aimed at his adversary.

"Hey, just watch it," the newcomer yelled angrily.

Tables and chairs were knocked askew as the fight continued. Other than the three women in the corner booth, the saloon's patrons gathered around, though staying back far
enough to elude the melee.

The guy was as big as Luke and just as strong, he realized.
But he was quicker on his feet and getting in a lot more
punches. The exhilaration of adrenaline kept him fast and
coolheaded. He connected a hard fist with the guy's face, and
the man sank to his knees.

Luke stood there rubbing his knuckles, which were bruised and hurting like hell. Moving to the bar, he picked up a cocktail napkin and dabbed at his bleeding lip. Just then the door burst open and two deputies walked in. In seconds they sized up the scene. One chair was broken, two tables were overturned and there were some shattered glasses on the floor.

"He started it," Pete said with an accusing finger pointed at Luke.

"Benteen threw the first punch," one of the fishermen volunteered, which was the first time Luke had heard the name of the man he'd fought and beaten to his knees.

"Doesn't matter who started it," a deputy said calmly. "Pete, are you pressing charges?"

"Damned right. Look what they did to my place. This is a decent place, and I ain't putting up with drunken brawls."

The door opened and Judd Hensley walked in. "What's going on in here, Pete?"

Pete was only too glad to relate the story. "Jim Benteen was on his way out, almost to the door, when this guy here jumped him."

Judd's stern gaze went to Luke. "Luke Rivers. Now, why doesn't this surprise me?"

"Maybe because you surprise easily," Luke retorted grimly.

Lori Bains did a double take at Luke's name. Sitting beside Melva in the booth, holding a napkin she'd filled with ice cubes from the drinks on the table to Melva's bruised eye, she mumbled, "Oh-oh." She had met here with Louise and Larry Hawkins, friends who just today had learned they were going to have a baby. Her celebration drink had been a glass of white wine. Larry's had been beer and Louise had ordered sparkling water. But they'd been talking so excitedly about the baby, Lori simply hadn't noticed Luke come in. Then, once the brouhaha had gotten started, she had rushed to soothe Melva rather than watch the fight, which she wouldn't have watched anyway, as men pounding on each other sickened and disgusted her.

But Maris wasn't going to like her hired man brawling in a public place and getting himself arrested. She sighed.

Jim Benteen staggered to his feet, saw Luke and charged into him again.

"Jesus!" Luke yelped, taking the man's weight in the gut. The deputies rushed to pull Benteen back with warnings to cool down.

"Put the cuffs on him," Judd commanded. He looked at Luke. "Cuff him, too. Charge them both with drunk and disorderly, and public brawling."

"I'm not drunk," Luke said angrily as his arms were yanked behind his back and the cuffs slapped on his wrists.

"No? Well, we'll find that out at the station. Pete, we'll make sure someone pays for the damage in here tonight."

"Lock 'em both up," Pete said disgustedly.

The deputies escorted Luke and Benteen through the door and to a police car. Judd ambled over to the booth with the women. "Melva, let me see your face." Lori lowered the ice-filled napkin so Judd could check the damage for himself. His mouth tightened; Melva's right eye was bruised and swollen. "Melva, are you going to file charges this time?"

The woman's uninjured eye dripped tears. "I know I should," she said bitterly.

"We all know that, but are you going to do it?"

"I...don't know. I need to think about it. Lori, let me out. I wanta go home."

"Would you like me to drive you?" Lori asked gently.

"No, I can get there myself. But thanks."

Lori got up and Melva quickly slid from the booth, gathered her purse and made a hasty exit. Larry had come over to the booth. "Are you okay, honey?" he asked his wife.

Louise slid from her side of the booth. "I'm fine. Lori, we're going to leave. I'll call you, okay?"

"Yes, do that."

Judd's stern eyes rested on Lori. "Sit down and talk to me for a few minutes."

"Sure, Judd."

They sat on opposite sides of the booth. "I'd like to hear from you what happened in here tonight," Judd said.

"I'll tell you what I can, Judd. It all happened very fast. One second everything was quiet and peaceful, and the next..." She took a breath. "I guess Luke came in when I wasn't looking. At any rate, I wasn't aware of him sitting at the bar. I could tell Melva and Jim were arguing, but I really wasn't paying them any mind. Anyway, he hauled off and hit her. There was no mistaking the sound of the blow. Melva started crying. Jim got up and started for the door. By then me and everyone else were stunned and watching. I still didn't recognize Luke, as his back was to the room, but he tapped Jim on the shoulder and said something to him. Jim threw a punch and the fight was on. That's really all I know, Judd. Melva won't file charges, will she?"

"I doubt it. She never does." Judd got to his feet. "Thanks, Lori."

Lori was frowning. "Judd, are you going to call Maris?"

"I don't know. Probably not. It's late, and a night in jail won't hurt Rivers none. Maybe he'll call her. See ya, Lori."

After Judd walked over to the bar to talk to Pete, Lori left the booth, got her purse from the table where she'd been sitting before the fracas and quietly left the Sundowner. Outside she drew in a breath of fresh air and walked to her car. Behind the wheel she sat there chewing on her bottom lip. Maris should be told. Maybe Luke would call her and maybe he wouldn't. Should she, Lori, keep her nose out of it? She'd suspected the day Maris had introduced Luke that there were feelings between the two of them, though Maris had been quick to deny any such thing.

Feeling uneasy, Lori pondered the problem. She and Maris were close, but Maris always held some portion of herself in reserve. During her and Ray's marriage there'd been times when Maris had needed to talk, times when she'd sounded off, but even when she'd been angry and hurt and at her most communicative, Lori had always sensed something held back. The truth was that Maris might resent anyone's assuming she would care that Luke had been arrested for public brawling, even Lori.

She was still sitting there, when Judd came out of the Sundowner. To reach his car he had to pass hers. He came around to the driver's side. Lori rolled down the window.

"I've been thinking, Lori. Maris should be told. Are you planning to call her?"

"That's what I've been sitting here debating," Lori admitted. "Judd, maybe she should hear it from you."

Judd nodded. "All right. If Rivers doesn't call her, I will. Good night, Lori."

Maris awoke to rain on the roof. It sounded nice and she lay there for a few minutes just listening. Then, for some reason, she turned her head and glanced at the clock on the bedstand, which read 11:25. Almost eleven-thirty. Maris frowned. What had awakened her? Maybe Luke's truck returning?

Climbing out of bed, she walked through the dark house to the kitchen window. Though the hard rain obscured the compound, she could see that Luke's truck was still absent. Her nerves tautened as well as her mouth. How many nights had she worried and lost sleep because Ray wasn't home?

Whirling, Maris returned to her bedroom and crawled under the covers. Damned if she was going to lose sleep over Luke!

Luke had been locked in a tiny cell with bars on three sides. He could see Jim Benteen in another cell some distance away. One of the deputies had dabbed Luke's cut lip with antiseptic and given Benteen an ice pack for his bleeding nose. Luke had again stated, rather fiercely, that he wasn't drunk and demanded a test to prove it.

The test proved negative, so he couldn't be charged with drunk and disorderly, only disorderly and brawling in public. In his present frame of mind he didn't give a damn *what* they charged him with. Sitting on the cot in his cell, he glared at the drab cement floor. If he ever saw a man hit a woman again he'd do the same damned thing, arrest or no arrest.

The sheriff came into the cell block, the heavy metal door clanging loudly behind him. He stopped at Benteen's cell. "Anyone you want to call, Jim?"

"I already did," Benteen said sullenly. "He'll be down to bail me out."

"I'm surprised you didn't call Melva," Judd said dryly.

"I'm through with that bitch," Benteen mumbled.

"I think I've heard you say that before. This time I hope you mean it. You'd be doing Melva a big favor." Judd strode the corridor down to Luke's cell. "You're entitled to a telephone call, Rivers." Luke slanted him a glance but said nothing. "Did you understand what I said?"

Luke smirked. "You're speaking English and there's nothing wrong with my hearing. Yes, I understood what you said. So what?"

"So, is there anyone you want to call?"

"No."

Judd studied the man in the cell for a long moment. "What about Maris?"

"What about her?" Luke's voice was flat.

"Well, you're working for her, damn it. Don't you think she might wonder where you are?"

"In the middle of the night? We don't sleep in the same bed, Sheriff," Luke drawled sarcastically.

Judd's skin reddened. "I never thought you did. Wait, let me rephrase that. I never thought of *Maris* that way."

Luke turned his face toward the one solid wall of the cubicle until Judd realized he wasn't going to prolong that line of conversation.

The metal door opened and a deputy entered the area. He unlocked Jim Benteen's cell. "You're outta here, Benteen."

Luke watched the man stagger to his feet. "Bet he didn't test negative," Luke muttered.

Judd merely shook his head and followed the deputy and Benteen from the cell block.

Stretching out on the cot, Luke crooked an arm over his eyes to block out the bright lights. He swore he'd stay in this god-awful place for the rest of his life before he'd ever call Maris and ask for her help.


Maris was still awake, listening to the rain and pondering the misery of life in general, when her phone rang. Frowning, she sat up, switched on the bedstand lamp and picked up the phone. "Hello?"

"Maris, this is Judd."

A chill went up Maris's spine. Judd didn't phone at midnight just to chat. "What's wrong?"

"Has anyone else called you tonight?"

"No one. Judd, what's going on?" A note of panic had entered Maris's voice.

"It's just something I figured you'd want to know. Luke Rivers has been arrested. I've got him here in jail."

"In jail! What on earth for? What happened?"

"He was brawling in the Sundowner Saloon. Pete's filing charges."

Maris's shoulders slumped. Brawling and drinking, no doubt. God, she hated drinking. Alcohol turned some people into fools or, worse, bullies. Sober, Ray had been reasonably amiable; drunk, he'd been belligerent, quarrelsome and mean. What if Luke was the same?

Still, the thought of leaving him in jail was abhorrent. "Judd...uh...how drunk is he?"

"He isn't drunk, Maris."

A dizzying relief rocketed through her. "In that case I'll be down to bail him out."

"Figured you'd say that," Judd said on a sigh. "But I won't be here, Maris. I'm beat and heading for the barn. Deputy Rawlins will be on duty. He'll take care of the paperwork."

"Thanks, Judd. Talk to you soon."

"You're acting like you'd rather I hadn't gotten you out of jail," Maris said, taking her eyes from the road to send Luke's stony profile a resentful glance. "Did you enjoy being locked up?"

"Of course I didn't enjoy it, but Hensley shouldn't have called you."

"Why not?"

Luke jerked his head around and glared at her. "Because what goes on between you and me is no one else's business, especially his."

"Well, your being in jail could hardly be *my* business unless someone told me about it, now could it?"

"I didn't want you involved. My truck's parked in front of the Sundowner. Take a right."

"I know where the Sundowner is," Maris snapped. "Why didn't *you* call me?"

"I just told you. I didn't want you involved."

"I don't believe you. You didn't call because you're angry with me. You left the house angry and you drove away angry.

You were angry all day—don't deny it—which is probably the reason you risked your damned neck riding Bozo."

"I rode Bozo to break him, not for any other reason," Luke retorted sharply. "Damn, women are something."

"Meaning?" Maris sent him a glowering look.

"Meaning you've got me going in circles," Luke muttered darkly. "Why in hell wouldn't I be angry? Besides, if you'd care to remember, when we talked about my breaking the horses you laid down some pretty stiff rules."

"What I said was no drinking or women on the ranch. Obviously you went elsewhere to do your drinking."

"I had one lousy glass of beer, for your information."

"But you got into a fight. Looks to me like your anger got a little out of control."

"You have no idea what happened, so don't go making any snap judgments, Maris."

"Fine, I won't. In the meantime, why don't you fill me in?"

Luke was staring straight ahead. The wipers were slapping away the heavy rain on the windshield. "I don't want to talk about it. There's my truck. Pull over."

His ungrateful attitude infuriated Maris. She had gotten out of a warm bed to drive through a dark and rainy night to help him out, and he hadn't even said thanks. She stopped her car next to Luke's truck. "Thank you, Maris," she mimicked. "Why, you're very welcome, Luke."

Luke had his door partially open, and was ready to hop out. He stopped to look at her. "You're right. Sorry. Thanks for coming to the rescue. See you at the ranch."

Maris's anger suddenly drained away. "Luke, I know you don't understand me, but I really don't mean to make you angry. You said that I've got you going in circles. You should know that I'm feeling pretty much the same about you."

Without warning, he slid across the seat, clasped the back of her head and pressed his mouth to hers. It was a hard, rough kiss that set Maris's heart to pounding. Her body responded immediately, and she attempted to gentle the kiss by parting her lips and seeking his tongue.

He broke away and narrowed his eyes on hers. "Why did you kiss me back?"

She swallowed. "Why did you kiss me at all?"

He muttered a curse. "You're driving me crazy." With that quixotic message, he slid back across the seat and got out in the rain, giving the door a hard slam behind him.

Perplexed, Maris sat there until he had gotten into his truck and started the engine. Then she slowly pulled away and headed for home.

Obviously they were driving each other "crazy," because her heart still hadn't settled down from that wild kiss and now she was wondering if it ever would again. God help her, she thought dismally. She had to be falling in love with Luke, and if that wasn't asking for trouble nothing ever would be.

Luke drove about a hundred feet behind Maris's car during the rainy miles to the ranch, his shoulders hunched forward, his features grim. He had given a part of himself to Maris Wyler that he'd never given to any other woman, and he didn't know how to get it back. Call it heart, call it soul, he thought resentfully, angrily, but when he left the No Bull after the horse auction, he'd be leaving without it.

It was the strangest sensation he'd ever experienced, but he couldn't think of one single way to alleviate its sting. That damned IOU had brought him more pain than any one man deserved, physical as well as emotional. Right now his split lip hurt like hell—a sane man wouldn't have kissed a woman so hard with a split lip—and the bones in his body that he'd broken in his fall last year were aching and throbbing, probably from both the fight and the damp weather. He felt like a bag of weary, hurting old bones, and he could hardly wait to reach the ranch and crawl into bed.

They finally got there. Maris parked the truck, got out in the rain, ran over to Luke's pickup and yanked open the door before he could. "Are you okay? I was thinking on the way home that you might need some aspirin or something."

Nimbly Luke crawled out of the truck, keeping his numerous aches and pains to himself. "I don't need anything, thanks." He started for the barn.

Frowning, Maris watched him for a minute, then shivered from the cold rain penetrating her clothing and ran for the house. But instead of going directly to her room, she stood at the kitchen window and tried to see the barn through the downpour. Eventually a light came on in the loft, appearing as a ghostly beam in the dreary night.

Sighing unhappily, she left the window and went to bed.

# Fifteen

It was still raining in the morning. Luke and Keith put on waterproof ponchos and went out to work with the horses, while Maris sat down and began making calls to the business offices of Wyoming's telephone company. She got nowhere. "Sorry, ma'am, but that information is not available," she was told repeatedly. All she wanted was to know if there was a telephone under another name at Katherine Willoughby's old address, but apparently the telephone company considered that privileged information.

Finally, frustrated and irate, she dialed the sheriff's office and asked for Judd. He came on the line.

"Sheriff Hensley."

"Judd, this is Maris. Listen, I need a tremendous favor. Can you go through legal channels or contacts or however you do these things and find out if a certain address in Wyoming has a telephone? I've been on the phone for hours trying to get the information, but no one will give me an answer."

"I can try, Maris. What's the address?" She recited the data. "Might take a while. I'll call you back when I know anything. Incidentally, Rivers has to appear before Judge Mathews on Thursday at 9:00 a.m. Did he tell you?"

"Your deputy told us both last night. Luke will be there. Judd, if Luke paid for the damage to Pete's place and he dropped the charges, wouldn't that be the end of it?"

"Pete's pretty upset, Maris. I doubt if he'd drop the charges for any reason."

"Hmm." Maris was thinking hard. "Well, thanks, Judd. I hope you have better luck getting that information than I did."

"What do you need it for, Maris?"

"You know the horses Ray bought? Well, I located the bills of sale and they were signed by a Katherine Willoughby with that address. I want to speak to her about the horses' ancestry. Luke thinks there's some good blood in the herd, and if we could prove it my horses would bring a much better price at the auction. But there's no phone in her name and I thought it might be listed under someone else's name."

"I'll do what I can, Maris. Talk to you later."

Maris got up from her chair with a determined expression. While Judd was throwing his legal weight around on that address and telephone number, she was going to take a little drive into town.

Walking into the Sundowner Saloon took courage for Maris. She wasn't accustomed to visiting taverns by herself, and seldom had even done so in the company of others. At least there were very few patrons on this rainy day, she thought gratefully while going to the bar.

A pudgy middle-aged man behind the bar came over to her. "Hello," Maris said with a smile. "I'm looking for Pete Riddick."

"You found him, ma'am. What can I do for you?"

Maris extended her hand over the bar. "I'm Maris Wyler."

"Wyler? Uh…would you be Ray's widow?" Pete shook her hand.

"Yes. Mr. Riddick, there was a fight in here last night, and one of the men involved, Luke Rivers, works for me."

Pete's face lost most of its friendliness. "Mrs. Wyler, I try to keep a nice, peaceable place here, the kind of place a man can bring his wife for a drink and feel comfortable."

"I understand." Maris glanced around. "It's very… pleasant." She looked for damage and couldn't spot any. There was a row of booths along the far wall and tables and chairs separating the booths from the bar. Her gaze returned to Pete Riddick behind the bar. "Let me get right to the point, Mr. Riddick. If I paid you right now for whatever damages were incurred by that fight, would you consider dropping the charges against Luke?"

Pete cleared his throat. "You'd pay right now?"

Maris withdrew a handful of cash from her purse. "Yes, right now."

"I have a list of the damage," Pete said, as though issuing a warning.

"May I see it?"

"Just a second. I'll get it." Pete walked to the back bar and picked up a piece of paper. Returning, he handed it to Maris.

She read it quickly: *Two tables...$250. Three chairs...$150. Glasses...$30.*

"I'm gonna ask the judge for an extra two hundred for the trouble of having to order new things," Pete said.

"So we're talking about six hundred and thirty dollars," Maris said with a wince she couldn't completely conceal. She'd brought the last of the cash from the yard sale with her, never dreaming the cost of the damage would require nearly all of it.

But her bills were current and the bail money she had handed over to the deputy last night—two hundred and fifty dollars—would be returned if the charges were dropped. The values that Pete Riddick had placed on his things were much too high, considering that every stick of furniture in the place showed evidence of longtime usage.

She wasn't going to argue values, however. Not when there was a chance Judge Mathews would make an example of Luke and sentence him to some jail time. The summer was waning. Labor Day was only a week away, and Maris wanted desperately to stick to her plan of a horse auction at the end of September. Luke had to be free to finish his work with the horses, and besides, she really couldn't bear the thought of him sitting in jail and coming out with a record that would follow him ad infinitum.

To whet Mr. Riddick's appetite for immediate payment, Maris counted out the correct sum and laid it on the bar. "The truth is, Mr. Riddick, I need Mr. Rivers at the ranch, and Judge Mathews might not be in a benevolent mood on Thursday."

Pete rubbed his mouth, his gaze on the neat stack of cash. "Well, I don't like causing a widow lady undue stress, Mrs. Wyler. Ray used to drop in now and again, you know."

"Yes, I know." Ray had "dropped in" at every saloon and tavern in the Whitehorn area on a regular basis. The Sundowner could have been the place in which he'd done his drinking the night of his fatal accident. Maris had never attempted to find out which establishment had allowed him to walk out too drunk to drive, because, in truth, she never had blamed anyone else for anything Ray had ever done. Her philosophy had always been that adult human beings were responsible for their own actions. Which she'd sort of been forgetting, she thought with an inward wince, recalling how she'd been looking for someone to blame for her own recent behavior.

"Well, what do you say, Mr. Riddick? Do we have a deal?"

Pete eyed the money again. "Would you tell Rivers that he's not welcome in here again?"

"If that's what you want, yes. Mr. Riddick, what really happened last night?"

"Rivers started the fight, Mrs. Wyler."

"Do you know why?"

"All I know is that Jim Benteen was on his way out and Rivers stopped him with some remark about pond scum." Pete shook his head in disgust. "They weren't even sitting anywhere near each other, Mrs. Wyler. Jim was in that corner booth and Rivers was sitting at the bar, just about where you're standing now."

Maris tried to visualize the scene. Why on earth would Luke leave his seat and start a fight with a man he didn't know? There wasn't any sense to be made out of something so irrational, but then she remembered that Luke had been in a foul mood when he'd left the ranch and maybe that was all the incentive he'd needed to pick a fight.

She sighed. There was an awful lot she didn't know about Luke, though in God's truth she never would have thought him the type of man to engage in barroom brawls. She especially wouldn't have thought him capable of *instigating* that kind of trouble.

"There were women in the place, too," Pete said, as though the presence of the fairer sex increased Luke's crime a hundredfold.

Maris felt as though the wind had just been knocked out of her. A woman. Of course. She should have figured that out for herself. Jealousy clawing at her insides startled her, and she suddenly wanted this over and done with. Pushing the money forward, she asked again, "Do we have a deal, Mr. Riddick?"

Pete hesitated, then reached for the cash. "Yeah, we do. I'll call the sheriff and tell him to drop the charges." He folded and tucked the money into his pants pocket. "Just be sure and tell Rivers to stay away from here."

"Gladly," Maris said coolly. "May I have a receipt?"

Driving into the ranch compound, Maris saw that the corral was vacant. The rain, coming down in sheets, had apparently driven Luke and Keith inside. She went into the house, calling, "Keith?" When she got no response, she figured Keith was with Luke.

The phone rang, and she picked up the kitchen extension. "No Bull Ranch. This is Maris."

"This is Judd. Pete Riddick called and dropped the charges against Rivers."

"He said he would."

"How'd you talk him into it?"

"I didn't do much talking, actually. But I did lay cash on the bar to pay for the damages."

"Rivers didn't gain any respect from me by sending you to do his dirty work," Judd growled.

"Luke doesn't even know about it."

"He doesn't. Well, now, seems like you're taking mighty good care of your hired hand, Maris."

"Judd, please. I need Luke out here, and..."

"Yeah, I think maybe you do. About that information you asked me to dig up—there's no longer a telephone at that address you gave me, but there's a Katherine Willoughby living in Sheridan. Got a pencil handy?"

"Right here." A little sick at heart over Judd's comment about her "needing" Luke—it certainly hadn't been said in a flattering tone of voice—Maris wrote down the address and telephone number Judd recited in her ear. "Thank you, Judd. I really appreciate this."

"You're welcome. I've gotta go, Maris. Another call." The phone went dead.

After hanging up, Maris sat there feeling rather numb. Obviously Luke and Jim Benteen had fought over a woman. Judd believed she and Luke were carrying on an affair, which they were. Sort of. And now she had to tell Luke what she'd done about getting his charges dropped, and she suddenly wasn't so sure that she should have done anything without discussing it with him first.

Well, there really wasn't any reason to rush out into the rain to impart the news. Grim lipped, Maris dialed Katherine Willoughby's Sheridan number. It was answered on the third ring.

"Hello?"

"Is this Katherine Willoughby?"

"Yes, it is." The woman's voice was melodious and pleasant.

"My name is Maris Wyler, Ms. Willoughby. About four months ago you sold ninety-three horses to my husband, Ray Wyler. Do you recall the transaction?"

"Certainly. And please call me 'Katherine.'"

"Thank you. Um... those horses were very green, Katherine, and I have a man breaking them. He's quite familiar with horses and mentioned that some of them appear to have excellent conformation and might be from a good bloodline. That's why I'm calling. Do you have any information on the herd's ancestry?"

"Not at my fingertips, Maris. Your husband, Ray, was apprised of the situation at the time of the transaction."

Maris took a breath. "Ray died shortly after buying the horses, Katherine. I'm sorry to have to bother you with this, but he told me nothing about the herd and I really do need any information you might have access to."

"Oh, you poor dear. Please accept my condolences. Losing a loved one is most difficult and very trying to the spirit. Well, let me begin at the beginning. Those horses belonged to my father, who became very ill about three years ago. I moved out to the ranch to care for him, and with him being gravely ill for so long, the horses were certainly my last concern and totally ignored. That is the reason they were so completely untrained. They grew up on the range without any human contact whatsoever. Your hired man is correct in his assumption that most of the herd has good blood, and I know Dad kept excellent records regarding their lineage. However, after Dad died I sold the ranch, lock, stock and barrel, and I can't think what I might have done with those records, or even if I kept them."

"Ray didn't inquire about the herd's lineage?"

There was a lengthy silence in Maris's ear. Finally Katherine said, "I honestly can't remember, Maris. But it seems only sensible to assume he didn't, or I would have given him the data. Are you certain you don't have it?"

"Very certain, Katherine. I've gone through everything in the house and really only found the bills of sale a short time ago."

"Well, I'm glad you have those, at least. Maris, give me a few days to gather my wits and think about those records. I was quite shaken over my father's death, even though I knew it was coming. At any rate, there are blanks in my memory connected to those unhappy days and the ensuing weeks when I was selling Dad's property. Give me your telephone number. I'll call you one way or the other."

Maris recited her phone number. "I can't tell you how much I appreciate your cooperation in this, Katherine."

"I think I understand, Maris. Besides, it's information you should have . . . if I can just think what I might have done with those records. Goodbye."

"Goodbye, Katherine, and thank you again."

"You're quite welcome, my dear. I'll be calling."

Maris put down the phone with excitement pumping through her system. Luke was right; her horses weren't just run-of-the-mill range animals. If Katherine found those records and they could be presented at the auction with each horse, the value of the animals would increase greatly.

This was very good news, and Maris became anxious to tell Luke about it. Besides, he might even look upon her talking Riddick into dropping those charges as good news. Sometimes she was such a pessimist, she chided herself. Why on earth *wouldn't* he be relieved over not having to appear in court?

Going to the kitchen door to brave the rain in a run for the barn, Maris stopped to frown at the wall hooks and what they contained. Keith's poncho was hanging there, and why would he have brought it to the house, then returned to the barn without it?

She gave her head a small shake to clear it. These days everything seemed like a problem of one sort or another. But Keith running around in the rain without his poncho was hardly a major crisis.

Yanking up the hood of her own rain jacket, Maris left the house and jogged to the barn. Inside she lowered the hood and called, "Luke? Keith? Anybody here?" Luke's pickup was parked in its usual spot, so the question was merely to let them know she was in the building.

Luke appeared at the top of the ladder. "I'm up here."

"Figured you were." Maris started up. "It's really pouring out there."

"We had to quit working."

Maris reached the second floor. "So what're you two doing to pass the time, playing cards or something?"

"Keith's not here."

"He's not? He's not at the house, either. Where is he?"

"Don't get panicky. Jessica McCallum came along and took him for a ride."

Maris heaved a sigh of relief. "Oh, thank goodness. I couldn't imagine where he might have gone on foot in this downpour."

The loft was chilly and damp. "Come on into my room. I've got the electric heater going," Luke said.

Maris followed him into his room. Luke closed the door. "You know who Jessica is, don't you?" Maris said.

"I figured it out the first time she came around."

"Yes, well, she must want to talk to Keith about something." Maris loosened her jacket. "She comes out to see him every so often."

"Have a seat," Luke offered.

"I'm too excited to sit. Luke, I finally made contact with Katherine Willoughby." Maris related what Katherine had told her about her father, his ranch and his horses. "So if she can locate those records, we'll have proof of their lineage to present at the auction. Isn't that great?"

"It'll only be great if she *finds* the records, Maris."

"Yes, but I have a very strong feeling that she's going to find them."

Luke grinned slightly. "Woman's intuition?"

Maris grinned back, until she remembered what else she had to tell Luke. "Um...I went to see Pete Riddick at the Sundowner, Luke."

His grin disappeared. "To do what?"

Deciding to present this news as though he couldn't possibly be offended, Maris put on a big smile. "I paid him for the damages to his place and he dropped the charges against you. Isn't that wonderful?"

"You paid him? How much?"

"Luke, the amount doesn't matter. But now you don't have to appear in court. The whole thing's over. Aren't you thrilled?" He didn't look thrilled, she saw with a sinking sensation. "Don't tell me you're upset because I just possibly might have saved you from spending some time in jail, for pity's sake!"

"I wouldn't have gone to jail," Luke said stonily.

"How can you be so certain?"

"Because of the circumstances."

Maris's lips thinned. "Oh, is two men fighting over a woman acceptable behavior these days? If it is, I certainly haven't heard about it."

Luke's eyes narrowed on her in a hard look. "Who told you that?"

"No one had to tell me. Pete said there were women in the place when the fight broke out, and I can put two and two together as well as anyone else."

Folding his arms across his chest, Luke leaned his hips against the bureau. "So you've got it all figured out, have you? You know something, Maris? I'm beginning to understand why Ray drank."

Her eyes widened in shock. "How...how dare you say such a thing to me?" she said hoarsely, on the verge of tears. There was no way she could defend herself against such an unfair accusation, but as quickly as her throat had filled with tears, just as quickly the urge to cry vanished and was replaced by cold fury. "You bastard," she said, her eyes shooting daggers. "There are a lot of things I will never put up with from a man again, and mental cruelty is one of them."

Luke wasn't exactly calm, either. "What the hell do you think your assumption that I fought with Benteen over a woman was, if not mental cruelty? Clean up your own act before you start judging mine, Maris."

"Are you saying a woman was not the cause of your fight last night?" Her words dripped skepticism.

"Actually a woman *was* involved, but not in the way you're thinking." Luke pointed an angry finger at her. "I didn't have to go to court to get tried and convicted, Maris. You did that all by your lonesome. And you're far from perfect, lady, damned far, *too* far to be acting so superior. You know what your biggest problem is? You're afraid of being human."

"And just what is that supposed to mean?"

"You know what it means, as well as I do."

"You're referring to our... our..."

Luke raked his hair into a mess. "For crying out loud, say it like it is. We didn't commit murder, Maris. We made love. Making love doesn't make you a criminal. You've got nothing to be ashamed of. You're a good and decent woman."

"Decent women do not go to bed with the hired help," she snapped.

Luke's lips thinned. "Sometimes you talk like a damned fool."

"And you're a jerk!" Maris started for the door, then stopped. "Since you asked, I paid Riddick six hundred and thirty dollars, *which* I'll be only too happy to deduct from that three thousand I never owed you in the first damned place!"

She stormed out. For a second Luke was dumbfounded by the staggering sum she had paid Pete Riddick. But then he bounded from the room and caught Maris by the arm before she could start down the ladder. "Do you know what was broken in his place last night? One damned chair. A few tables got knocked over, but I would swear on a Bible they weren't damaged. Oh, yes, a few glasses got shattered. Does one chair and a few glasses add up to six hundred and thirty bucks to you? They sure don't to me, sweetheart, and besides, Benteen should have paid half the damages, *which* he would have been forced to do if you hadn't stuck in your nose and stopped us from going to court!"

Maris jerked her arm out of his hand. "Don't you ever touch me again, and don't worry about me doing you any more favors, you... you ingrate!" Her bravado was all on the outside, however. Internally she was cringing because Luke was right. Benteen *should* have paid half the damages. She *should* have kept her nose out of it.

But she had pictured Luke as guilty and drawing a jail sentence from a coldhearted judge, and she needed him to finish breaking the horses. It was all too much, and she suddenly felt her legs giving out. Moving to one of the heavy beams that supported the roof of the barn, she leaned against it, all her fighting spirit gone.

"Oh, damn," she moaned, turning to hide her face from Luke.

He looked at her forlorn figure and felt his own anger losing impetus. "Maris, it's done. Just forget it," he said wearily. "Deduct the sum you paid Riddick from the three thousand. I just don't give a damn about it anymore. I'll finish breaking your horses and get the hell out of Montana the minute they're sold." He hesitated, then added, "And I'm sorry I made that crack about why Ray drank. I don't know where it came from, because it's not how I feel about you at all."

His apology didn't alleviate the pain his remark had caused Maris, but she stopped hiding her face and turned around. He looked utterly miserable, she saw, which, perversely, made her feel even worse than she had. "I . . . I'm sorry, too. I thought I was helping by going to see Pete Riddick. And I'm sorry I called you names. I seem so on edge lately." She ran her fingers through her damp hair, pushing it back from her face. "I'd like us to get along for the remainder of your stay here. Do you think we can manage to do that?"

"We can try," Luke said quietly. Even though she was damp, a little disheveled and unquestionably upset, Maris made him think of sex. He'd rather kiss her than fight with her any day of the week. He took a long breath for caution, because in the back of his mind was a question that wouldn't go away. If he made a pass right now, would she melt as she'd done before? Or would a sexual advance from him at this point finish destroying their already deteriorating relationship?

Maris was again thinking of the mystery woman who had caused the fight, though "not in the way she'd been thinking." What had Luke meant by that? However badly she wanted to know, she couldn't bring herself to ask.

"I'm going to the house," she said, sounding tired and defeated.

"Put your hood up. The rain is still coming down hard."

She looked Luke in the eye. "Maybe I will and maybe I won't. Don't give me advice, Luke. I don't like it any more than you do. And maybe I do talk like a damned fool sometimes, but so do you."

"Aw, hell." Luke groaned. Turning on his heel, he returned to his quarters and slammed the door behind him. If that was Maris's idea of getting along, she must have slipped a cog.

He frowned at that notion. She hadn't been that edgy when he'd first gotten to the ranch. In fact, she hadn't been that edgy until today. Maybe his getting arrested had upset her a lot more than she'd indicated last night when she'd bailed him out. But that conclusion didn't seem completely accurate, either, not when she had gone out of her way today to make sure he didn't spend some time in jail.

Standing at the window and watching Maris running through the rain—with her hood up—to the house, Luke shook his head and admitted that he knew only two things for sure with this peculiar lady. One, he never stopped wanting her, and two, as he'd told her last night, she was indeed driving him crazy. Sad to realize, there couldn't possibly be a cure for what ailed him as far as Maris went. Not when he couldn't even give the disease a name.


Glancing at the clock every few minutes, Maris made supper. Jessica keeping Keith this long—a good three hours—had never happened before and didn't feel quite right to Maris. Worrying that something was wrong, she browned a chicken, then put it in the oven to bake, along with three large potatoes.

Her thoughts weren't only on Keith, however. What woman had been involved in Luke and Jim Benteen's brawl last night? And *how* was she involved? Why hadn't Luke come right out and explained? Did he think it was none of her business and never planned to tell her about it? What was strange was that Pete Riddick's explanation of the fracas hadn't pinpointed a woman. He'd merely said that he didn't like that sort of thing occurring in his place with women present.

At five-thirty, the normal dinner hour, Luke rapped on the kitchen door and walked in. "Isn't Keith back yet?"

"No, and I'm getting very worried. Did Jessica say anything about keeping him so long?"

"All she said was that she needed to talk to him and would he please take a ride with her."

"I see." Maris thought a moment. It was possible that Jessica was seeing to Keith's supper, though it really wasn't at all like her to be inconsiderate of Maris's routines. Regardless, Keith wasn't the only mouth to feed on this ranch and Luke was probably hungry. "Everything is ready, Luke. We may as well go ahead and eat. I can warm the meal for Keith if he hasn't already eaten when he gets home."

# Sixteen

They weren't at the table more than five minutes, when a motor noise announced an arriving vehicle. "It's them," Maris said with obvious relief. Rising, she went to the window. Though true nightfall was still some hours away, the rain and heavy cloud cover darkened the area. Still, Maris could identify Jessica's car. "It's them," she repeated with a glance back at Luke.

Luke had started eating, but he laid down his fork. "Don't wait," Maris said. "Keith will be right in." She resumed her place at the table, anticipating Keith bounding in at any moment and plopping into his chair.

But minutes passed and then more minutes, and still Keith didn't appear. They could hear the idling engine of Jessica's car and Maris began worrying again. "Something's wrong," she murmured, more to herself than to Luke. Maris wondered if she should go outside and speak to Jessica, then argued herself out of it. If Jessica wanted to talk to her, she wouldn't be sitting in her car.

Finally the door opened and Keith walked in. Maris stood up and smiled, although Keith's down-in-the-mouth expression really didn't invite smiles. "I'm glad you're home," she said to the boy. She saw him swallow and noted the paleness of his face. "Is anything wrong, Keith?" she asked gently.

"Jessica wanted to come in with me, but I told her I could do this. My dad died."

"Oh, Keith. What happened?"

"He died in his sleep last night. The doctor said he had a heart attack." Keith held out a folded piece of paper. "Jessica wrote this just now so I could bring it in to you."

Jessica's writing her a message was the reason Keith hadn't immediately come in, Maris thought, accepting the paper.

"Shall I read it now?" she asked Keith. "Dinner's on the table. Are you hungry?"

"I'm not, Maris, thanks. I think I'll go to my room, if you don't care."

"Of course I don't care." She went to Keith and put her arms around him. "If or when you feel like talking, I'll be here."

Luke had gotten to his feet. "So will I, Keith."

"Thanks, Luke." The boy shuffled from the kitchen with his head down.

Maris slowly sank to her chair. Luke returned to his. They looked at each other across the table, empathy and sympathy mingling on the path of their gazes. "I had better read this," Maris said quietly, indicating the note from Jessica:

Maris,
I tried calling you several times today, but you were apparently out. Now Keith prefers going in and telling you about Terrance by himself and I feel as though I should honor his request. He hasn't cried, Maris, which maybe is only to be expected, given his sad and abnormal relationship with his father. He has also said very little today. We went to the prison, then to a funeral home to make arrangements for Terrance's interment. I'm sure it was all quite traumatic for Keith, though he showed very little emotion throughout.

At any rate, I will be calling tomorrow. Keith is going to have to wade through this on his own, Maris, though it will be enormously therapeutic for him to know that we all care about his pain and that he has friends who will remain constant.

Jessica

Maris lifted her eyes to Luke's. "Would you like to read it?" He nodded. "If you don't mind."

She handed the paper across the table. It was while Luke was intent on Jessica's handwriting that Maris felt the first gush of tears. Sniffling, she got up for a tissue and blew her nose. But once flowing, the tears wouldn't stop. Standing with her hips against the sink counter, she wept silently and wiped away tears.

Luke started to say something as he raised his eyes from the paper, but stopped short when he saw Maris crying. "Did you know Terrance Colson?"

"No. I recognized him on the street, of course, but I never knew him personally."

"Then you're crying for Keith."

"I . . . I guess so." With a fresh tissue, she wiped away another spate of tears. "I didn't cry for Ray," she said, and covered her face with her hands.

The unhappy, embittered tone of her voice startled Luke almost as much as what she'd said. He got up, rounded the table and gently pulled her into his arms. She wept into his shirt and accepted the comfort he was offering. What she'd said was the God's truth. Instead of sorrow over Ray's untimely death, she had felt resentment that he would die so unnecessarily. Before his death she had cried too many times to count, but after the accident and even at the funeral her eyes had contained deeply rooted anger instead of tears.

Luke's natural warmth lessened the chill in her soul. It felt good to be held and soothed and treated as someone special. Her thoughts turned from sorrows the world over to the immediate present, to how she felt in Luke's arms. It wasn't shocking anymore to think about falling in love with him, though remembering that his time here was running out created an almost unbearable ache in the vicinity of her heart.

Jessica's comment in her note about Keith's having to wade through this by himself rang true for Maris, as well. She, too, had something to wade through. Foolishly she had become emotionally involved with a wandering man, and she would pay for it, possibly for the rest of her life.

She stepped back, though Luke's hands remained on her shoulders. His eyes contained concern and caring, which touched her deeply. "Are you all right now?" he asked softly.

"Yes, I'm fine." It was a lie, but if she said, "No, I might never be all right again," he would force her to talk about old events and hurts that she didn't even want to think about, let alone discuss. "Finish your dinner, Luke. Wait, let me put your plate in the microwave for a minute." Darting away from him, she whisked his plate of food from the table and into the microwave to reheat.

They sat at the table, though neither had much appetite. Maris was despondent and showed it. "Is it best to leave Keith be, or should one of us go to his room and talk to him?"

"I think we should give him some space for a while, Maris. When he's ready to talk he'll come to us."

"He's so young to be all alone in the world." Maris's eyes filled again.

"He's not alone. He has you and he has me, too, if he wants me."

"But you're not going to be around much longer." Maris bit down on her lip. Keith would miss Luke, too. He had started out shy and reticent around Luke, but she'd known for some time now that the boy enjoyed working with Luke and being in his company. Then Maris remembered Mrs. Colson, Terrance's mother. "Keith has a grandmother somewhere. I'm sure Jessica must have notified her."

Luke acknowledged the information about Keith's grandmother with a nod, though his mind was strangely stuck on Maris's remark about his impending departure. The thought of driving away and putting Maris, Keith and the No Bull out of his life was intensely disturbing. But what could he say? *Maris, I've been thinking about staying.* How would she receive such a remark? Their arrangement ended in September. Once the horses were sold she and Keith could easily care for the few beeves on the ranch. She'd mentioned turning the No Bull back into a cattle ranch, but that would take time, and resources she didn't have. Unless the horse auction was a rousing success, that is, which was a distinct possibility should Katherine Willoughby locate her father's breeding records.

They finally stopped pretending to eat and pushed their plates back. Tonight Maris was in no hurry to clear the table and get the dishes washed. By the same token, she noted, Luke didn't appear in any hurry to leave, probably because of the weather. Before it started raining he'd been going out to the corral or one of the pastures after dinner to work with the horses till dark, and tonight's heavy rainfall pretty much eliminated any outside activity.

Absently she toyed with the salt shaker, turning it around and around on the table with the tips of her fingers. "Where will you go from here?" she asked in a very low and quiet voice.

Luke blinked, as though suddenly coming awake. "I don't know."

"Where's the next big rodeo in October?"

"I don't know that, either."

"Haven't you done any checking into it?"

"No, I haven't." Luke leaned forward. The ceiling light was reflecting in Maris's hair, appearing as shiny golden and reddish highlights. "Maris... I said some things to you today..."

"And I said just as bad to you, Luke. Let's not start apologizing again. Not tonight."

He could see the unnatural glistening of her eyes, the pallor of her skin. Old Terrance's death had affected her very strongly. Oddly, it had also brought Ray's death closer and somehow made it more grievous for Maris.

"All right," he agreed, getting to his feet. "I'll say goodnight." He glanced at the dirty dishes on the table. "Unless you'd like some help with the dishes. In fact, why don't you let me clean the kitchen and you go and lie down?"

As though jerked to her feet by an invisible hand, Maris stood and began stacking dishes. She wasn't an invalid, for heaven's sake, just shaken up. "Thanks for the offer, but I'd rather keep busy."

Without another word Luke left. He and Maris had no real relationship and why did he keep thinking they did? There was an ache in his gut, a sadness, that he didn't know how to combat. It was for everyone on the No Bull, for Keith and what he must be going through, for Maris and her strength and her weaknesses, so at odds with each other, and for himself, a man who had mindlessly drifted for nearly twenty years and now realized that he would never again be content with that careless, freewheeling life-style.

After the kitchen was back in order, Maris sat in the living room. She kept listening for some sound from Keith's room, some indication of his presence. There was nothing, and she couldn't stop thinking of him in there alone. The mantel clock ticked off the minutes, then the hours. Finally she got to her feet. Unnerved or not, she couldn't sit up all night.

Passing the door to Keith's room on the way to her own, Maris stopped to listen again. Unable to bear the silence any longer, she slowly turned the knob and pushed the door open only enough to see into the room. Keith was fully dressed, wide-awake and lying on top of the bed covers, with the nightstand light burning.

"Keith? Are you all right?"

His head turned on the pillow to look at her, then, abruptly, he swung his feet to the floor and sat up. "I don't know, Maris. How does a person know if he's all right?"

This was not a child speaking to her, Maris realized as she entered the room and sat down on its one chair. She had thought of Keith as a boy since Jessica had first brought him to the ranch, but he had lost the last remnants of childhood today and looked and sounded like a man.

"Good question," Maris said quietly. "I'm sure it's one that most people ask themselves at one time or another. There's so much stress involved with losing a family member that days of confusion aren't at all out of the ordinary. It happened to me when my parents died."

Keith lifted his eyes to look at her. "And when Ray was killed?"

Maris took a breath. "There was stress at that time, yes, but it was different than when my parents died."

"Different how?"

Maris thought for a moment. Keith needed honesty right now, but how much honesty was she strong enough to give him? His eyes looked old and weary, she saw. He was obviously struggling with his own private memories of his father, and quite possibly feeling guilty because he hadn't loved Terrance. It was that guilt Maris wanted to eliminate.

"I didn't love Ray, Keith. I was sorry he died, but the sorrow was for his wasted life, not for me. I believe that when someone dies whom you love very much, then the grief you feel is for yourself. You know how much you're going to miss this person, and you actually torture yourself by remembering the good times you'd had together. That's the way it was with my parents. With Ray..." Maris paused, realizing that this was the first time she had said these things aloud. "With Ray I almost felt a sense of relief. He had caused me a great deal of heartache and unhappiness, and I felt . . . I thought . . ." Her voice faltered. There were so many aspects of her marriage she couldn't tell this young man about. She shaped a shaky little smile. "I think I've said enough for you to understand."

"Dad never loved me," Keith said in a voice so low Maris could only just hear him. "He probably never loved anyone. He was never nice, Maris, not to anyone, not the way you and Luke are."

Maris stood up to pull her chair closer to the bed. Seated again, she reached for Keith's hand and looked directly into his eyes. "I want you to know with all your heart and soul that this is your home. I'd like you to consider me as family, Keith. Is that possible?"

He nodded. "I'd like that, Maris. When I went to see my dad that day, he said he wanted me to live with him when he got out of prison. I didn't want to. I didn't believe he had changed. Luke said for me to tell him to stay sober for a year and then maybe I would live with him again."

"Luke said that? Then you discussed it with him."

Keith nodded again. "Luke's great, Maris." Keith's eyes dropped and his old shyness suddenly reappeared. "I wish *he* were my dad."

Sitting back, Maris took a long breath. Reminding Keith of Luke's approaching departure at this emotional moment would be cruel. Luke might be nice in Keith's eyes, but he had his faults, make no mistake. Barroom brawling was one that Maris could hardly overlook. For a second the faceless woman involved in that brawl flashed through Maris's mind, and her lips thinned slightly. Luke might not be a Ray Wyler or a Terrance Colson, but he was far from perfect.

But disenchanting Keith by saying so would only hurt the boy and he already had enough pain to deal with. Besides, Keith may as well remember Luke as being only "nice" after Luke was gone.

Sighing, Maris patted Keith's hand. "Feeling any better?"

"I guess so."

"It will take some time, Keith."

"Will . . . will you go to the funeral with me? It's set for the day after tomorrow."

"Absolutely. I'll be right by your side every minute." Maris saw the mist forming in Keith's eyes. He was trying hard not to cry, but she could see that the dam was finally breaking. It was what he needed to do, to just let go of his tightly contained emotions and bawl.

But her witnessing his breakdown would only embarrass him. Briskly Maris got to her feet. "I'm going to bed. If you need me in the night for anything, knock on my door."

"Thanks, Maris." Keith's voice was thick with tears.

"Good night, honey," she whispered, and bent over to kiss his cheek. "I love you like the son I never had. Remember that. Always."

She hurried across the room to the door, then stood in the corridor and felt her own influx of tears and sorrow.

The sun was bright the next morning. Maris prepared breakfast and was pleased when Keith made an appearance. Luke came in and they sat at the table.

"How're you doing, buddy?" Luke asked the boy.

"All right, Luke. I want to work today."

"Good. I really need your help. There's only a handful of unbroken horses left in the big pasture, and I'm planning on starting the training process with each one of them today."

Maris's heart skipped a beat. "Then we're going to meet the deadline?"

"No question about it," Luke replied. "I'd get some advertising out about the auction, if I were you."

"I'll work on it," Maris murmured.

Two hours later she was painting signs announcing the auction, when the phone rang. "Maris, this is Katherine Willoughby. I located Dad's breeding records. I'm shipping them to you today—it's quite a bulky package—so watch for it, dear."

Maris's knees went weak and she had to sit down. "I can't thank you enough, Katherine. I'll reimburse you for the shipping cost if you'll let me know the amount."

"I'll put a little note in the parcel. I hope the records will be of some help to you, Maris."

"I'm sure they will. Thank you again, Katherine."

Elated, Maris put down the phone and let out a yell. "Ya-hoo!" She started for the door, anxious to tell Luke the good news, but the phone rang again and she returned to answer it.

"Is this Maris?"

"Yes, it is."

"Jim Humphrey here." He chuckled in her ear. "Bet you thought I was never going to pick up that Corvette. I got tied up with other things, but I'll be there this coming weekend. Just wanted to let you know."

"That's wonderful, Jim." Another burst of elation had Maris grinning. This was a good day, a *great* day.

Again she started for the door and again the phone rang. Maris looked back at it with a disbelieving expression. What next?

"Maris, this is Jessica. How is Keith doing?"

"Surprisingly well, Jessica. He's out working with Luke today. Would you like me to call him in so you can speak to him?"

"No, that's not necessary. You can pass on my message. Maris, the county will pay for new clothes for Keith to attend his father's funeral. I'd like to pick him up and take him shopping this afternoon."

"The county?" Keith was not a charity case, damn it! Not to her, he wasn't. "Jessica, I will buy Keith whatever he needs for the funeral."

"That cost is not your responsibility, Maris."

Maris thought of that two-hundred-fifty-dollars bail money sitting at the sheriff's office, which she hadn't yet picked up. It would be more than enough to buy a suit of clothes for Keith, which was something she should have thought of before this.

"I want to do it, Jessica. Keith has become very important to me."

"He really is an exceptional young man, isn't he? I have very high hopes for his future, Maris."

"So do I, Jessica."

"Well, I can see he's in very good hands." Maris could hear the pleased smile in Jessica's voice. "Until he turns eighteen I will have to keep an eye on him, but I have a very good feeling about Keith now. And it's all your doing, Maris. Thank you."

"It's I who should be thanking you, Jessica. You brought him into my life, and I couldn't be happier about it. One thing has come to mind, though, Jessica. Has anyone contacted Keith's grandmother?"

"I called and spoke to her sister, Maris. Mrs. Colson is very old and unwell. Her sister said she barely recognizes anyone anymore, and she couldn't possibly make the trip to attend the funeral. I told Keith about it yesterday."

"I see. I just wanted to be sure she'd been notified."

After a few more words, they hung up. This time when Maris started for the door to go outside, the phone remained silent. She had a marvelous idea, and she could hardly wait to pass it on to Keith.

He was in the corral with Luke and another Appaloosa. Maris leaned on the fence and called, "Hey, you two, I've got a whole slew of things to tell you. Can you take a break for a few minutes?" They were both working without shirts, but it wasn't Keith's youthful torso that had Maris mesmerized. Luke's skin was as dark as a hazelnut and glistening with perspiration in the bright sunlight. The core of her felt every rippling muscle of his beautiful body as surely as if he were touching her, and the sensation literally took her breath.

At that very instant, while Luke was removing his gloves and Keith had already started toward her, a thought struck Maris nearly dumb: she had missed her period. It had never happened before. She'd rarely ever been even a day late, and now she had completely missed a period and she'd been too preoccupied with other things to notice something she had never failed to keep very close track of.

She began trembling and had to hang on to the fence to at least appear steady and in control of her senses. But this could be the real thing. She could be pregnant. Oh, Luke, she thought with a remorseful look in his direction. Tricking a man as she'd done with Luke was unforgivable.

But it hadn't seemed so terrible before falling in love with him, she realized with panic eating a hole in her stomach. If it was true, would she tell him now?

Oh, God . . . oh, God . . .

"What's up?" Luke asked, strolling over to the fence, which Keith had already reached.

"Uh...uh..." Maris's mind was so full of unconnected topics, she couldn't settle on one.

"You said you had something to tell us," Luke reminded her.

"I did. I do." Gratefully her dizzy brain remembered Katherine's call. "Katherine Willoughby found her father's breeding records and is shipping them to me."

Luke's face lit up. "Hey, that's great."

"Yes...yes, it is. Oh, Jim Humphrey called and he'll be here this weekend to pick up the Corvette."

Luke was grinning. "You're just full of good news. Anything else?"

"Something for Keith." She was beginning to calm down, thank God. "Keith, I'd like you to have some new clothes for the...for tomorrow."

"You would? I was just gonna wear my jeans."

"Would you rather just wear jeans? I was thinking of a suit." The boy smiled shyly. "I've never had a suit."

"A suit and tie would be very appropriate," Maris said.

Keith looked at Luke. "What'll you be wearing, Luke?"

With a glance at Maris, Luke cleared his throat. "A suit and tie." He hadn't given the subject one second's thought, but if Maris wanted Keith in a suit and tie, then he'd go along with it, though it probably surprised the heck out of Maris that he even owned a suit and tie.

"Okay," Keith said. "How much will it cost? I've got about fifty bucks..."

"I'm paying for it, Keith. Now, here's the big question. Do you want to go shopping by yourself or would you like someone to go with you?"

Keith's boyish smile flashed. "I'd like someone to go with me." Maris smiled broadly, thrilled that he would want her company and advice. "I'll go call Susie right now and see if she can go," Keith said, hopping the fence and heading for the house at full speed.

Maris's mouth dropped open. "I thought he meant me."

"Susie's his girlfriend," Luke said calmly.

"The girl he took to the movies that night? But they only had that one date, didn't they?"

Luke shrugged. "Apparently it was enough."

Maris sucked in a slow breath. "Well, this is a surprise."

"Don't let it get you down, honey," Luke said gently. Reaching across the fence, he laid his hand on her shoulder.

Maris brought her gaze around to him and it hit her again. She could be pregnant with his baby and he was leaving in less than a month.

Luke's hand slid up under her hair to the back of her neck. "You look beautiful today," he said huskily.

The words came out of her mouth before she could stop them. "So do you."

He laughed, softly, sensuously. "Maybe after Keith leaves we can . . . talk."

"Keith!" Maris began backing away. "There's something I have to tell him."

"Well, hell," Luke muttered, watching her hurrying to the house. For a minute there her mood had been the one he liked. Liked, hell! It was the one he *loved*. The one in which she got all dewy-eyed and excited and game for anything.

But then he relaxed. Keith would be leaving and maybe, just maybe, he could coax her back into that sweet, female mood.

Maris went into the house calling, "Keith?"

He came out of his room wearing clean jeans and shirt. "She can go, Maris. I'm going to pick her up in half an hour."

"That's wonderful, but there's something I need you to do before you pick up Susie. It won't take but a minute. Stop at the sheriff's office and they'll give you two hundred and fifty dollars in cash."

"How come?" Keith looked completely mystified.

"Uh . . . it's money they owe me. Use what you need of it for a nice suit and accessories. I would suggest a white shirt and a tie in subdued colors. Get some shoes, too, some *real* shoes."

Keith grinned. "No boots or sneakers, huh? Okay, I'll stop and pick up the money." He started out, then did an about-face. "Thanks, Maris. You think of everything."

Maris collapsed onto the nearest chair. She came up with everything, all right, she thought disgustedly, even devising that awful plot to get pregnant without Luke's knowledge.

But then the thought of a baby refired her earlier elation, and she sat there and fantasized about having a child in the house and in her own arms, until she remembered that she had to call Judd and tell him to release that bail money to Keith.

Jumping up, she dashed to the phone.

# Seventeen

When Keith drove away in Maris's pickup, Luke washed up at the corral faucet, dried himself with his shirt, draped the shirt over a post fence, strode to the house and walked in. Maris was just hanging up the phone, and he went to her, took her by the hands and brought her to her feet.

Her eyes became very wide and startled. "No, Luke."

"Look me in the eye and tell me you don't want me," he said gruffly.

"I..." Her blood was suddenly racing. "It would be a lie."

"That's what I thought." Bending, he placed his hand behind her knees and scooped her off the floor and against his chest. "Which way to your bedroom?"

She buried her face in his neck. "Down the hall. Last door on the right." It was no use, she thought. She'd tried keeping Luke from doing something like this and had obviously failed. Maybe, without realizing it, she'd even been inviting one more repeat of their tempestuous lovemaking before he went away.

Today he seemed in a hurry. He set her on her feet next to her own bed and began undressing her. "Go slower," she whispered. Their eyes met, and the grim expression in his evolved into warmth and desire.

"Sorry." Gently he tugged her forward and pressed his lips to hers. Maris felt his kiss all the way down to her toes. A strange mixture of joy and misery made her feel reckless, and she snuggled closer and thrust her tongue into his mouth. After he was gone she would remember each time they had made love, and maybe he deserved the same cruel fate. She would make today as memorable as she could. He would not drive away without memories, not after today.

His naked chest seemed to beg for attention, and Maris ran her fingertips, her nails, over his smooth, dark skin.

"Baby," he whispered raggedly. "Why do I want you so much?"

She'd been asking herself the same question, only in her case the answer was becoming acutely evident. Apparently Luke wasn't thinking beyond the pounding beat of his own blood, which was sort of sad. And yet, if he said right now that he was in love with her she would be aghast. Heaven knows she had long stopped comparing him to Ray, but there were still worrisome similarities, such as fighting in a bar and, for that matter, going there in the first place. What else did a person go to a tavern for but to drink? Then there was the biggest similarity of all, rodeo. Luke's obsession for rodeo actually surpassed Ray's.

No, she didn't want to hear that Luke loved her, or that he would drop in and see her if and when he ever returned to this part of Montana. His departure after the horse auction had to be final and the end of their relationship.

Even with those thoughts deeply entrenched in her mind, Maris sighed seductively and responded to his desire with every cell in her body. She kissed him as demandingly, as passionately, as he kissed her, and her caresses were as bold and intimate as his.

Suddenly it was she who seemed in a hurry. Groping for the buckle on his belt, she opened it and then the zipper of his fly. He unbuttoned her blouse and pushed it from her shoulders. Their kisses had become hungry and greedy, landing willy-nilly on noses and chins and lips. She pushed down his jeans and undershorts while he did the same with her jeans and panties.

But their clothing got hung up on Luke's boots and her shoes, and they separated to hastily rid themselves of the obstructions. Naked then, Maris drew back the spread and blankets. They tumbled to the bed, legs entwined, to kiss and touch and explore each other's bodies.

"You're so beautiful," Luke whispered. His mouth opened on her breast. His tongue teased her nipple until it had formed a rigid peak, causing an unbearable ache between her legs. He seemed to know, because he slid down in the bed and began kissing her inner thighs, gradually going higher. Moaning softly, eyes closed, Maris curled her fingers into his hair, all she could reach of him. His tongue was like hot satin on her most sensitive spot, and in minutes a starburst of pleasure began in her lower abdomen.

"Luke...Luke..." she whimpered, needing his arms around her at this unique and special moment.

He heard and understood her cry. Moving up in the bed, he gathered her into his arms and kissed her lips. He held her against his chest until her trembling had ceased.

Then he tipped her chin and looked into her eyes. The mist of tears and the softness he saw touched his soul. Tenderly he kissed her. "Maris . . . we need to talk," he said hoarsely.

"Not now. Please . . . not now." If he talked about love she would fall apart and confess how much she cared for him. She would tell him that nothing mattered but loving him, and it wasn't true. Or it wouldn't be true once this incredibly sensual interlude was over. But in her present mood she would say foolish things, things such as his need for the excitement of rodeo being no detriment to their relationship, and that she didn't care if he hung out in bars and got into fistfights and was arrested. She did care. Those things caused her great pain, and she didn't want to tell romantic lies because of his sexual power and then regret them later.

For a moment Luke nearly forced the issue. They *did* need to talk. He wanted to understand why she'd become so important to him, and why she made love with him if he wasn't equally as important to her.

But he was unmercifully aroused and talking could come later. Maris surprised him by sitting up. But she wasn't eluding his embrace, he realized, not when she smiled mysteriously and then straddled his hips. He sucked in a huge breath of air as his excitement increased to the bursting stage.

Leaning forward, she feathered kisses across his lips. Her long hair caressed his shoulders and the sides of his face. The crests of her breasts softly touched his chest, and she deliberately moved them back and forth in exquisite torture.

His eyes were partially closed, his breathing deep and labored. "What're you doing to me?" he said thickly.

"Do you want me to stop?" she whispered with a seductive smile.

"No way."

Laughing softly, she took his sexy bottom lip between her teeth and gently nibbled. Luke's hands rose up to cup her bottom. "Incredible," he murmured.

"What's incredible?"

"Your...uh, hips." Her nibbling at his mouth was driving him crazy. "If you raise up just a little..."

"Yes? If I raise up just a little you'll do what?"

"Do it and find out," he growled.

Maris appeared to be thinking very hard. "Could it be this?" Lifting her bottom, she reached down to his manhood and held it upright, positioning them both for a perfect union. Very slowly she took him inside herself, until she was sitting precisely on the juncture of his thighs.

"That's it," Luke said with his eyes closed and supreme pleasure all over his face.

He was fully inside of her, lying flat on his back, and the sensation was unbelievably exciting for Maris. "I kind of like this," she said playfully, albeit in an unusually husky voice.

"I kind of like it, too."

"It makes me feel quite powerful."

Luke's eyes opened. "Like you're the boss?"

"Like I'm in control."

His eyes were dark and smoldering. "You are. What are you going to do now, boss?"

"Hmm. Maybe this." With her hands on his chest she slowly raised her hips and then slid down again. "How was that?"

"That was good. That was *very* good. Do it again."

"Again? Once wasn't enough?"

Her teasing tone delighted Luke. Never had she teased him about anything. Nearly every day Maris let him see another side of her. A lot of the time the side she exposed wasn't altogether pleasant, but he was beginning to realize she was a many faceted woman. A complex woman.

But he could tease, too. "Well...maybe once *was* enough. I'll let you decide. You are in control, you know."

Her teasing expression vanished. "So I am. Maybe I'll keep you in this position for hours."

He laughed, a trifle grimly. "I wouldn't last for hours, baby, but give it your best shot."

She fell forward and whispered into his ear. "I know what you want, you devil." Then she straightened and began moving her hips up and down, using her knees on the bed to propel herself.

He clutched at her thighs. "That's it. That's fantastic. Don't stop. Don't even slow down." His right hand crept over his own belly to locate and then stroke the core of her pleasure.

"Luke...oh, Luke," she gasped, stunned that she would be this needful so soon after the heights she had just reached no more than ten minutes ago. It was almost laughable that she had decided to give him a memory about today that he would never forget. *She* was the one who would never forget this day, and didn't she already have enough incidents to suffer over after he was gone?

But there was no stopping now. Nor, as Luke had pleaded, even a chance of slowing down. She was caught by the rhythms of their intense lovemaking, soaring and feeling more alive than ever in her life. She loved this man, adored him, and she just might die when the day came for him to drive away in his fancy pickup.

Her eyes flooded with tears, and when the powerful and beautiful spasms of release began, she fell forward, too dazed even to wonder if Luke had come to the same dizzying fulfillment.

He had, and he held her in an embrace so tight he marveled that she didn't complain. "Straighten out your legs, honey," he whispered. Mindlessly she obeyed. Luke turned them to their sides. "Do you want to get up?" Damn, he thought. He hadn't used protection again. What in hell was wrong with his brain? When he was hot for Maris and she cooperated, everything sensible simply disappeared.

She was starting to come out of that magical haze, starting to think again. "Uh...yes, I'd better." Still dazed, she slipped from his arms and got off the bed. Somehow she made it to the bathroom without tripping over anything, though how she'd accomplished it she would never know.

Automatically she refreshed herself, then, standing before the bathroom mirror, she studied her reflection and saw the dejection in her eyes. Her heart was already broken and Luke was still here. How would she bear it when he wasn't?

Wrapping a large bath towel around herself, she returned to the bedroom. Luke had stacked the pillows and was lying against them with his eyes closed, and wearing an expression of utter satisfaction. Hearing her come in, he lifted his lids and smiled at her.

"Hi, baby." Maris didn't smile back and his spirit deflated. Every damn time they made love she got depressed right after. "Don't do this, Maris."

"Don't do what?" Listlessly she began picking up her clothes.

Luke sat up. "I think you know." He watched her gather clothes for a moment. "Maris, come over here. Please."

She heaved a despondent sigh. "Luke, I don't like myself very much right now. Just get up and go, please."

Leaping off the bed, Luke grabbed her by her upper arms. "We're going to talk. Come and sit down."

"Talk about what?"

"About us, damn it! What else would I want to talk about?"

"Don't shout at me," she said sharply.

"Then talk to me. Right now, right here." He began pushing her toward the bed. "Sit down."

She shook off his hands. "Don't give me orders." She wasn't yelling. In fact, her voice had become steely, steady and lethally quiet.

Luke took a breath. "I'm sorry. Maris, would you please sit down and talk to me?"

Apparently this "talk" was inevitable and it may as well be now as later, she thought. "Yes," she said, and marched to the closet for a bathrobe, which she put on with her back to him. Then she went over to the room's one chair and sat down. "Go ahead."

Luke scrambled for his jeans and yanked them on without bothering with his underwear. He turned to look at Maris. "The first thing I wish you'd tell me is why you get angry and depressed every time we make love."

A snotty retort nearly made it to her lips, but she decided against it. It was time for the truth with Luke. "I like you more than I should. I don't want to like you. I don't *want* to sleep with you. I don't want anything between us but our original deal. Second, I have never casually slept around. I turn into someone else with you, the kind of woman that I have never respected or even wanted to know. I believe that only people deeply in love with each other should be making love. I believe that it's up to the woman to say no to a man, because men can and do sleep around and it means nothing to them. Nor does the woman mean anything to them. I..."

"Whoa," Luke said, sounding as breathless as if he'd been the one making that long speech. "Let's start with why you don't want to like me."

Maris's left eyebrow went up. "I think that's perfectly obvious. You're leaving in a few weeks, aren't you?"

Luke hesitated. "That's been my plan all along, yes. But let me ask you this. Don't you ever let yourself like anyone who isn't living on the ranch?"

"We're not talking about ordinary liking, and you know it," Maris said with cutting asperity.

"Ah, that's good." Luke nodded enthusiastically, surprising her. "Now we're getting somewhere. You don't just *like* me. It's possible that you even—" he cleared his throat "—love me."

Maris's face drained of color. "Don't presume too much, Luke. However I feel about you, it's going to come to a screeching halt very soon now. I'd just as soon not get in any deeper than I already am, and if you had any feelings at all for me you wouldn't even be mentioning the word *love*."

"Because you and I couldn't possibly have a future together, right?" He practically stopped breathing, almost praying for some word, some sign from Maris that would indicate otherwise. She disappointed him.

"That's *exactly* right. Let me tell you something, Luke. I will never again make any sort of commitment to a man who has not only completely settled down in one place, but who wouldn't have it any other way."

"A man like Judd Hensley." Just saying the sheriff's name caused Luke's spine to stiffen.

Maris scoffed. "Don't bring Judd into this. I don't have to explain my friendship with Judd to you, nor do I intend to try."

"Don't expect me to believe Hensley hasn't made a pass, Maris," Luke said with some sarcasm.

"Judd has *never* made a pass," she said with icy distinction. "You're exactly like Ray was. You simply cannot visualize a nonsexual relationship between a man and a woman."

Luke's face shut down. "I'm *nothing* like Ray was."

"Nothing! Good grief, do you take me for an idiot? He couldn't enter enough competitions to satisfy his obsession with trying to kill himself in a rodeo arena, and he was forever fighting in bars. Usually over a woman, I might add."

Luke's lips tightened into a thin line. He looked at her for a long time, then said brusquely, "So you feel that my career choice and one fight in a bar make me like Ray. Maris, what's your friend Lori's telephone number?"

Maris blinked. "What?" Walking over to the telephone on the bedstand, Luke repeated the question. "Why do you want Lori's number?" Maris asked incredulously.

"Because she was at the Sundowner that night and I'd like you to hear from her what really happened."

"Lori was there? I don't believe you. She would have called me . . . or something."

"She was there, Maris. Believe it." Luke picked up the phone and pointed it at Maris. "Call her."

Perplexed, Maris stared at the phone in Luke's hand. Lori had been there? She'd seen the fight and what had caused it? If that was true, why hadn't Lori called and told her about it?

Maris lifted her chin. Lori was a very busy woman and many times weeks passed without either of them calling the other. It could also be that Lori simply didn't want to carry tales. "Why don't you leave Lori out of this and tell me what happened yourself?"

"Because I don't think you'd believe me. I don't think you believe *anything* I say. For some crazy reason you've got me mixed up with Ray. It's like Ray went away and I showed up and nothing had changed."

"That's the most ridiculous thing I've ever heard." But the sneer in Maris's voice wasn't nearly as definite as she'd meant to convey. Without question she had lumped Luke and Ray in the same untrustworthy category many times. By the same token, she had also recognized their differences. Ray had been as lazy as they came and no one could ever accuse Luke of shirking responsibility. As far as his work with the horses went, anyway.

She had only discussed Ray with Luke in general terms, and maybe it was time to get specific. Maris stood and went to the window. "You're not like Ray. I'm sorry I said you were. Oh, there are similarities, make no mistake, but you're not mean or lazy or unkind, and he..." Her voice cracked. She was getting painfully close to the very memories she had diligently avoided since Ray's death.

"He what, Maris? Tell me, please."

Maris sighed. She had opened this can of worms all on her own, whetting Luke's curiosity, and maybe he *should* hear the facts of his friend's true nature.

She turned to face Luke. "You and Ray were good friends, weren't you?"

"Uh... let's just say we ran into each other quite a lot."

"At various rodeos."

Luke nodded. "Yes, but that didn't make us good friends, Maris. What were you going to say a minute ago?"

"Are you sure you want to hear this?"

"I'm positive. Maris..." Luke moved close enough to touch her and very gently brushed a strand of hair from her cheek. "Tell me your secrets, honey, and I'll tell you mine."

"You have secrets?"

"There's one that's been eating a hole in my gut for weeks now."

Instinctively she knew his "secret" was about her. He was going to talk about love, and she was just stupid enough to listen and then confess her feelings for him. He was right. Ray had died, Luke had shown up and nothing had changed.

But that wasn't completely true, either. *She* had changed, and she'd meant what she'd said about never again committing herself to an unstable man. Yes, she would tell him her secrets, and if that didn't get her point across to Luke, nothing ever would.

"Very well." Needing some space between them, Maris went to the other side of the room. "When Ray and I were married, I was very deeply in love with him." She noticed Luke's flinch but let it pass without a reaction from her. "He brought me here and I immediately found a second love, the ranch. He showed me around the place and I was so starry-eyed I only barely noticed the evidences of neglect. It was around the middle of September and we had a beautiful fall that year. Every day was sunny and warm, and Ray was full of smiles. We drove somewhere to eat out almost every night. We slept late in the morning. He always had something fun lined up for the day and I rarely had any free time to even do any housecleaning. 'We're on our honeymoon,' he'd say if I mentioned that the carpets needed vacuuming or the laundry was piling up. And he never did any real work outside. Once in a while he'd go down to the barn and putter around for an hour or so, but that was about it.

"The weather changed. There was no snow, but it got very cold very fast. One morning I awoke and heard the cattle bawling. You know how far the pastures are from the house, so it was a muffled sound, but incessant and disturbing. I couldn't figure out what was causing it, so I slipped out of bed, put on some warm clothes and went out to investigate. It was bitterly cold. The thermometer read five below zero. I hurried to the fields and found the animals milling around the water ponds, which had completely frozen over.

"It seemed like a simple enough problem to me, and I rushed back to the house to wake Ray and tell him about it, assuming, of course, that he would take the news as I had. Obviously holes had to be chopped through the ice so the animals could drink.''

Maris drew a breath. "He became enraged when I shook him awake and explained the situation. Cursing and throwing things around, he got dressed and stormed out of the house. I was so stunned I didn't know where to put myself. Would he want my help outside? Would my presence anger him further?

"I made a pot of coffee and worried myself sick. Had I done something to anger him? To that point I hadn't seen him angry and it scared me. Would he calm down outside and come back in sweet as sugar? I realized that awful morning that I really didn't know my husband.

"Well, he didn't come in at all. About three hours later, from the kitchen window, I saw him getting into his pickup and driving off. He got home around midnight that night, so drunk he could barely walk. I helped him into bed, then I sat up the rest of the night, crying and accusing myself of doing something to make him angry enough to drink himself into a stupor.''

Maris went to the chair and sat down. ''That was the beginning. Ray was never the same after that. He told me he hated the ranch and he was no longer very fond of me. He started going off by himself, to one rodeo or another. I chopped through the ice when the ponds froze over. I delivered hay to the fields when there was too much snow for the cattle to paw through to reach the grass.

''I knew what my options were—leave Ray or stay and take whatever he dished out. I hated fighting and did everything I could to avoid dissension. But he got mean when he drank, and he—'' She stopped to swallow. This was something she had never told anyone. ''He started hitting me.''

''Hitting you!'' Luke looked as though someone had just hit *him*. ''And you still stayed?''

Maris didn't answer. Instead she said, ''I had wanted a baby from the day we were married. One night he told me that he'd had a vasectomy *after* we were married. He laughed about it. He had let me hope and pray for a child. He had watched me taking my temperature to check for my fertile times, and all along he'd known he couldn't become a father.''

''Mental cruelty,'' Luke mumbled. Clearly he was dumbfounded by Maris's history. ''He must have loved you to marry you, so what changed him?''

''I disappointed him, Luke. He wanted a playmate, which was exactly what I'd been during his courtship. But you see, I took marriage seriously and Ray did not. He didn't want to run the ranch the way it needed to be run. He didn't want to be tied down by a wife who thought animals should be properly cared for. I honestly don't know how the ranch survived after Ray's father died and Ray lived here alone. He must have worked sometimes, however erratically or begrudgingly, probably doing only what absolutely had to be done to keep the place together. When I finally faced reality and took a really good look at everything, the signs of neglect were everywhere. Fencing was falling down. Every building needed repairs and paint.''

Maris threw up her hands and got to her feet. ''There's so much more I could go on for the rest of the day. But I'm sure

I've said enough for you to understand why I get depressed, as you pointed out, every time we make love. No, you don't seem to be like Ray in temperament. But you do have some of his traits, and that scares me, Luke. I admit to being weak with you. I admit that I'm enormously attracted to you, but you have to do a little admitting, too. One, you're always going to be a traveling rodeo rider. Two—"

"Stop." Luke spoke quietly, but the intensity of the expression on his face was enough to stop Maris from enlarging her list. "It's time you heard my secrets."

"I...I'm not sure I want to," Maris said falteringly.

"Fair is fair. I listened to yours—now you listen to mine." Luke walked a small circle in the middle of the room, taking in a long breath at the same time. Maris watched with her heart in her throat. He finally stopped and looked at her. "Here goes," he said in a tone of voice that sounded as though he were preparing to dive into an erupting volcano. "I'm thirty-five years old, I've traveled thousands of miles, I've met hundreds of women, and until coming here I thought everything was great. Oh, sure, I was broke, but I figured I'd collect that three thousand from Ray and make a new start."

He narrowed his eyes on Maris, who was standing stock-still and staring at him rather nervously. "Did I ever tell you *why* I was broke?"

"No," Maris said cautiously.

"I took a bad fall about a year ago and broke several bones. My horse broke his neck and had to be put to sleep. He was the best cutting horse..." Luke looked away for a moment, embarrassed to find himself on the brink of tears. "Anyway, I used up my savings in getting well. You know, if I hadn't had that accident I might never have remembered Ray's IOU."

"This happened while you were competing in a rodeo, right?" There was sudden frost in Maris's eyes. "I'm sorry about your mishap and your losing your horse, but a man risking his neck in rodeo just doesn't make any sense to me."

"It's no damned different than any other sport! Do you hate football players, too?"

Maris's jaw dropped. "I never thought of it that way."

"Well, try, okay? Maris, the only reason you hate rodeo is that Ray used it to get away from the ranch. After what you just told me, he might even have used it to get away from you.'' At her hurt expression, he took the sharp edges off his voice. ''Honey, I'm trying to tell you something. I feel ... different now. I've been trying to figure it out for weeks. It's you. It's Keith. It's working with the horses. It's watching you do your gardening, and the way you worked your tail off on that yard sale. It's the way you run the ranch and take care of the cattle. It's how you treat Keith and how much he likes and respects you. It's...''

He chewed on his bottom lip. He shoved his hands into the pockets of his jeans and yanked them free again. He raked his hair and darted nervous glances at her. And finally, when she was starting to think of dashing out of the room and probably the house altogether to avoid what was coming, he blurted, ''I'm different because I love you.''

Maris wilted. ''I don't want to hear this.''

''You already did, but I'm going to say it again. I love you and I'm pretty sure you love me, too.''

Sinking weakly to the edge of the bed, Maris hid her face behind her hands. ''I knew you were going to do this to me—I just knew it. Luke, go away. I mean, pack your things and *go away!*''

''Not on your life, sweetheart.'' He knelt beside her. ''It took every ounce of courage I could find to tell you my secret, and now that it's been said I'm sure as hell not going to disappear.''

Dropping her hands, Maris jerked her head up. ''Not until you get the itch to wander again. And it will happen, Luke. Maybe I've gone overboard with my dislike of rodeo, but don't expect me to believe that you've suddenly lost a lifelong yen to compete.''

''That's exactly what I expect you to believe,'' he said softly. ''You know what my big problem is now? I don't have anything to offer you.''

''Offer me?'' Her voice was as unsteady as she felt inside, all quavery and woozy.

''Maris, I'd like to stay here and help you run the ranch. But I don't have anything to contribute. Why would a woman want to marry a man who has only two assets—a six-year-old pickup and an uncollectable IOU?''

"Marry?" She was going to faint, she could feel it starting in her midsection and working its way up to her brain. She strove for clarity. "Uh . . . you're going to collect on that IOU after the horse auction."

"Let's talk about that after we decide on the marrying part of this conversation."

She tried to swallow the massive lump in her throat. "Luke, I can't . . . I can't marry you. And it's not because of your assets. I explained about Ray . . ."

"I'm not Ray. I won't yell at you because the ponds freeze over. I won't leave you alone to chase after either a rodeo or another woman, and I will never, never lay a hand on you. Except to make love." He managed a hopeful, lopsided grin. He'd laid his heart on the line with Maris, something he'd never done with any other woman. "Those are promises, Maris, vows. You're the only woman I've ever talked to like this, the only woman I've ever been in love with."

Maris's chest was so tight she could just barely breathe. Didn't Luke understand anything she had told him? Ray had made promises, too. Ray had . . .

*No!* Ray hadn't promised anything. Ray had led her into love and marriage with no more than a sexy grin, a persuasive personality and a dishonest glibness. She probably knew Luke ten times better right now than she'd known Ray on their wedding day.

It scared her that she was weakening, leaning toward Luke's unusual marriage proposal, forgetting about him fighting in the Sundowner, forgetting that he'd lived a restless, roaming life and, probably most important, that very few people possessed the strength of will to change lifelong habits and routines.

She looked into his eyes, then raised her right hand and laid it on his cheek. He had told her—begged her, actually—to call Lori and hear from her best friend what had really happened at the Sundowner. She had to call Lori anyway, to ask her to pick up one of those home pregnancy tests at Tully's Drugstore for her. She would also ask Lori about the fight.

"Luke," she said quietly. "I'm not saying no, all right? But I need some time to think about it."

He closed his eyes for a blissful moment, then buried his face in her lap. "You'll say yes," he whispered. "I know you will."

Maris heard, but said nothing. She merely stroked his hair, very gently, very tenderly. Whatever decision she finally came to, she was in love with Luke.

That love could be either a blessing or a curse. Only time would tell.

# Eighteen

Keith, with Susie's help, bought a handsome dark-gray suit and the correct accessories. Maris was impressed by their choices and said so, though she hadn't yet met Keith's young friend. The next day Luke, Keith and Maris dressed up for Terrance Colson's funeral, and they drove to the somber event in a hushed mood, using Maris's truck.

The saddest part of it for Maris was that other than the three of them, the only person at the service was Jessica McCallum. If Terrance had had any friends, they weren't announcing it by attending his funeral. Maris mentioned Susie to Keith and he said, "I asked her not to come. I didn't want her here, Maris."

He seemed so grown-up, Maris thought. The suit and tie added years to his appearance, but it wasn't only his clothes that made him look older. Maturity was in his eyes, in the set of his mouth and shoulders. Giving him a small smile of understanding, Maris curled her hand around his arm.

Later, after the brief service was over, Jessica spoke to them all, though her message was unquestionably for Keith. "If you need anything, please let me know."

The drive back to the ranch was almost as silent as the drive out. Maris felt Luke's emotional tension much more than she felt Keith's, and she was relieved when the trip was over. Keith had every right to introspective sobriety today; Luke was tense because of their conversation yesterday. Every time he looked at her, which was often, she felt his head in her lap again, her hand in her hair. Each time she remembered what he'd said. *You'll say yes. I know you will.*

Possibly she would. Possibly she wouldn't. Weighing Luke's hopes and her ambivalence from every angle didn't seem crass to Maris. She had vowed never to marry again. While that oath might be a bit overboard, vowing to avoid another unstable man was not, and certainly she had done that, too.

No one discussed plans for the balance of the day, but Maris immediately went to her room to change clothes. When she walked into the kitchen a short time later, Keith was on his way outside. He stopped for a few words.

"Thanks for being there, Maris."

"I wouldn't have had it any other way." Her gaze flicked over his jeans and boots. "Are you going to work?"

"Luke needs my help."

Maris glanced out the window and saw Luke down by the corral, also wearing jeans and boots. The men on the No Bull were both hard workers and even on a day like today would not evade responsibility. Was there a chance the three of them could actually become a family?

Maybe she should be thinking in terms of the *four* of them, Maris thought uneasily. She would call Lori the minute Keith was out of earshot.

He grabbed an apple from the bowl of fruit on the table and left through the kitchen door. Maris sat down and eyed the telephone. Love wasn't enough to guarantee harmony between a couple, she reminded herself, thinking of Luke and Ray and everything in between. But was she judging Luke too harshly because of her years of unhappiness with Ray?

Slowly, reflectively, Maris picked up the phone and dialed Lori's work number. The receptionist asked her to hold for a few minutes, as Lori was busy with a patient. With the silent telephone at her ear, Maris doodled on a pad and thought about Luke and his many promises. His concern about having nothing of a material nature to contribute to their relationship was touching, though anyone's net worth had never been of great significance to Maris. Still, she could see why he might have doubts about that aspect of his proposal.

She heaved a long-suffering sigh. Nothing was ever easy. If she said yes to Luke she might regret it within months, as she had with Ray. If she said no, she might regret it for the rest of her life.

"Maris?"

"Lori, hi. Have you got a minute to talk?"

"I have *fifteen* minutes to talk. I'm on a break. How've you been? I've been meaning to call for weeks, but the baby business is booming these days and I've been working practically nonstop."

"I've been meaning to call you, too. So much for good intentions, right? Lori, do you recall our conversation about that home pregnancy test?"

"Sure do. Are you ready to try one? Maris, if you're certain of your condition now, you really should make an appointment with your doctor."

"I'm not certain, and I think I'd rather try the test first. Could I impose on your busy schedule and ask you to pick one up for me?"

"I'll do it today. Are you hoping to get a positive reaction? I know you've always wanted a child, but you're alone now and single parenting can be very trying."

"Trying or not, I'm hoping very much that the test will turn out positive, Lori."

"Then I hope it does, too. So...what else is happening on the No Bull? How's Keith?"

"His father died. Did you hear?"

"No, I didn't." Lori paused. "I suppose I should be sorry, but I really can't muster up any sorrow for a man who did what he did to his family. How did Keith take it?"

"Quietly. I don't think he can muster up much sorrow, either."

"Understandable. Well...how's Luke? He's still working for you, isn't he?"

"He's still here. Lori, about Luke...he said you were in the Sundowner the night he got into that fight with Jim Benteen."

"I was there with Louise and Larry Hawkins, Maris. Judd called you that night, didn't he? I was going to call, but when he said that he planned to, I decided to stay out of it."

"He called, Lori, but... Well, no one's told me what really happened."

"Luke didn't?"

"When I questioned him about it, he said to call you."

Lori laughed. "He did, huh? Well, I suppose he's not proud of being arrested, but after it was over and I grasped what had happened, I was very proud of him. He's quite a guy, Maris."

"Tell me about it, Lori."

"Sure, glad to. I was sitting with my back to the bar, yakking with Louise and Larry, and I honestly didn't see Luke come in and sit at the bar. You know the layout of the Sundowner, don't you? Well, Melva Waterman and Jim Benteen were sitting in that back corner booth. Those two have lived together off and on for a good ten years, Maris, and when they're in an off mood, they fight. That's what they were doing that night, hissing at each other like two spitting cats, and drinking heavily, to boot.

"All of a sudden this loud cracking noise came from the booth. Melva let out a wail and everyone in the place knew that Jim had struck her. He got up to leave and was nearly to the door, when Luke stopped him. Something was said between them. I didn't hear what it was, because Louise and I went over to Melva to see if she was all right.

"The next thing I knew, Luke and Jim were fighting, knocking over chairs, trying to kill each other it looked like. Pete called the sheriff. I'd made a makeshift ice pack out of napkins and ice from the drinks on the table, and was holding it to Melva's eye.

"The deputies arrived, though the fight was pretty much over by then. Benteen was on his knees and Luke was leaning against the bar, blowing on his bruised knuckles. Sometime along in there Judd walked in and I realized who Luke was. It all happened pretty fast, but I would give Luke a pat on the back any day of the week for what he did, Maris. There were other men in the place and none of them did one blasted thing about Jim hitting Melva.

"That's the story, Maris. Apparently Luke doesn't like men beating up women."

Recalling Luke's shocked reaction when she'd told him that Ray had hit her, Maris bit down on her lower lip. "Apparently not," she said after a moment, her voice husky and emotional.

"I wonder why Luke didn't tell you about it himself," Lori mused.

"He said it was because I wouldn't believe him. He added that I doubted everything he says," Maris said quietly.

"Do you?"

Maris took a rather shaky breath. "Maybe it seems that way to him. I haven't always been...kind to Luke." *Not only that, I tricked him into making me pregnant.* Maris felt about two inches high. "Lori, thanks for the story. I'll let you get back to work now."

"I'll drop off that test sometime today, probably this evening."

"Thanks, Lori. See you then." Maris nearly hung up, then said, "Lori? Are you still there?"

"You darned near lost me," Lori said with a laugh.

"I'll pick up that test myself."

"Really? What about John Tully catching on and spreading it around town?"

"To hell with what John Tully or anyone else might think," Maris said emphatically.

"Good girl. See you when I see you, okay?"

"Bye, Lori."

Maris put down the phone. Ray had fought in bars just for the hell of it; Luke had fought to protest Benteen's treatment of Melva. There was a world of difference between Ray's temperament and Luke's. And Judd himself had told her Luke hadn't been drunk. She'd been too quick to judge, and who was she to judge anyone's ethics or behavior, anyway? It took a pretty sneaky woman to make love with a man just so she could get pregnant, and in the process make plans never to let him know about his own child should her deceitful plot be successful.

But she hadn't only made love with Luke to get pregnant. She must have fallen in love with him very early in their relationship to have made love with him that first time. Hadn't she stood around outside, trying to look busy, just so she could watch him working without his shirt? He had affected her right from the first and she had fought and denied the feelings developing within her as hard as she could, simply because he was a rodeo rider.

Getting to her feet, Maris went to the window over the sink. Luke was in the corral with a reddish brown horse; Keith was nowhere to be seen, probably putting the already trained horses through their paces in one of the pastures.

Maris's pulse began a faster beat. Her own nerve astounded her. Going to the back door, she stepped outside and shouted, "Luke?"

He turned his head toward her. "What?" he yelled back.

"Could you come to the house?"

"Yeah. Be right there."

She went inside to quiver and tremble and pray she was doing the right thing.

Luke loped from the corral to the house and went inside. "What is it?"

Maris's legs felt about as steady as a bowl of gelatin. "I . . . I love you."

His eyes widened, but surprise didn't prevent him from closing the gap between them in two long strides and pulling her into his arms. "I love you, too, baby."

Her face was against his bare chest, and she could smell the musky maleness of his sun-heated skin. "There's something I have to tell you," she whispered tremulously.

"Tell me anything."

"You're not going to like it."

"Try me."

"Yes . . . I have to." Maris pushed herself free of his embrace. "I . . ." She couldn't look at him. "I think I'm pregnant."

He was stunned for a moment, but then a slow grin broke out on Luke's face. "Maris, that's great! Why would you think I wouldn't like it?"

She swallowed nervously. "Because I . . . I planned to lure you into making me pregnant, knowing you were going to leave in September. You never would have known about the baby."

He sat down. Rather, he plopped into the nearest chair as though every ounce of strength in his body had suddenly deserted him. "I don't believe you'd do something like that," he mumbled.

"It's true, Luke," she whispered with her eyes cast downward.

"Why are you telling me about it now?"

"Because I'm ashamed. And sorry. I always had so much to say about your . . . uh, faults, or what I considered faults, and then I did something worse than you've probably ever done."

"But you really are pregnant?" Luke asked, as though needing to hear it again.

"I'm not a hundred percent sure yet, but I think so." He still looked shell-shocked, she saw with a sinking sensation. Maybe he didn't want children. Oh, God, why hadn't she considered that before calling him in to confess her sin?

But no, he'd declared her pregnancy great. What had stunned him was her deceit. He probably hated deceit and anyone capable of it.

The strangest sense of calm suddenly descended upon Maris. She wasn't any more perfect than the next person. She was willing to overlook Luke's flaws and only he could decide if he was able to accept hers.

"If you don't love me now, I won't be angry, Luke," she said quietly.

He jerked his eyes toward her. "Don't love you? Do you think my feelings for you are that shallow? There are only a few things that could destroy my love for you, lady. One of them is infidelity and the others ... Well, I can't think of them right now, but it would take something pretty damned serious to turn me off on you."

Thrilled at his attitude, Maris opened her mouth to say that she felt the same about him, but the front doorbell rang before she could express herself. She nearly jumped out of her skin. "Who on earth could that be?"

Luke got up. "Why don't we go and find out?"

It was a deliveryman with a large cardboard carton. "I have a delivery for Mrs. Maris Wyler," he said cheerfully.

"I'm Mrs. Wyler."

"Sign here, please." The man held out a clipboard containing a receipt.

Maris glanced excitedly at Luke. "It's the package from Katherine Willoughby." Quickly she signed the receipt and the deliveryman tore off a copy and handed it to her. Luke picked up the carton. "Thank you," Maris told the man.

"You're welcome. Have a good day, Mrs. Wyler." Whistling, he walked off to his truck.

Luke carried in the carton. Maris quickly closed the door and followed him to the kitchen. "Set it on the table. Do you have a knife?"

"Right here." Luke pulled a jackknife out of his pocket. The box was opened in no time, and they could both see that it was crammed full of file folders.

Maris took out the top folder and read its label. "'Satin Dolly.' Oh, my goodness, Luke, it just occurred to me. How will we decide which horse belongs to which file?"

"We'll figure it out." Luke picked up a folder and began thumbing through the papers in it. He smiled. "Everything's here, sire, dam, grandsire, grandam, and even farther back than that. Physical descriptions, time of birth..." He looked at Maris. "Do you realize what you have here?"

"Uh...records?"

"Damned good records. I wonder why Ray neglected to ask for these files when he bought the horses."

"I think the key word in that statement is 'neglected,' Luke."

Their gazes meshed for a long moment. "If you hadn't taken care of this ranch, there wouldn't be a No Bull, would there?" Luke said.

"I'm sure the ranch would still be here, but I wouldn't own it." Maris smiled a trifle grimly. "Me and the bank, that is."

"You said you planned to go back into the cattle business, once the horses were sold."

"That's true."

Thoughtfully Luke looked at the carton of breeding records. "How about raising horses instead?"

"Luke, I understand the cattle business. Raising horses is a whole other ball game."

His gaze pinned her with its intensity. "*I* understand horses."

Maris's heart skipped a beat. "We're talking about you and me now, aren't we?"

"We're talking about a lot of things, Maris, mainly our future. Are you going to marry me? I said I didn't have much in the way of assets to offer you, but there's one I didn't think of until now. There's very little I don't know about horses." He laid his hand on the carton of records. "With these we could breed and raise the best cutting horses in the country. There's always a demand for good cutting stock, Maris. Ranchers use them as well as rodeo riders. I paid ten thousand dollars for Pancho and he was worth every cent. That's the kind of price you could get for properly trained cutting stock."

"Ten thousand!" Maris drew a startled breath. "Do you mean to say that my horses are worth..." She multiplied ninety-three times ten thousand and gasped. "Nearly a million dollars?"

Luke chuckled. "No, I don't mean that at all, though it would be great, wouldn't it? I'd say that about half your herd has the traits needed for good cutting stock. What I would do is keep the best and sell the rest, which would result in enough animals to get started in the horse breeding business *and* the cash to keep the ranch going through the winter. By spring I'd have some of those horses so well trained, ranchers and rodeo riders would be begging to buy them."

"We would still hold the auction," Maris said, a little breathless over Luke's ambitious and exciting ideas.

"Definitely. With these records of ancestry, any of your horses will bring a good price. But some of them will never be more than what they are right now. A good cutting horse needs to possess three qualities, Maris—the ability and desire to learn, a lot of endurance and a natural freedom of movement. I could go on and on about that subject, and I will if you think my idea is worth pursuing. But our first decision isn't about the horses, is it?"

She knew what he meant. "No, I guess it isn't," she said quietly, though her heart had started beating double time.

"It seems relatively simple to me," Luke said almost casually. "I love you and you love me. Maris, I'm asking you to be my wife." His nonchalance vanished. "I'm also asking you to believe in me, aren't I?"

"Yes," she whispered. "But that coin has two sides. Can *you* believe in *me* after what I did?"

"You really weren't going to tell me about the baby?"

"No," she said meekly.

"Last night you said you needed time to think about my proposal. What changed your mind?"

"I called Lori and she told me why you fought with Jim Benteen. Lori's proud to even know you, and Luke...so am I." Tears were beginning to blur Maris's vision. "I love you. I fought it so damned hard. I kept telling myself you were like Ray, but you're not. You're not like anyone else I've ever known."

A corner of his mouth turned up in a wry little half smile. "I can say the same about you, believe me."

She couldn't help laughing, though it came out rather shaky. "I guess that's a compliment."

Luke moved to pull her into his arms. "Here's a much better one. You're a beautiful, sensual, intelligent woman, and I want to spend the rest of my life with you. If you want to sell every horse on the place and raise cattle, that's what we'll do. If you want a dozen babies, that's what we'll have. Marry me, Maris. Make me the happiest man on earth." He grinned then, surprising Maris. "Make my mother the happiest woman on earth. She's always wanted me to settle down. 'Like normal folk' is the way she puts it. Think what a favor you'd be doing her by marrying her son."

"And giving her grandbabies?" Maris threw her arms around Luke's neck. "Oh, Luke," she said on a sob.

He squeezed her tightly to himself. "Was that a yes, honey?"

"Yes . . . yes . . . *yes!*"

# Epilogue

Luke asked Keith to be his best man at the wedding and Lori acted as Maris's matron of honor. It was a quiet affair, with just a handful of Maris's closest friends in attendance. The bride was indeed pregnant, having seen a doctor for verification of what she already knew. Keith was bursting with pride over his role in the affair, and actually strutted during the small reception held at the ranch after the ceremony, Maris saw with great affection. Of course Susie was there, and Keith's machismo was directed at her. She was a pretty little thing, but what Maris really liked about her were her plans for her future.

"Oh, yes, I'm definitely going to college," she told Maris while they chatted over a cup of fruit punch. "Keith has been talking about Montana State U, in Bozeman, so I'm also considering that school. He told me that Luke really gave him a pep talk about going to college."

Maris sent first Keith then Luke a pleased glance across the room. "Is that a fact? Montana State U, hmm? That's my school."

After the wedding there was a lot of work to do to get ready for the horse auction. School had started for Keith, but as long as he kept up with his homework, Maris and Luke thought it was fine for him to continue working with the horses.

Maris worked hard on the piles of records that Katherine Willoughby had sent. Finally, she and Luke managed to figure out which records belonged to each horse in their herd. As they had planned, Luke picked out the best of the lot for breeding. He was pleased with their bloodlines and temperament, and assured Maris that they had the start of a fine stock.

As she worked with Luke through the last weeks of September, Maris was thrilled not only by the thought of the growing life inside her, but by the wonderful new future she and Luke were building together with each passing day. Luke felt badly that he wasn't able to give his bride what he called a "proper honeymoon," but she felt those first days—and nights—of their marriage couldn't have been happier, or more satisfying.

The auction was a great success, with buyers coming from miles around and the bids flying fast and furiously. Next to her wedding to Luke, Maris thought it had to be the most exciting day of her life. Luke himself ran the auction with impressive professionalism and flare. Maris was thrilled as the high-figured sales totaled up, and feeling quite proud that day to be Luke's wife.

With the proceeds from the auction and the money received from Jim Humphrey for the Corvette, Maris set about making some much needed repairs on the ranch. And there was still enough extra money for Luke and Maris to fly to Texas. The trip was not only their honeymoon, but Maris wanted very much to meet Luke's mother. Lila Rivers actually wept when Luke introduced his bride, then she wiped her eyes and served them a sumptuous home-cooked meal.

They didn't sleep at Lila's house, however. There was a very nice motel in that small Texas town and they rented a room for the five nights of their stay, the time they had allotted themselves to be away from the ranch, as there was so much to do before the cold weather set in. Their honeymoon days would be spent with Lila, but they wanted to be alone at night, which Lila Rivers understood and graciously accepted as only natural for a newlywed couple.

Maris had splurged on some lovely new nightgowns, and she picked what she thought was the most appealing to wear on their first night in the motel. She came out of the bathroom all perfumed and pretty for her husband, and saw Luke already in bed. One small light was on, casting the room in soft shadows.

His gaze washed over her, ardent and loving. "Stand there for a second and just let me look at you," he said huskily. Maris got warm all over from the heated head-to-foot inspection she received. "Damn, you're beautiful," he whispered. "Come here." He held up the sheet in invitation.

Maris slid into bed and was immediately brought into a feverish embrace. "I love you, baby," Luke said hoarsely.

"And I love you." She wrapped her arms around him and held on tightly, almost fiercely. "I love you so much it scares me."

He nuzzled his mouth in her hair. "It scares you because you loved Ray and it didn't last. We're going to last, Maris. Count on it. I don't want you scared or worried about anything. I'm always going to be there, honey, always. You can talk to me about anything. Let's make a pact right now. I saw this in a movie a long time ago and even then it made good sense to me. Let's never go to bed angry. If either of us does something to annoy or anger the other during the day, let's talk about it and make up before we go to bed."

Maris smiled tremulously. "That's a wonderful idea, Luke. I swear I'll do my part."

"And I'll do mine. We'd be fools to let anything undermine what we have, Maris." He tipped her chin to look into her eyes. "And we're not fools, either of us. We're going to have the best marriage ever, honey." His mouth covered hers in a passionate, loving kiss, and in seconds neither was thinking of anything beyond the ecstasy and joy of being together.

Before they left Texas they told Lila about the baby. Again she shed tears. Maris took her mother-in-law's hands in her own. "Will you come to the ranch when the baby is born?"

"May I?"

"Lila, you may come anytime you wish, but I would be particularly pleased if you were there when the baby is born." Maris smiled. "And as I said before when I was telling you about Keith, you have to meet him. Luke and I both think of him as our son, which sort of makes him your grandson."

During the flight home, Maris put her head back and thought of her incredible happiness. She felt Luke take her hand, and she turned her head to smile at him. "I love you," she whispered. Then she realized that he was pressing something *into* her hand, a small piece of paper. "What is it?"

"Take a guess."

Instead of guessing, she unfolded the little square of paper and looked at it. It was Ray's IOU, and across the face of it Luke had printed in bold letters PAID IN FULL.

Her lips twitched with a smile, then she gave a little laugh. But when Luke laughed, too, she began giggling. They lost it then, both of them laughing so hard that other passengers started smiling at them.

They finally calmed down. Maris looked at the IOU again. "I'm going to frame this and hang it in our bedroom."

"You're kidding."

She leaned over and kissed his lips. "Without this little piece of paper, you never would have come to the ranch. It's a keepsake, my love. I might not hang it on the wall, but I'm definitely going to keep it." Her eyes took on a teasing twinkle. "And when the No Bull Ranch is famous for its marvelous cutting horses, bred and trained by that also famous handler, Luke Rivers, no less, and we've been rich for so long we can't even recall when we weren't, then I'm going to take out this ancient IOU and remember that it brought us together."

Luke grinned. "Incidentally, there was so much going on before we left the ranch, I don't think anyone told you that Blackie is going to have pups."

Maris's jaw dropped. "How did she get pregnant?"

"The usual way, I suppose," Luke said dryly.

"But she's the only dog for miles!"

"Apparently not."

Maris settled back with a contented smile. "Do you realize that you changed my entire life?"

"Do you realize that you changed *my* entire life?"

They looked at each other for the longest time. "It was fate, wasn't it?" Maris said softly. "We were destined to be together."

"I think that's as good an explanation as any," Luke murmured, leaning forward to kiss her sweet, sexy lips. "I wish we were alone right now."

"Patience, my love," she whispered throatily. "We have the rest of our lives."

And indeed they did.

\* \* \* \* \*

# MONTANA MAVERICKS

*continues with*

*SLEEPING WITH THE ENEMY*

*by Myrna Temte*

*Available in October*

*Here's an exciting preview....*

# One

Taking a moment to consider the wisdom of confiding in Maggie Schaeffer, Jackson Hawk studied her face. Her looks had never failed to get to him, from the first moment she'd walked into his office.

But even more, she cared deeply about the people on this reservation, he was certain of that. She'd even earned herself a nickname—Maggie the Little Fed Who Actually Listens, which was indeed high praise for an outsider who'd been here such a short time.

But could he trust her with information as sensitive as this? Well, shoot, if Little Fed kept poking around on her own, she'd probably hear the rest, anyway.

"Have you ever heard of Jeremiah Kincaid?" he asked.

She nodded. "I've met him once. In Congressman Baldwin's Washington office. He's the president of the local Rancher's Association, isn't he?"

"That's right. He's pretty much run the whole county for the last thirty years. His father ran it before that." Jackson sighed and leaned back in his chair. "Mr. Kincaid and his pals got in pretty thick with our Bureau of Indian Affairs and were granted long-term land leases at rock-bottom prices on almost half the land on this reservation."

"Can't the leases be revoked?" Maggie asked.

"They're due to expire on the first of June. But when I informed Mr. Kincaid that the tribe would not renew those leases, the Rancher's Association filed a lawsuit against us."

"On what grounds?"

"Guys like Kincaid don't need solid grounds, Maggie. They buy judges and congressmen and even U.S. senators."

"Now wait a minute. Are you implying that my boss takes bribes?"

She was quick, all right, Jackson thought with a grin. And so damned earnest. "I don't know. But what was Jeremiah Kincaid doing in Baldwin's office?"

"I don't know, and I wouldn't tell you if I did. I have some integrity, you know." She shot him a huffy glare that dared him to challenge her last statement. "Constituents visit him every day. That doesn't mean he takes bribes."

Jackson shrugged. "You're right. But I have to tell you it makes me damn nervous to find out Kincaid's been to see him. And frankly, I'm worried about the congressman's sudden interest in us. It was clever of him to send you here."

"You think he's using me somehow? To harm the tribe?" She gaped at him for a second, then firmly shook her head. "He wouldn't do that. I know he wouldn't."

"For God's sake, Maggie, how naive are you?" Jackson stood and paced the length of the room and back.

"Come on, Jackson. I don't see how anyone could use my work to help Kincaid. I was asked to report the truth about conditions here. That should help you, not hurt you."

Jackson shrugged his broad shoulders. "Maybe that has nothing to do with your report. For all I know, your boss might be drafting legislation to force us to renew the leases, and he wanted you out of town, so you wouldn't find out about it."

"That's pretty paranoid—"

"I'd rather be paranoid than stupid."

"Well, gee, thanks a lot." Maggie rose and walked stiffly to the doorway.

"Wait a minute." Jackson hurried after her. She turned to face him, unable to disguise the pain that showed in her eyes.

It was hard to believe, that after everything Jackson Hawk had put her through, she still thought him handsome—the handsomest man she'd ever seen. His smooth, coppery skin stretched over a blade of a nose, sharply defined cheekbones and firm jaw and chin. His long black braids did nothing to detract from his masculinity; he was so tall, his shoulders so broad, his voice so deep and rough, she doubted anything would be able to do that.

But it was his eyes that affected her most. Black, black eyes, shining with intelligence, glittering with anger. Eyes that looked into the darkest corners of her soul. And so often, just like to-day, found her wanting.

Jackson reached out and touched her arm. "I didn't mean that the way it sounded. I'm just afraid you're too trusting."

"Well, it's obvious you don't trust me, either," she said. "After all, I *do* work for the evil congressman."

She was so damn cute when she was furious, Jackson had to grin. "Actually, I kind of admire your loyalty to your boss. I only wish I knew how much loyalty you feel toward the people here. You don't have any real connection to us."

She raised her chin to a proud, almost haughty angle. "I'm as Northern Cheyenne as you are, Jackson Hawk. And I happen to have a very direct connection to the Laughing Horse Reservation."

"What are you talking about?"

"Take a look at your tribal rolls. I'm listed as Margaret Speaks Softly. My mother was listed as Beverly Speaks Softly."

Jackson frowned. He'd heard that name before—recently, in fact. When the memory surfaced, he had even less reason to trust Maggie. "I've heard of her. She left over twenty years ago and never came back. Married some big-shot white man, didn't she? The guy who owns all those motels?"

"That's right. My father's name is Calvin Schaeffer."

"Then you're half-white? You don't look—"

"No. My biological father was Northern Cheyenne, too. He abandoned Mama before I was born. When he died, Cal adopted me. He's been a wonderful father, Jackson. I love him very much."

Well, that explained a lot of things about Maggie Schaeffer, Jackson thought. "You never even said you were Cheyenne. Why the hell didn't you tell me this before?"

"You were so busy judging me and telling me I didn't belong here, I didn't think it was any of your business. I'd appreciate it if you wouldn't spread this around. It's no one else's business, either."

"You have family here, Maggie."

"I know, but I'm not sure I want to meet them. My mother must have had her reasons for staying away. Until I find out what they were, I'd rather not have any contact."

It was too late for that, Jackson thought, grimly shaking his head. She'd already met her grandmother, Annie Little Deer. Annie's husband of fifty years had died a month ago, and Jackson remembered her mentioning with regret her long-lost daughter. She knew Annie would cherish the knowledge that Maggie was her granddaughter. But it was Maggie's decision to make.

"All right," he said. "You can trust me not to tell anyone."

"Thank you." Maggie nodded, lowering her gaze. "But you still don't trust me, do you?"

"Should I?"

"Yes, damn it. What have I done to make you believe I would ever willingly hurt anyone?"

"Nothing," he said. "But I told you, I have to focus on these leases. I can't afford to deal with legal hassles right now."

"Just give me the information I need. I know I can help."

Jackson had to smile. She had that look in her eyes again, like a mama grizzly protecting her cubs, and he pitied the poor man who had to face her down. He led her to the next office and dug out the appropriate file from one of the cabinets. She scanned the contents and tucked the folder under her arm. Jackson shook his head in bemusement as she left his office with a cheery wave.

Maggie Schaeffer had a healthy temper, and she wasn't afraid to show it. But when an argument ended, she didn't seem to hold a grudge. He liked that about her. That and a lot of other things.

In fact, the only thing he didn't like about her was her boss. Damn it, an Indian woman as intelligent and educated as Maggie had no business working for a jerk like Congressman Baldwin. She should be working for her people in some capacity. So why the hell wasn't she? They could use her talents right here.

"Forget it," Jackson muttered. "Calvin Schaeffer's daughter would never live on a reservation. Not in a billion years."